BE
happy
& free
TODAY!

COMPLETE EMOTIONAL HEALING GUIDE
FROM SOUL WOUNDS

BE
happy & free
TODAY!

COMPLETE EMOTIONAL HEALING GUIDE
FROM SOUL WOUNDS

Start A *joy* Chapter In Your Life

IŞIK ABLA

This book is dedicated to all God's daughters, and to my own beautiful daughter

thank you

I thank Jesus for healing my wounds and setting me free. I'm very thankful for my family and great friends for being part of my "freedom journey." I am also deeply grateful to Kathleen for her loving support, diligence and wonderful help.

Contents

introduction

part one

part two

part three

Introduction

My Journey to Freedom & Happiness

I lived twenty-eight years of my life in darkness and misery as an abused Muslim woman.

I was born and raised in a Muslim family in Turkey. I was considered inferior from birth just because I was a girl. My father was a womanizer. He was a mean and angry man, all the time. My mother was always sad and depressed. She experienced constant nervous breakdowns because of my father's many affairs, and basically lived on antidepressants—most of them illegal.

In this dysfunctional environment, I had to grow up quickly. I never had a childhood. I was abused by both of my parents physically, verbally and emotionally. Beginning at age five, I was sexually molested by a relative. After many years, I learned that my parents knew all about it and didn't do anything to protect me.

Because I experienced deep wounds of rejection from my parents, I became addicted to pleasing people, desperate for their acceptance and approval. I just wanted to be loved and accepted. For that reason, I always ended up with controllers and abusers in my life.

Like everyone, I looked for significance in life, and found mine in studying and trying to prove to others, especially my father, that I was not stupid, even though I was a girl. I became a bookworm at an early age and started living in the dream world of stories. They were my escape in life, especially when I was being abused.

As I grew older, I began to find my significance in studying Islam and trying to become a good Muslim. In our family and community, my great-grandmother was an authority on Islam. Along with the teachings of the Quran, she also practiced witchcraft, as well as white magic for the sick. She took me under her wing and started mentoring me.

Education, diplomas and seminars cannot solve our problems! Only the power of God can!

I was insecure, angry, hurt, unforgiving and hateful, and my newfound devotion to Islam didn't help. On the contrary, various aspects of Islam and our culture made things worse for me. I believed myself to be inferior to men—a belief rooted in our religion, culture and family. My parents celebrated my brother's birth when I was fourteen. Everyone congratulated them that they had finally had a son.

My father told me I was nothing to him and that my mother could do the job of raising me. At one point in my life, I wanted to kill and die for Allah. I thought that would be the most heroic and significant thing for someone who had nothing to lose!

I went to college at age sixteen, and at nineteen graduated with a bachelor's degree in literature. Then I began attending another prestigious University in Turkey, studying business administration at night for a postgraduate degree. Moreover, I attended many seminars and conferences to learn about marketing, branding, leadership and how to manage employees and companies. I wanted to prove myself so badly—to prove that even as a woman, I could be someone important. I had dreams. And as I studied more and worked harder, I started climbing the career ladder. But substituting freedom and happiness for career, diplomas and education left me even more empty and unfulfilled. The more I ran away, the more I was going deeper into a dark pit of my captivity.

My escape from darkness would not come easily. As a teenager, I married a Muslim man who started beating me up almost every other day. At times he physically tortured me on a daily basis. When it became a life-and-death situation, with the help of a lawyer friend I was able to get out of the marriage and escape to America for my freedom. It is another miracle story. When I look back now, I can see the hand of God in that situation. It was a complete miracle—and I thought that finally, as I escaped to the United States, I would find my dreams coming true.

Wherever You Go, There You Are

With my divorce certificate in hand, I fled to America immediately after my divorce was final. I was afraid that if I stayed in Turkey my ex-husband might kill me, as he'd threatened to do many times. I reasoned that by going to America I could be free. I *wanted* to be free. I *dreamed* freedom. But even in a free country, I was still a captive. I had a lot of unforgiveness, anger, hurt, lies and deception. I needed freedom from many chains! I fled to a free country to be free, but I was a prisoner.

I always say, "Wherever you go, there you are." Unless God comes and changes your inner self, you are the

> Unless God comes and changes your inner being,
> *you take the same person with you wherever you go.*

same wherever you go. You can change your house, your hair, your car and even your country. You can change basically everything externally. But you can't change *you* without the transforming power of God.

What Do You Need?

I was in America, but still with the same mentality. I still needed a man to tell me who I was and what to do with my life. I needed a man to tell me what to eat, drink, say and wear. I believed I could not exist without a man! As a divorced woman, I had no self-worth, and prayed constantly for a husband. I was lonely in this new country and didn't know the language well, which only made my neediness worse.

After much prayer for a man, and with a friend's help, I met someone right away. We got married and had a beautiful little girl—but I was experiencing a whole new type of misery and abuse. As soon as we were married, I found out he was a drug and alcohol abuser. I was in depression and didn't know it at that time. I wasn't aware that I hadn't recovered from my past hurts, or that I carried open wounds. The expression "basket case" is probably an understatement to describe my condition at the time!

My new husband didn't like to be home. He had another life outside of home. He was always out with his friends, partying, drinking and living a different life, avoiding spending any time with me or our daughter. When he was home, he was drinking, mean, and full of rage. He was addicted to pornography and also having affairs. I was trying to survive once again, this time with a little baby in my arms. I was almost numb to pain, trying to block any feelings of hurt.

Desperate to be free of my misery, I turned back to study and found a very bad friend myself, who tried to destroy my life even more.

If you are too hardheaded, you don't really "get it" until you hit bottom. I was very hardheaded—and so I hit bottom—and hit it hard.

On New Year's Eve, the year 2000, my husband came home high and drunk. He took me, our daughter and my former mother-in-law in the car to a family dinner. As he zigzagged up the highway, we were all terrified.

I wanted to drive, and he wouldn't let me. We started to fight—and then he stopped the car and kicked me out.

He left. I was in the middle of nowhere on the side of a highway, crying, screaming and yelling at God for putting me through all this misery.

That night, a very kind lady stopped her car to help me. I had no idea she was the beginning of a miracle. She took me to her friend's house. Next day, I went to pick up my daughter with a police escort.

Working Hard To Survive

Now a single mother, my thinking and lifestyle went downhill fast. Thank God, the one thing I was good at was working hard, and I found a job at a Christian company. The employees had a Bible study every day. I attended just to please my boss. In my heart, I believed Christians were infidels and evildoers. The Quran ordered Muslims to rid the earth of them. However, despite my beliefs, I started to like the Bible studies— especially as I would hear about the unconditional love of Christ Jesus. I was falling in love with Jesus more and more each day. Yet, at that time, it was impossible for me to leave Islam and become a Christian. My beliefs were just too deep-rooted.

"I would prefer to die than become a Christian," I said.

I often told myself that I would prefer to die as a Muslim than become a Christian. Christians called Jesus the "Son of God"—what blasphemy that was to a Muslim! I thought it was stupid even to think of God having a son. But inside, I felt like I was dying. There were times I would recite and recite surahs from the Quran. But doing so was of no help to me at all.

Suicidal thoughts began to come. The voice of the enemy was telling me, "You are not good enough. You are a failure. You can't make it in this life. It is better to die than to suffer in this life." I felt like I had nothing

I was hearing the voice of the devil as the first person's voice and didn't know it. I thought suicidal thoughts
were my feelings and inner voice.
Now I can see how the voice of the enemy was telling me, "You are not good enough. You are a failure.
You can't make it in this life.
It is better to die than suffer like this."
And I was believing in that voice!

to give—to my daughter, to myself or to the world. After two divorces, my family was ashamed of me. In our culture, even one divorce was unacceptable! I believed I was no good for anybody, not my daughter, not even God.

One morning, I woke up with heavy suicidal thoughts. I was too tired and broken to fight them anymore. I started planning my suicide in my mind.

That day, I took my daughter to day care and went to work. In the restroom at the office, I released my anguish to God—what God I was praying to, I didn't really know. I just wanted final closure with God before ending my life. I don't know if I would actually have done what I was thinking and planning to do—I want to be honest here. All I know is I had a dream and a plan to end my life that was all but consuming me.

God Wants To Meet Us At Our Crossroads!

When I came back to my seat after that prayer, my boss called me to his office. I thought he was going to fire me. He was very serious and spoke slowly. He told me God had spoken to him and that he had to be obedient. Then he told me that God had heard my prayer in the restroom. God knew all my thoughts about suicide. Jesus knew my pain and hurt.

I could hardly believe my ears. The things my boss was telling me were secrets in my own heart—no one else knew them.

Jesus revealed Himself to me in a miraculous way!

I felt the presence of God as my boss spoke, and he asked me if I wanted to receive Jesus Christ as my Lord and Savior. I didn't think about it even for a second. I just fell on my face to the ground, started crying bitterly, and said a simple *yes* to Jesus.

At that moment, I felt the tangible presence of Jesus with me, with an awareness of His love and grace that is hard to describe. I knew I had been changed at that very moment. I knew something supernatural had happened. I felt as though a ton of weight was lifted off my shoulders.

At that moment, I knew I was forgiven. Jesus had touched me and changed me.

Into The Supernatural

In only a few minutes, that suicidal woman from the morning was gone. I was full of supernatural joy and a love I could not describe. I went to my daughter's day care, picked her up, and kissed her and kissed her and hugged her in tears. This time they were happy tears. She had a new mom.

From that day, Jesus started radically changing my life. But I had so much stuff that God had to deal with! On one level, Jesus had set me free instantly—but I still needed freedom in areas I didn't even know about. I would say I was a very worldly Christian at the beginning. The way I acted, thought, dressed, spoke and carried out all kinds of things needed to be transformed by heaven.

As I became more desperate for truth, Jesus taught me His ways. He healed my many wounds. He taught me to be a better mother and to learn that I could live without a man defining me. I started giving my testimony at churches, and began serving in the church and studying the Bible. I was very dedicated to the Lord and to the ministry. I went to a school of ministry and many Berean Bible courses, hungry to learn more and more about my new faith.

My parents, who were bitter toward me at first because of my decision to become a follower of Jesus, started seeing the difference in me. They started seeing love instead of hatred. They treated me with contempt for about two years, but as I changed more and more, they accepted me and stopped insulting me. My father even responded to my altar call when I was preaching at a church in Turkey! My mother started reading the Bible. I could never have imagined such things in the beginning!

New Life; New Dreams

I made many mistakes as a new believer. My beliefs were mixed up with my old religion, and I lacked knowledge and understanding of the Word of God. At the beginning of my walk, I failed God in many ways with my worldliness and mediocrity. I was still craving love, which I was seeking from men. I was lonely and depressed from time to time. But Jesus was gracious and loving toward me. He took me by the hand, teaching me *His* ways versus mine. He was very kind and gentle to me.

After awhile the Holy Spirit started teaching me how to be happy and whole without a man. He made me secure in my singleness. Maybe you have heard this before, that when you surrender a desire or a dream to God, He gives it to you—if you have truly surrendered. That is exactly what happened with me. I completely surrendered the desire to get married. I was married to Jesus, and for the first time, felt whole and happy without a man in my life. I was not interested in anyone and was settled with the thought that it was perfectly fine if I never got married again.

Then, after some time and when I least expected it, I met a Christian man in the church choir. I didn't know it then, but he had been praying about me for a long time, as God had told him I was the one for him! He was never married before, and was waiting for the right one. He knew my testimony, as I had shared in the church. He waited and prayed for a year before approaching me. Making the story short, after awhile God spoke to me about him several times. I didn't want to get married, and dismissed the voice of God. I was waiting for a big sign, since I didn't want to get married—I was happy with Jesus, with the ministry He had called me to, and with my daughter. God had to work in my heart before I became open to marrying again.

My husband and I sought the Lord about marriage for a year, and when He gave us peace, we got married in our home church. But believe me, it was not a "happily ever after" story. We both brought into our marriage more baggage than we could ever have imagined. But by the grace of God and a lot of hard work, prayers and counseling, we made it to "happily married." The last thing I want to do here is paint you "a perfect final marriage" picture. That would be a huge lie. We both needed freedom and the healing touch of Christ for our many wounds and past hurts.

In the meantime, God raised me up in the secular corporate world. First I became the chief financial officer of a multi-million-dollar European company, and was then promoted to president and CEO. My dreams were finally coming true. But I still had invisible chains preventing me from being free and happy. I must admit that Jesus was revealing and healing some of my wounds, as I sought Him. However, I didn't know how to be *intentional* in getting rid of all my chains to enjoy my freedom.

An Unexpected Calling

Then one day, when I was sharing with a church group, a missionary heard my testimony and recommended me to the president of a Christian TV station that was broadcasting to Turkey. They were looking for a female preacher from a Muslim background who wouldn't hesitate to show her face on TV, even with as much danger as was involved.

Well, let me tell you something: I didn't care if all Muslims went to hell. I had no burden in my heart for them. I honestly didn't care if Muslims got saved or not. My heart was hardened, and I was still angry inside.

As you might guess, the Holy Spirit started dealing with my heart. One day as I was having a devotional time with Jesus, He spoke to my heart clearly and told me He was going to use me to set the Muslim world free. I told Him that He would have to give me a burden, then, because I couldn't do it without a burden. That very morning, Jesus gave me a burden for the Muslim world, and I accepted God's calling to be on TV, preaching the gospel.

God started moving in the Muslim World *using a former abused woman like me.*

As CEO for another company, I started using my yearly vacation time to record TV programs for Turkey. It was hard work. I would fly to another town, go into the TV studios and produce eighteen programs in three days. I can't explain how I did it other than by the grace of God. Once He calls you, it is amazing how everything unfolds in His way and His timing! Those programs became very successful and popular. We started receiving hundreds of e-mails and letters, which later became thousands.

My dreams had grown and changed. Now I dreamed freedom, not only for myself, but also for the nations!

As the programs went out, I received many insults and threats, but was also receiving many messages from those who were hungry and thirsty for truth.

At that time, I had a good career, and my husband had his own company. We had a blessed financial life. However, as the responses increased and the influence of the programs grew, we started praying about doing the TV shows full time.

After six months of praying, I received an offer to become a full-time TV minister. The offer didn't include my husband, and yet we would both have to leave our careers and move to a new place, far away from our home.

My husband said we didn't even have to pray about it. It was an answer to prayer. We accepted the offer, took our daughter and moved immediately.

A Whole New Vision

Right after our move, I started filming live TV programs every week, which were broadcast to Turkey and then to Iran. The responses multiplied. High demand was coming from all over the Muslim world, and later from the Western world as well. Then I expanded the broadcasts into the languages most spoken by Muslims. Over time, God has given us a tremendous increase, and has enlarged our ministry's borders.

Big Visions Need Free And Happy People

I am not alone in this work! When God has called you for a big task, you need healthy people around you. You need free and happy people to be in the Father's business instead of those just trying to survive in their pity parties and miseries.

People are needed who share that big vision in unity with you to achieve what God has called you to accomplish. Because of our growth rate, we are always short of staff, but God has brought incredible people to work with me. Each member of our "Dream Team" works heart and soul for the Kingdom. We cannot afford to have mediocre people on the team. We are facing the giant of Islam. We face warfare, tests and trials as we persevere to break down the walls of radical Islam, and break the chains of bondage. We face many challenges, and can only make it with a strong prayer life and being deeply rooted in the Word.

Prayer Life As A Foundation And Stabilizer

We have a prayer ministry that makes Jesus the center and foundation of everything we do. Faithful prayer covering by a ministry chaplaincy ensures each team member is walking in Christ's freedom and joy. Our prayer team prays for every one of us, and for those who request prayers from us.

From the very beginning, you need to know that the enemy hates you. The enemy hates us and what we are doing, and will do anything to try and stop us from fulfilling our destiny in Christ. But our God is greater than the devil. All we need to do is to seek God and use our authority in Christ to stand our ground. We are in the battlefield. We can only win this battle on our knees. In this book, I will be showing you how to be free through prayers, as well.

I was in the ministry and needed freedom myself!

In my ministry to Muslim women, I have spent years trying to help free them from their chains. But soon I discovered that Muslim women were not the only ones who needed freedom from bondages. As I began to minister in churches, I started meeting many women—Christian women!—who were clearly in chains as well. I had a problem with understanding people of God who claimed to know Christ as their Lord and Savior, being in chains. It puzzled me. I didn't want to accept the fact that women in Christ could be captive. I could accept Muslim women being chained, but I couldn't accept Christian women being in bondage! Weren't they God's daughters? Shouldn't that mean they were free in Christ? While I was asking these questions, God was gently showing me my own chains and bondages, even after I had become a child of God. My journey to freedom helped me understand, relate to, and better minister to these women.

You want women to be free. Yet, *you are not completely free yourself.*

I started seeking the Lord about why women in the churches were under so much bondage. One day during a prayer meeting with a couple who were in a deliverance ministry, Jesus spoke to me and said, "You want to see women free, yet you, yourself, are not completely free."

That was shocking to me! You know you are hearing from the Holy Spirit when you hear what you least expect to hear! I was not expecting to hear those words. *But they were completely true.*

I had many chains in my life that needed to be broken. Two of them were insecurity and inferiority. Having grown up as a Muslim in Turkey, with a father who wanted nothing to do with me for many years, I had felt inferior to men all my life. That carried into my life as a Christian, and even into the ministry. I also believed many other lies about myself. Insecurity and inferiority had opened a wide door for the enemy to creep in.

Moreover, I was not free in the area of forgiveness. Not only had I not truly forgiven my parents, I also hadn't forgiven myself for past mistakes. I was angry and bitter with unforgiveness.

I needed complete freedom to help people to be free.

Through prayer time with that couple, I was set free from these chains, and supernatural joy started coming in as I sought the Lord more and more for my freedom. I learned more about the voice of the enemy and how even Christians often follow his voice instead of God's. And most importantly, I gained a deeper understanding of the true freedom that Christ offers.

Galatians 5:1 tells us why Jesus has set us free: it is for freedom! Freedom is the reason Jesus went to the cross. It is the reason He brings us out of the kingdom of darkness and into the kingdom of light. Sometimes Christians doubt that God really wants them to be free. But all we have to do is look at the Scriptures! When Jesus began His ministry, He stood up in the synagogue and told the people that God had sent Him to open prison doors and set the captives free (Luke 4:18–19). That is still His purpose today! Perfect freedom is God's will for you and me.

As I continued to minister in churches and on TV, God had a special purpose and plan for me to experience His complete freedom so I would be able to deliver His freedom message to others. As I ministered, the Holy Spirit trained me to see people's chains, and where they were lacking freedom. Once your spiritual eyes are open to His truth, it's amazing to see how many people are chained to so much bondage, even in the Christian world—even ministers, preachers on TV, and pastors! Once the curtain was removed, everything became more and more clear under His light.

You bear more fruit if you are free and happy

Today, our ministry has millions of followers, mostly Muslims, in the world of social media. We receive thousands of e-mails and messages. Our programs are uploaded onto the Internet and viewed by millions of people in the Middle East and all over the world. We are asking God for Muslim nations as our inheritance. I thank God for what He is doing, and I give Him all the glory and praise. I can never forget how far Jesus has brought me.

But what would happen if I was not free and happy? How could I do the work God has called me to do with chains? Many people, even ministers, are just trying to survive their daily lives by working, raising a family or leading a ministry.

I don't know your story, but I am here to tell you that if you read this book carefully, pray the prayers of receiving with a believing heart, you too can be free and happy. It is time to say, "Enough is enough!" to your chains, and enjoy your life fully, as your Maker intended you to.

Now It Is Your Turn

If you are a daughter of the King of kings, He has adopted you! That means you are a princess, and you need to learn to live like one. Maybe you need to get free from the past. Maybe you need to get free from lies people told you that you believed. Maybe you need to get free from lies you tell yourself. So many of us need to learn that we are pretty, that we are loved, and that we are significant to God. We need to learn who Jesus is for us. Maybe you need to get free from legalism, spiritual dryness or a religious spirit.

The Bible says it is *for freedom* that Christ has set us free! That means if you are living in bondage in any area of your life, you have not yet experienced the fullness of what Christ did for you. There is more. And you *can* experience it.

In this book, I want to share what I have learned about living like the King's princess. I want to share what I have learned about the chains around our lives and how our Father wants to break them off! I want to teach you some of the truths that have changed my life—and that can change your life, and the lives of the women in your life, and women in every part of America and the Muslim world and every other place where human beings live. I want to share some of the vision that is burning in my heart for you.

In these pages, we will look at freedom from many things: from pain and depression, from bitterness and anger, from wrong identities, shame, and labels of the past. We will see how to get free, how to stay free, and how to grow in freedom.

I pray that you will be blessed and set free!
IŞIK ABLA

TODAY!

COMPLETE EMOTIONAL HEALING GUIDE
FROM SOUL WOUNDS

part one

Steps to Your Freedom

Chapter 1

Identifying the Invisible Chains!

This story I once heard illustrates our situation perfectly:

The Circus Elephant

In a town far away, there was a very talented elephant. This elephant was the possession of a famous circus. He was the centerpiece of all the acts, because he could do tricks that no other animal could do. When the circus traveled, they always announced the famous elephant act first and foremost. His show was number one.

At one of the stops on the circus' route, the wealthiest man in town heard about the elephant's famous act. As he was an animal lover, he decided to go see it for himself. He was truly amazed by the talent of the elephant. After the show, he walked behind the circus tent to congratulate the elephant trainer. But as he approached the elephant's cage, he was shattered by the brutal treatment the elephant was receiving from his owner. He immediately rushed to the scene and told the owner that he wanted to buy the elephant. The owner told him this was not possible, as the elephant was a moneymaking machine and was the only reason people came. But the wealthy man offered an amount of money that the owner of the elephant couldn't decline.

So the rich man took the elephant to his mansion. He hired people to build the elephant a nice shelter, with lots of space to roam, all the food and water he could want . . . and no chains.

However, after a few days the new owner noticed that the elephant was not eating or drinking. He tried everything, but could not get the elephant to eat or drink. Finally, he searched out a great veterinarian who had a lot of knowledge about elephants.

When the veterinarian examined the elephant, he called the kind man and said, "Here is the problem. The elephant's shelter is over there, and his food is a few yards away. He is not walking the few yards to eat his food because he still thinks he has chains."

In shock, the new owner exclaimed, "But he doesn't have any chains! Why can't he just walk over and eat his food and drink his water? He is free now!"

The veterinarian replied, "He still has chains in his mind. He can only go as far as the length of his old chains. They are not visible to you. But they are visible to him. For him to eat and drink, you need to bring his food and water near to him."

Invisible Chains

Just like this elephant, many of us were set free by Jesus Christ on the day we received Him as our Lord and Savior, but we are still bound by invisible chains in our minds and hearts. The enemy has no right to keep us bound—but we don't know it!

I know a lot of people who know how to put on a happy face and are like clowns—the entertainers of their families or friends, but deep inside they are unhappy, and carry their invisible chains everywhere they go. Others live under masks of success or beauty or even "holy living." Some don't even try to hide their bondage. We invited Jesus into our hearts, and He gave us a new life. However, many of us still live under the bondage of our invisible chains. We still listen to the enemy's voice and believe what he says.

Therefore, many people around us are hurting and miserable. Some of them are mean and unhappy people. The world looks at us and asks why they should become Christians when so many believers are living their lives in bondage.

Step 1: Proclamation

This step is very powerful and important. First, you need to proclaim who you belong to and who you are in Christ. If you accepted Jesus Christ as your Lord and Savior, you believe *in your heart* that He died on the cross for your sins, sicknesses, curses and bondages, and rose from the dead on the third day, you are a child of the living God. You are born again and the Holy Spirit lives inside of you.

> *But before we go any further . . .*
> *If you haven't accepted Jesus Christ as your Lord*
> *and Savior, here is who Jesus is and why He is*
> *extremely important to know and receive into*
> *your heart for your eternal freedom.*

- Because of Adam and Eve's disobedience, sin and a curse entered the world which resulted in death. **Romans 5:12**
- God sent us the law to teach us how to live, but the law was powerless to save us. **Romans 8:3**
- All sinned and fell short of the glory of God! **Romans 3:23**
- We cannot save ourselves through our good works. We can only be saved through our faith in Jesus Christ by His grace. **Ephesians 2:8**
- The wages of sin is death. **Romans 6:23**
- Without the shedding of the blood, there is no forgiveness for sin. **Hebrews 9:22**

- If you declare with your mouth, "Jesus is Lord," and believe in your heart that God raised Him from the dead, you will be saved. **Romans 10:9**

God came down to earth in human flesh, and by going to the cross and shedding His blood, He paid the penalty we would have had to pay for our sins. He rose on the third day and overcame death.

Now if you'd like to receive Jesus as your Lord and Savior, pray the following prayer with faith:

Dear Lord Jesus,

I believe that You came down to earth to save me from eternal punishment for my sins. I believe that You died on the cross for me and rose from the dead on the third day. I believe that You are the Son of God. Please forgive my sins. I invite You into my heart. Come and be the center of my life. I confess that starting today, You are Jesus my Lord and Savior. In Your Powerful Name I pray.

Amen.

If you prayed the above prayer earnestly from your heart, you are born again and you are a child of the living God. You have a Perfect Father in Heaven who loves you unconditionally. You belong to God's family through the sonship of Jesus Christ. I also want you to know that declaring who you are and to whom you belong is very powerful, and brings breakthrough.

Step 2: Identify & Acknowledge

The first step to your freedom is to identify and acknowledge your chains. Do you have a sore spot? What offends or hurts you the most?

Usually what gets you the most is where your deeper wound is hiding. Is it rejection? If someone is not returning your call or saying "hello" to you, does it hurt you and anger you very much?

I used to get very angry with pushy and controlling people. When I brought it up before the Lord, He showed me that I was raised by a controlling mother who dominated me with guilt trips and manipulation. When someone else employed those same tactics with me, I would put up with it for awhile because it was familiar to me. But then anger would start building up and I would have an explosion. The person in front of me would say, "What is the matter with you? What have I done?" Once I had identified the root of the problem, brought it before the Lord, confessed it and forgave my mother for the wound she had caused, I was free. I could establish healthy boundaries without being angry at people who had similar behavior patterns as my mother.

Now, answer the following set of questions:
- *What is angering or upsetting you?*

- *What is hurting you the most?*

- *Is there an open wound?*

- *Do you have a broken heart?*

- *What makes you react irrationally?*

- *What is stealing your joy?*

Then answer the second set of questions:
- *Who or what event is the root of your anger or sadness?*

- *When you look back, where and how did it start?*

You don't have to think very hard to come up with something. Remember you lived this. When you are giving reactions to certain situations instead of responding maturely, most likely you are wounded. You don't have to live like that. When you ask God, He will show you. It is there, embedded in your memory, and the Holy Spirit will reveal it to you.

There may be a few that come up for you right away. But if there are more chains that you're not aware of, the Holy Spirit will continuously reveal them to you and show you any bondages in your life.

> *You will know the truth, and the truth will set*
> *you free.*
> JOHN 8:32

This process can be painful. But don't give up. Get on your knees again and again and ask the Holy Spirit to show you the areas you need to be free, and the very roots of those chains. You want to ask Jesus Christ to remove those chains from their roots.

Holy Spirit is Called the Spirit of Truth

> *When the Spirit of Truth comes, he will guide*
> *you into all truth.*
> JOHN 16:13

If you pray and ask the Holy Spirit, Spirit of Truth, to reveal those areas you need freedom from, He will show you. You need a quiet place to do this, because the enemy will do anything and use anyone to distract and interrupt you.

Holy Spirit, Spirit of Truth,
Please reveal to me any bondages and chains in my
life that are hindering my freedom and happiness.
In Jesus' name I pray,
Amen.

Wait as Holy Spirit reveals to you. Also ask Him to reveal the root of that bondage. For example, if Holy Spirit is showing you that you have a hurt of rejection, ask where this hurt is rooted. Ask God which event and person planted this seed in you. How did that event make you feel?

Step 3: Confession

To be free, you first need to be honest and transparent concerning the areas where you need freedom. As I always say, **"The problem is not the problem. Denial of the problem is the problem."** For you to receive your freedom, first you need to identify, acknowledge, then confess to God those areas where you are bound. Whatever you cannot confess, is your enemy. What shakes you the most to talk about, is your enemy. And the devil loves for you to keep it secret, so you can be bound forever. This is one of the ways he can steal your freedom, destiny and happiness.

Make a list if it will help you. My list was very long when I started seeking freedom. So don't be discouraged or hard on yourself because you have so much to deal with. Remember, Jesus died on the cross to set you free from the chains that bind you. We all need Him and His freedom.

Just to give you an idea, here are the chains that were on my list: insecurity, inferiority (from growing up in a male-dominated culture where women had no worth), worthlessness, anger, unforgiveness, lies and deception (not only lying but also believing in lies of the devil about myself and others), self-hatred, hopelessness, lack of faith, double-mindedness, selfishness (self-absorption and self-pity is in this group; always being in the ME zone, which is a form of idol worship), fear and worry, victim mentality, and many more.

Dear Lord Jesus,

I confess that I need freedom in the areas of anger, dealing with rejection, fears, worries, insecurities, seeking approval of people, boundaries, poor self-image, inferiority, materialism or idolatry, __[fill in the blank]__. (One at a time) This bondage entered into my life when _____ happened. I receive your healing and freedom in this area, dear Lord. I forgive the person who hurt me. I also repent of believing the lies of the devil because of that incident. Please forgive me Lord for allowing this lie to enter into my heart. I believe You, Jesus, that You died on the cross for me to be free from all these chains. Today I come to You, Lord, asking You to set me free. I believe and receive Your freedom.

Amen.

Stay in prayer to make sure you are receiving your freedom. There is no doubt that Jesus came to set the prisoners free according to Isaiah 61. It is God's promise! As a believer in Jesus Christ, you need to take God at His Word. You need to believe and receive for the promise of freedom to be effective and alive in you. If you need more faith to receive it, then pray for more faith and repent from doubt and unbelief.

Step 4: Renounce and Repent

Confession is a huge step to your freedom, but confessing, itself, is not enough. You need to hate that bondage to renounce it.

Dear Lord Jesus,

I renounce my inferiority, rejection, feelings of being unloved and not good enough, (list) _____ and believing lies about myself and _____. I repent from making an agreement with the enemy's lies about me and others. I choose Your truth instead of those lies. Please forgive me for my sins and for making wrong choices because of past hurts. In Your Name, Jesus, I pray.

Amen.

Step 5: Forgiveness

Unforgiveness is a stronghold that can keep you in bondage and hinder

God's blessings, joy and fulfillment in your life. Whoever hurt you, betrayed you, abandoned you, rejected you, bullied or belittled you, or has done any other wrong to you, you must forgive in order to have complete freedom in Christ. Unforgiveness is poison to your emotional and even physical health. You also need to forgive yourself from your past mistakes, and make peace with yourself, with others and with God.

Just to give you an example, I had two abortions before I accepted Jesus Christ as my Lord and Savior. After my salvation, I still had a hard time receiving forgiveness from God and forgiving myself for murdering my two unborn babies. It took me awhile to acknowledge that I was still carrying guilt and shame. I could not be free and happy until I received God's forgiveness completely, which meant forgiving myself as well.

I also had to forgive my parents, who abused me and messed me up with their dysfunctional and cruel treatment. Then I had to forgive my first husband, who beat me and some days tortured me physically. So, I had a long list of people who had done wrong to me. I had to forgive them to move on.

In the same way, you need to forgive those who hurt you, including yourself.

Step 6: Casting Out the Enemy

Through our sins, the tragic events in our lives, our traumas and wounds, we unintentionally open doors to the enemy. We invite his lies, his false comfort and his wicked ways, and even demons are able to come through those open doors and enter into our lives and souls. Many people don't realize the dark power of the enemy they engage through believing his lies and deceptions. Also, a wounded soul or a broken heart can open a wide door to the enemy to reign and rule in our minds, our hearts and our actions, without us even knowing it.

In a little bit, I will be writing about a wounded soul and will lead you to a prayer for healing and restoration of your soul. Now it is your turn to evict the enemy from his residence in your mind and soul, and gain complete control over your life through the authority Jesus Christ has given you.

Dear Lord Jesus,

I thank you Lord that You shed Your Blood at Calvary for my sins, sicknesses and chains. I thank You that I overcome the devil by Your Blood and by the Word of my testimony which is that I am a child of God. You also have given me authority according to Mark 16 to cast out demons and trample upon serpents in Your Name. Based on Your Word, I now cast out the enemy in the Name of Jesus Christ. I command you devil and any impure spirits to leave me right now in Jesus' Name. I don't ask you to leave. I command you to leave, because I am a child of the Living God and I am under the Blood of Jesus Christ.

Amen.

Step 7: Putting Everything Under the Blood

There is power in the Name and Blood of Jesus Christ. You need to receive your freedom, then sign and seal it with the Blood of Jesus, with the following prayer.

Dear Lord Jesus,

Thank You for setting me free today. I cover myself and the freedom I just received with Your precious Blood. I declare that everything I confessed and have been set free from is under Your Blood. I declare that I am free and will keep my freedom in You all my life. In Your Name I pray, dear Jesus.

Amen.

Know Your Enemy

You need to understand that the enemy hates for you to be free, and he will fight to incarcerate you. He will tell you his lies: "Do you think you can get free this easy? Huh, what a joke! This is not working for you. Look, you are not feeling anything. This happens to others, but it is not happening to you. You have to be perfect or do this and that to receive your freedom." These are only some of his lies. He will come at you day after day to steal your freedom with his lies.

Can the devil steal your freedom? Yes. You have the free will to hand your freedom to him by buying into his lies and putting your handcuffs back on. So don't you believe in his lies! Reject them and always plead the blood of Jesus over yourself, your mind, your healing and your freedom.

During years of a deliverance ministry, I have learned that the demons cannot stand two things:

1. *The Name.* Jesus Christ has power. The devil shrinks and becomes powerless when the name of Jesus Christ is exalted.
2. *The Blood of Jesus Christ.* The blood that Jesus shed on Calvary has cleansing power, protecting power, saving power, delivering power and healing power. This is why I plead the blood of Jesus over myself, my family, the ministry, my friends, our ministry team, and everything else you can think of every single day.

I cast out demons and set people free in the name of Jesus Christ and with the blood of Jesus Christ. Revelation 12:11 says, "They overcame the devil by the blood of the Lamb and by the word of their testimony." What is the word of testimony? A testimony exalts the name of Jesus Christ. When you testify, you put the devil under your feet. This is why I may decline speaking engagements, but I try never to decline giving my testimony. It is the ultimate exaltation of the name of Jesus Christ. I decrease myself by telling others what a wretch and a bad person I was, and how good and amazing my Lord Jesus Christ is.

Receiving is a Gift!

Receiving is a gift. Many people have a hard time receiving a gift, even when that gift comes from God. To receive, you need to have faith.

> *Without faith it is impossible to please God.*
> HEBREWS 11:6

Believe that Jesus Christ died on the cross to set you free.

It is for freedom that Christ set us free.
GALATIANS 5:1

Once you accept the areas where you need to be set free, then with a prayer, receive God's gift of freedom:

Dear Lord Jesus,

I open my heart to You right now to receive Your freedom and inner healing in the following areas: _____. I believe that You shed Your blood on the cross for me to be completely free. I receive it in Jesus' name.

Amen.

------ ❧ ------

What Holds You Back from Receiving Your Freedom? Doubt and Disbelief!

Doubt and disbelief are the biggest hindrances to becoming free. To receive your freedom, you need to believe it is available to you, and you need to embrace it. The enemy of your soul will bring doubt and disbelief into your mind to prevent you from seeking or receiving your freedom in Christ.

Just like the serpent asked Eve in the garden, "Did God really say that?"—he will bring you questions like, "Do you really think it is this easy for you to be free?" The answer is "Yes!" If you are truly open to receiving your inner healing and becoming free, you must believe that Jesus will do it, because He died on the cross for your freedom.

"If you can?" asked Jesus.
"Everything is possible for one who believes."
Immediately the boy's father exclaimed,
"I do believe; help me overcome my unbelief!"
MARK 9:23–24

Dear Lord Jesus,

I pray that You remove doubt and disbelief from my mind and fill me with Your faith. I repent from my doubt and disbelief. Please forgive me of my double-mindedness. I declare according to Your Word that nothing is too difficult for You. I ask You today to cancel the voice of the enemy, who is trying to put doubt and disbelief into my mind to keep me captive. I come against the voice of the enemy and bind his lies and deception in Your powerful name, Jesus. I am Your child my LORD God, and I am covered under Your blood, Jesus. I want everything You have for me. In Your matchless Name, Jesus, I pray.
Amen.

Protect Your Freedom

You must know that after you are free and delivered, you need to protect your freedom in Jesus Christ. Remember, the thief comes to kill, steal and destroy, as the Scripture states in John 10:10. After you are free, the devil will come bringing temptations for you to fall—to make you believe you are still captive after all, and that maybe you didn't receive freedom like you thought you did. You need to be on your guard against his wicked schemes. This is why Jesus tells us in John 15 that we must always remain in Him and He in us.

Freedom in Christ is a continuous walk, my dear friend. It is not a one-time deal.

You are a child of God, and you have every right to be free.
It is for freedom that Christ has set you free!

You need to be prepared by the Word of God and in the Spirit to protect your freedom. When the enemy comes to steal your freedom to make you a captive again, you can stand against his lies and temptations. You must protect your freedom by abiding in God and recognizing and obeying His voice.

It is for freedom that Christ has set us free.
Stand firm, then, and do not let yourselves be
burdened again by a yoke of slavery.
GALATIANS 5:1

The biggest deception we can have as believers is that once we are saved, we won't hear the voice of the devil anymore. Eve heard from the devil in the garden of Eden. Satan spoke to our Lord Jesus. What makes us think that we are immune from hearing the voice of the enemy? Many times, the enemy uses people around us, even church people, to speak his lies to us and steal our freedom. Your ears must be trained to hear the Good Shepherd's voice and to distinguish it from the voice of the enemy.

As soon as you receive your freedom in Christ, the enemy will bring doubt and disbelief into your mind, tempting you to open the door to him again and allow him to steal your freedom. You need to stand on the Word of God and seek the Lord daily to be able to live a free life.

So if the Son sets you free,
you will be free indeed.
JOHN 8:36

Now the Lord is the Spirit,
and where the Spirit of the Lord is,
there is freedom.
2 CORINTHIANS 3:17

Then you will now the truth,
and the truth will set you free.
JOHN 8:32

May God's joy and freedom be restored in your life! You will be His freedom song and story for the captives.

It is for freedom that Christ has set you free!

Created to Be Mine

I created you to be mine
My heart leaped with joy
When I saw your face
I loved looking at your little hands
I hemmed you in the secret place
I gazed upon your eyes
And planned a future for you happy and free
I picked the color of your hair
And selected your frame carefully
I created you to be my princess
When you fall and hurt
I will hold you, carry you, and heal you
I created you to be mine
Always sweet and true
Always near to my heart
Forever with me, I created you to be
The special one

Chapter 2

Who Are You?

Do you truly know your identity?

For you created my inmost being;
You knit me together in my mother's womb.
I praise you, because I am fearfully and wonder-
fully made.

P SALM 139:13–14

My Dear Daughter,

I want you to know your identity in Me. I called you for a purpose and a divine plan. You are not an accident. You are special to Me and precious in My sight. I want you to know your worth in Me. If you were the only person on the face of the earth, I would have come only for you, to rescue you and die on the cross for you. That is how valuable and precious you are to Me. No one else can give your worth and identity to you; no one can add it to you or take it from you. Be secure in My love, not in the love of others. Don't depend on other people's acceptance and approval. When you live your life only to please Me, you will see My best for you unfolding.

Never forget, My daughter, that I love you with an everlasting love. My love for you never changes or fails.

Dear Lord,

Thank You for loving me so much. I receive Your love and Your plans for my life. Please forgive me for focusing my eyes on pleasing others or seeking their acceptance and approval instead of Yours. From today on, I will embrace and cherish my identity in You, because this will please You, and I want to please You! I don't want to be someone else. I want to be who You created me to be. I receive Your plans and what You have in store for me with an open heart. In Jesus' name I pray.

Amen.

·······⌘·······

Do You Know How Beautiful You Are?

"Do you know how beautiful you are?" I asked a girl who attended one of my conferences. She was about thirty years old. I usually ask this question, because the reaction of most women is mind-boggling!

In typical fashion, she answered my question with three questions: "Who? Me? Beautiful?"

My dear sisters, we will never be free in Christ until we find our identity in Christ. And let me tell you: for most of us, that means learning to see ourselves very differently than we have before! Seeing ourselves the way God sees us is key to our freedom, because it is the truth that will set us free.

I looked back at that girl and said, "Yes, you are beautiful. Don't you know how beautiful you are? I am forty years old, and only began feeling beautiful for the first time in my life at age forty. Don't wait to be my age to feel beautiful and special!"

She was in tears. She hugged me and cried for awhile. I asked God, while hugging her, *What has the enemy done to women all these years? What is he still doing?*

God answered me, "He is the thief. I want you to come against his lies in my daughters' lives."

That is how this book was birthed in my heart—it was on that day that I was hugging an absolutely beautiful thirty-year-old girl who believed a lie that she was ugly and not good enough for anything or anyone.

If one million people told me I was beautiful, I wouldn't have believed them!

I was no stranger to that girl's struggle and the lies the enemy was telling her. As a young girl, I settled in my heart that I was not pretty. So I focused on studying and working hard to find my significance. Everybody looks for significance somewhere. I found it in trying to compensate for my physical ugliness with academics and success. My parents' cruel words always echoed in my mind—"You are ugly and stupid."

(Later on, they told me the reason they talked like that was that they thought if they told me I was ugly, I wouldn't focus on my appearance and become vain. They also said they called me stupid to motivate me to prove myself at school. How messed up is that?)

When people told me I was beautiful, I would think they were lying to me. I knew how ugly I was, and believed they were complimenting me out of pity.

A friend introduced Linda to me years ago, when I was still a new believer and didn't have much experience ministering to women. Linda was absolutely beautiful, to the point where men and women literally just stared at her. She was a model, so it was official that she was gorgeous! I just looked at her in amazement as she was telling me all her struggles. But now I look back and understand much better how much this precious girl was suffering and in bondage.

Linda was a dress size one and thought she was fat. When I told her she was very thin, her answer was, "No, I am not. But thank you for saying that." All she would talk about was how poorly she was doing on her diet and how she could improve her eating habits to lose weight. She had a perfect nose, and was planning to have plastic surgery to get it changed.

> My father left my mother and me when I was little.

Linda had chains that are familiar to many women today. Over the years, I have met many women who feel fat, old and ugly. Others think of themselves as stupid, lazy, worthless and no good. They are listening to the voice of the enemy.

As we talked, Linda revealed that her father was an alcoholic who left her mother and her when she was little. Later, when she was eleven years old, he came to visit them one day. Linda ran to her dad to give him a hug. In her mind, she thought she had to do everything possible to get him to stay. She thought if she was good or said the right things, he would definitely stay.

But as soon as she ran to her father, he pushed her away and said, "Don't hug me, kid, I am here to see your mom. Where is she?"

With a broken heart, Linda went to get her mother. She never saw her father again. For years, she thought if she had only been good enough or pretty enough, her father would have loved her. She believed there must be something wrong with her that her father didn't want anything to do with her. When she grew up, she went to bed with any man who told her she was pretty or that he loved her. She knew all of them were lying, but she wanted to believe in their lies, if only for a moment.

I talked with Linda and prayed over her. She cried and cried for a long time. Yet, she left as much in bondage as she came. I heard she underwent one plastic surgery after another.

Linda's story might be extreme in some of its details, but the bondage she lived with is common. Girls who don't have a good relationship with their fathers, or who are abused by their fathers, oftentimes end up with eating disorders. Most of the women I meet who were abused by their fathers are under the bondage of food. It is very easy to see it. The girl or woman in such bondage talks about food, diet and weight all the time. She notices other people's weight gain or loss. The weight-loss industry finds its success using the chains of bondage and misery that Hollywood brings into the lives of these women and many others, even those from healthier homes. It is a long and well-crafted setup of Satan, and many of us buy into it. I am sorry to say I don't know many women who are free from this, even in my circles.

Who Are You?

Many women and young girls suffer with insecurities deeply rooted in their past. Rejection, abandonment, trauma, physical and verbal abuse, and other tragic events cause many to have a very poor self-image. Of course, today's media promotes impossible ideals and sets up the standard for a certain look, size and shape for all females. It sets most of us up for failure! We women are almost programmed by the media to think we must look a certain way to fit into the ranks of the beautiful. Hearing other people's negative criticism causes more damage, even destroying our own opinions about ourselves.

The enemy creates false identities for us through the media, the words of others, our past histories and our own minds. But pay attention to this: *these identities are false.* The identities of insecurity, inferiority and low self-worth are false! They are based on lies, and that means the truth can free us from them.

Knowing your identity is key to your freedom.

Knowing your identity in Christ will free you from all the lies and deceptions about yourself that the enemy is trying to put over on you. But you must choose to believe God's Word to inherit what Jesus has planned for you. You have a free will to choose and believe.

It is crucial for you to know and receive God's Word in order to know your identity. Once you know who you are in Christ, nothing and no one can shake you.

If you know Jesus, here's what the Bible says about you:

Who Am I?

- I am God's child—**John 1:12**
- I am blessed and will have joy—**Ephesians 1:3**

- I am not an accident. I was chosen before the creation of the world—**Ephesians 1:4**
- I am holy and blameless—**Ephesians 1:4**
- I am adopted into God's family—**Ephesians 1:5**
- I am accepted. No matter who rejects me, I am accepted by God—**Ephesians 1:5**
- I am redeemed! My chains are broken by Jesus Christ, and I am set free!—**Ephesians 1:7**
- I am forgiven—**Ephesians 1:7**
- I am sealed with the Holy Spirit—**Ephesians 1:13**
- I have a purpose and plan in Christ—**Ephesians 1:9, 11**

If you know Jesus as your Lord and Savior, the Bible is very clear: your identity is that of a daughter, a princess of the King of kings! You can receive that identity and learn to walk in it. You are beautiful and loved by God.

If you don't know Jesus as your Lord and Savior, you can invite Him into your heart with one simple prayer. You only need to believe when you pray the prayer on the following page (turn there now):

Dear Lord Jesus,

I believe that You are the son of God. You died on the cross for my sins. You rose from death on the third day, and through my faith in You and in Your resurrection, I have eternal life. Please forgive my sins. I repent from all my sins, and from this day on, I make You the center of my life. I praise You for making me your princess. In Jesus' name I pray.

Amen.

If you prayed this prayer with faith, you are born again! You are a child of God. Your sins are forgiven. God is giving you a new heart and a new life. Now is a perfect time to begin to know your true identity. What you have believed in the past about yourself may not line up with the truth. It is time to embrace reality. You are special in the sight of God. You are beautiful and precious. You are God's masterpiece. You are fearfully and wonderfully made. You are created in God's own image. Any negative belief you may have about yourself is from your enemy, the devil.

From today on, study the Word of God through reading the Bible and believe who you are in Jesus Christ. Welcome to the family of God.

Dear Lord Jesus,

Please show me my identity in You. Please tell me who I am in You. I believe that You have a plan and purpose for my life. I open my heart to receive what You have for me. I know that everything You have for me is good, and I welcome my identity in You. I cancel the voice of the enemy, in Jesus' name, right now, so that I may hear God's voice.

Amen.

He has *blessed us* in the heavenly realms
with every spiritual blessing in Christ.
For *he chose us* in him before
the creation of the world
to be *holy and blameless* in his sight.
In love he predestined us for adoption
to sonship through Jesus Christ,
in accordance with his pleasure and will—
to the praise of his *glorious grace,*
which he has *freely given us* in the One he loves.
In him *we have redemption* through his blood,
the forgiveness of sins,
in accordance with the riches of God's grace
that he lavished on us.
With all wisdom and understanding,
he made known to us the mystery of his will
according to his good pleasure, which he *purposed*
in Christ,
to be put into effect when the times reach their
fulfillment—
to bring unity to all things in heaven and on earth
under Christ.
In him *we were also chosen,*
having been predestined according to the plan of him
who works out everything in conformity
with the purpose of his will,
in order that we, who were the first to put our
hope in Christ,
might be for the praise of his glory.

And you also were included in Christ
when you heard the message of truth,
the gospel of your salvation.
*When you believed, you were marked in him with
a seal,*
the promised Holy Spirit,
who is a deposit guaranteeing our inheritance
until the redemption of those who are God's
possession—
to the praise of his glory.
EPHESIANS 1:4–14, *emphasis mine*

Chapter 3

Do You Know How Special You Are?

You are special and beautiful,
even though you may not feel that way.

My frame was not hidden from you
When I was made in the secret place,
When I was woven together in the depths of the earth,
Your eyes saw my unformed body;
All the days ordained for me were written in your book
Before one of them came to be.
PSALM 139:15–16

My Precious Child,

Everything about you is beautiful to Me, says your Maker. I planned and created you with love. You are loved. You are cherished. You are not an accident. I created you in My own image. You are My masterpiece.

I know there are many times you don't feel special. Many times you may not feel cherished, even appreciated. But when you fix your eyes on Me, and seek my thoughts, not the thoughts of men or others, you will start seeing yourself through My eyes. Then you will feel My love for you.

> *Dear Lord,*
>
> *Thank You for creating me in Your own image. Please forgive my complaints about my appearance or other parts of myself. I have often complained about my looks and wished to look different in the area of _____ [name it, whether it's your weight or your nose or your wrinkles]. Today I repent of my complaints. Please teach me to see myself through Your eyes. Please set me free from any bondage in my mind that I am not aware of, in Jesus' name.*
>
> *Amen.*

When you truly know your identity in Me and feel safe and secure in Me, then you will be free from other people's opinions and negative criticism. I invite you today to run to My arms and feel the depth of My affection for you.

What Do You Believe About Yourself?

During one of my recent visits to my family in Turkey, I was able to spend some quality time with my brother and his wife. She is thirty-one years old and a very pretty woman. But every time I told her "You are very pretty," she would roll her eyes as if I was lying. On top of that, she would call herself names all the time. She would say, "I look like a squirrel. I look like this. I look like that." She always had something negative to say about herself.

I stopped her once and asked her, "You don't believe me when I say you are beautiful, do you?"

Her eyes got wet immediately. I continued, and said to her, "You are very pretty, and you should stop calling yourself names!" She admitted that she called herself names. I kept talking to her: "During my conferences, I talk about beauty. I speak to women about finding themselves beautiful. I want to tell you that because of some event in the past, many of those women have false beliefs about themselves. When do you think these false beliefs about yourself started?"

Now, I want to ask you the same question: When do you think you started thinking or believing negative things about yourself? Did it start with someone's negative comment or criticism? This is the case most of the time. Or was someone else praised more than you (a sibling, for example), making you feel less or inferior?

I want you to think about it. Whether it's about your looks or something else, ask yourself very seriously when you started wearing those labels.

"You look like a cow," said my father, seeing me for the first time in two years. I responded, "I missed you too, Dad."

My father and mother labeled me with many things all my life—ugly, stupid, an embarrassment. I remember returning to Turkey to attend my grandmother's funeral after not seeing my family for two years. My father was waiting for me at the airport, and the first time I put my foot back on Turkish soil, he said to me, "Wow, you just look like a cow." And I was like, "Thank you, Dad, I missed you too."

People measure each other all the time, and in the process, we give one another labels. Some are neutral, some are good, but many are negative, and we end up labeling each other with things the enemy can use. We label ourselves, as well—it's just the way we are. We sit down and talk, and we measure each other. "Oh, you make this kind of banana bread? I do that too." "Oh, my two kids are going to Harvard." "Oh, twelve years I have been working for this company." Somewhere down the line, you start feeling insignificant and saying, "Oh, I am just a mother, I am just a housewife, I am just a caregiver, I am just a student." And that is labeling too.

God Wants to Remove the Devil's Labels

I grew up with labels in my heart. Whether they're obvious or not, I would bet that you have them too. They may not be the same labels—yours and mine might be very different. But Jesus took them all on the cross and died with them to set you free.

After Jesus removed my labels, He called me to remove the labels of others. My husband and I worked in the inner cities of Florida at the time. We went to the streets and witnessed to drug addicts, dealers and prostitutes. We went to the halfway homes and delivered food and just poured love over people who never knew much about love.

One very precious brother named Roberto, had a label that he was not good for anything. He could never be something. He truly believed in this label.

I was the CEO of a company at that time, and Roberto had recently come out of jail and couldn't find a job. I needed some help, so I hired him. The day I hired him, I gave him four brand-new white polo shirts from Ralph Lauren and said, "Every day, I want you to come wearing these shirts." Roberto started crying because he felt unworthy to clean up! He felt unworthy to become someone. He felt unworthy to change. He thought that value was for someone else, not him.

"Mamma," he told me—he was fifty years old and calling me Mamma—"you wasted your money on these expensive shirts. They are for important people. I am not important."

I said, "You are Roberto. You are very special in God's eyes and mine. God just picked these shirts for you."

He took the shirts, and I noticed that his pants were sagging—pretty typical for his neighborhood! Before I left, I went and pulled his pants up. I said, "You don't wear them to show your boxers."

He said, "Oh, Mamma." I said, "Don't Mamma me. If you want people to respect you, you don't wear your pants like this. Pull them up." And he pulled them up.

Roberto worked faithfully for me for a long time. He straightened up his life with God's help and opened up three halfway homes. His labels were gone, and he wanted to help others remove theirs as well.

Back then, I also hired a young guy in his twenties who was under house arrest. His probation officer came to me and asked, "Why is a

God does not see people the way we do.
We label people as worthless.
He sees them as precious
and worthy of respect.

nice lady like you wanting to hire this guy? He is nothing. Why? You are wasting your precious time with these guys. These guys are trash." My answer was, "I was like them. I was trash, and God turned me into a treasure. I am paying it forward. Everyone needs a chance."

That officer's words were just one label after another! This is how the world sees people. But God doesn't see people the way we do. In this case, God told me to call this young man "sir." I would go to that young brother and say, "Sir, how are you today?" One day he just started weeping. "Why do you call me sir? Nobody calls me sir."

I answered, "I respect you, brother, because you are trying. God told me to respect anyone a whole lot if they are trying, so I respect you a lot." Over time, his labels started to fall off too. Instead of going back to jail, he went to college!

God wants to name you with His truth and His purpose for you.

When God starts removing our labels, our lives will turn around. God wants to take you to the next level. He wants to remove your labels today. Whatever they are, He wants to remove them from you. Jesus has set you free to live free, and that means living free of the false identities the enemy has created for you!

Whatever insecurities you have, you need to trust and believe God. You need to confess the truth. You need to say, "According to Psalm 139, 'You have searched me, Lord, and You know me. You know when I sit and when I rise. You perceive my thought from afar. You discern my going out and my lying down. You are familiar with all my ways. Before a word comes out of my mouth, You know it.' That means You know me intimately—You know who I really am. That means I'm special to You. And You know the desires of my heart, and You know what I want to be. Psalm 139 says 'You created my innermost being, and You knit me together in my mother's womb. I praise You because I am fearfully and wonderfully made.' That means I really am fearfully and wonderfully made! The labels are wrong. I am not ugly or worthless or stupid. I am a beautiful creation of God."

God wants this truth to become a reality in your life. Did he not take the orphan girl, Esther, and turn her into a queen? God wants to remove the labels from your life that say you are an orphan, you are forgotten or that you don't matter. He wants to name you with His truth and His purpose for you.

My daughter recently went to a training for the mission field, and someone gave her a word from the Lord that her new names are "The Peaceful One, Shalom, the Pure and the Righteous One." She has been through her heartaches and hurts in life, having divorced parents. She had her share of wounds that God had to heal. I tried as a mother to heal her, but it doesn't work that way. Each of us individually needs to go to the Father and ask for our new names, our freedom and purpose. Today may be your day to receive a new name from your Father in heaven, along with your freedom. If the Holy Spirit is leading you right now, take some time and pray to your heavenly Father about these things.

The Power of What We Believe

In the Bible, there's a tragic story in the Book of 2 Samuel. David's daughter, Tamar, was raped by her half-brother Amnon. The Scriptures say that she ran to her other brother's house and lived like a desolate woman the rest of her life. Why? She was the king's daughter! Justice was due to her. All of her riches and privileges were still hers. And yet, all Scripture says about her is that from that time on she lived like a desolate woman.

This shouldn't be your life story. God wants to complete your story with honor and love. He wants you to live like the King's daughter you truly are!

Tamar saw herself as desolate. She believed that label, and it came to define her life. It matters what we believe about ourselves. It matters what labels we accept. If we want to be defined by God's love for us and by our true worth in His sight, we must learn to drop the labels the enemy and the world have put upon us. What we believe about ourselves is powerful.

What do the labels in your life say about you? *Addict, incapable. Stupid and ugly.* These things were spoken over me. Such labels become curses, afflicting us and keeping us under. But for every label the enemy tries to give, God has a true name for us.

Labels And Lies

Powerless. That's a favorite label of the enemy. But Christ tells you, "Abide in Me, and I give you the power. You can do all things through Me. You have the power to do everything, and if you have faith as a grain of mustard seed, you can move mountains." Does that sound powerless to you?

Quitter. I was a quitter. I couldn't confront people, so I would quit instead. I would quit relationships because I wouldn't say how I felt. I would go under a controlling friend for awhile, then suddenly cut the cords and walk away. She wouldn't know why, because I wouldn't talk. I would just run away instead of confronting the situation, because I didn't have a backbone.

Sometime after I became a Christian, God began teaching me how to tell people the way I felt when they would act in a wrong way toward me or tell me to do something that was uncomfortable for me. He set me free from that label.

Are you wearing any of these labels? God can set you free!

Divorced. This was another label in my life. When I started speaking for the Lord, I would think, *How can I go on a platform and tell people that I was divorced twice?* That's how much this label defined me. For many years, I was in love with being in love, but nothing worked. I always chose the same type of men. I had a boyfriend between my two marriages who told me I was fat when I was a size one. He told me I would look perfect if I lost twenty pounds. The lie that I was worthless kept me bound in situations like that until God broke the power of that label over my life. In place of this label, God calls us *Beloved. Accepted.* He brings us into an eternal covenant with Himself, where He is forever committed and devoted to us.

The labels are endless. *No one likes you. Useless. Raped. Abused. Retarded. Gluten intolerant. Abuser. Inferior. Fraud. Pitiful. Alcoholic. Stupid. Gay. Gross. Hated. A mistake. Immature. Unsuccessful. Loser. Wimp. Hypocrite. Adulterer. Failure.*

Maybe, as you read that list, you hear the things you've believed about yourself. Maybe these are the labels you wear. Today, right now, Jesus says, "Give all of them to Me and just become My princess. Give all this junk to Me. Let Me make you beautiful, because you *are* beautiful in My sight."

Agreeing With God Is Empowering God In Our Lives

As I've already shared, it took me forty years to start feeling beautiful. But in a very real way, *God wants you to feel beautiful.* He wants you to love yourself—not in a narcissistic way, but in a way that agrees with God about your value instead of agreeing with the enemy's lies and labels. *God wants you to believe Him about yourself.* You can't love your neighbor as yourself if you do not love yourself. You can't have peace with yourself if you do not love yourself. To love yourself in a godly way is to agree with God about who you are—His beloved, precious, handcrafted daughter.

God wants you to believe HIM about yourself, not the enemy or the lies people have spoken.

One day I was talking to God, and Jesus told me, "I like your personality. You are fun." And I was like, "Thank you!" As you read this, open your heart to receive those compliments from the Lord. Let Him tell you things you never heard from your parents. Let Him tell you, really, who you are in His eyes.

Statistics show that 80 percent of women see themselves as at least fifteen to twenty pounds heavier than they are. Why?

Because something is speaking into your ear and telling you lies.

Now, even as you are reading, is the time to be set free. Jesus wants to set you free, to remove your insecurities and turn you into a truly humble servant. You won't say, "Oh, I am just this" or "I am just that," but you will say, "I am a servant of God. I am the King's daughter. I am His princess, and He lavishes His love over me. I am fearfully and wonderfully made. I have the mind of Christ and the crown of beauty." When you choose to receive freedom from Jesus, you'll agree with what God says. You'll accept the names He gives you and not the labels of the enemy.

It's A New Day

I was born into a house of mourning, and grew up with a lot of gray and earth tones, and dark colors. Even when I was seven or eight years old, my mother would buy me these outfits that were all gray and dark blue and black. In many ways, those colors were a picture of my whole life at that time, and I wore them like a label. I never had a Barbie girlhood.

But let me tell you something: It's a new day. If you come to my house, you'll find that I have a Barbie bedroom. God is giving me my childhood that was lost. He's giving it to me now. And I am enjoying it! I refuse to wear the colors of the old life, so to speak. I have exchanged the enemy's labels for the goodness of God.

I refuse to wear
the colors of the old life.

Whatever the colors and labels of your past, it's a new day. Maybe the enemy has told you that you are gay. Maybe he's telling you that you're ugly and worthless. Maybe he's rubbing your face in past sins. Maybe he's trying to put new labels of shame and guilt on you.

Let me tell you: You are not what the enemy is calling you. *You are not.* It's a lie. If right now you are living a faithful life, you do not need to carry that filth anymore. If you need to repent, repent. Jesus is washing you with His blood right now and telling you that you are free from shame, you are free from guilt. You are free. *You are free.*

Make peace with yourself today. You don't have to be someone else. You are you, and He loves you just as you are. It's time for the labels to fall away. God has named you as His precious daughter.

Lord Jesus,

I confess that I have believed the enemy's lies about myself and have worn his labels. I repent of that today and choose to believe what You say about me. I let go of the labels. I let them fall away. I gladly replace them with Your names for me: I am loved. I am your princess. I am beautiful in your eyes. In Jesus' name.

Amen.

Chapter 4
Emotional Healing is Not Optional!

"But I will restore you to health
and heal your wounds,"
declares the Lord.
JEREMIAH 30:17

My Beautiful Daughter,

Today, I clothe and cover you with My love and peace. I want to restore everything that was stolen from you and heal your wounds. Open your heart to Me and talk to Me. Tell Me the very burdens and struggles of your heart. I AM here to give you peace. I want to give you peace about yourself. I want to give you peace about your circumstances. I AM the Prince of Peace. If you come to Me, to your Maker, I will fill you with joy that surpasses all your understanding.

The LORD is close to the brokenhearted
and saves those who are crushed in spirit.
PSALM 34:18

Dear Lord,

I come to You with my wounds and burdens. I ask You to heal my heart from the very things that devastated and hurt me deeply. I give you my pain and my scars. [List what they are and the cause of them.] I accept and receive the truth that because of Your scars and wounds, I am healed. I receive my healing not only physically, but also emotionally, from You, Lord Jesus. Thank You for Your inner healing of my heart. Thank You for Your blood that was shed on Calvary for my healing and freedom.

Amen.

·······✤·······

He heals the brokenhearted
and binds up their wounds.
PSALM 147:3

Is Healing Possible?

In the last few chapters, we've talked about freedom, identity and labels. But right about now, some of you are asking another question:

Can you be free from your pain?

Is it possible to be not just free, not just renamed, not just brought into God's family, but *truly healed?*

The answer is yes, it is! In fact, for a princess of the King, it's not really optional! We need to be healed in order to represent our Father and to enjoy the freedom He has won for us.

You can be healed emotionally—and in many ways, it's simpler than you may think. Emotional healing takes place when you start receiving.

Recovering From The Unthinkable

Jesus looked at them and said,
"With man this is impossible, but not with God;
all things are possible with God."
MARK 10:27

Pam shared this testimony with me in writing so that I could share it with you:

> *I heard the front door close. I knew what that meant. Mom had left for work, and I would be left with Dad . . . and another night of horror. I had a simple beginning. My father was in the Coast Guard and my mother stayed at home until I was nine years old. I had an older sister and a younger brother. We moved often, so I didn't have any close friends.*
>
> *At the age of nine, I decided I wanted to know where babies came from and asked my mom. She told me to ask my dad. I did. He told me he wanted to teach me to be a wonderful wife for my future husband, so he was going to show me how babies were made. That was the beginning of sexual abuse for me. It was happening to my sister and brother as well, but I was unaware of that at the time. He would wait for Mom to leave and take me to the loft outside in our laundry room. Whatever you're imagining right now, it was that bad. I was raped every day for almost five years. Sometimes I fought, sometimes I didn't, but it was rape just the same.*

We still went to church each Sunday. Dad would go up front for prayer. I would pray the ceiling would drop on his head. It didn't. Therefore, I felt like the Lord wasn't there for me.

When I was nearly fifteen years old, our neighbor started asking what was happening to me. I had never told anyone because Dad would threaten many things as a consequence. Our neighbor had heard screams coming from the loft, and she pestered me until I told her what was happening. Well, God can use nosy neighbors! She took me to the youth bureau, and he was arrested the very next day. I thought all my troubles were over.

Through my teenage years, I didn't feel like I had much worth. I thought using my body was the only thing I was good at and so that's what I did. I became promiscuous. I wanted love but didn't know how to get it. Well, it didn't bring love, and it didn't bring happiness either. I knew I needed to do something differently. So I decided to get married and have children! That would bring love.

At twenty years old, I married a man who had his own wounding. His father had an illness, and Henry had prayed for his healing. His father still died. Henry chose to turn away from the Lord. He was mad that God hadn't healed his father. Henry had anger in him, and it came out many times when he felt I held him at a distance, which was often. I wanted children but not affection. I had my own wounding.

I had two miscarriages, and then at twenty-three, I had our first son. Three years later, I had our second son. I loved being a mom. However, as the years went by, I felt a heaviness and sadness inside I couldn't seem to get past. I tried to push the feelings down, but they kept popping up.

I got a call from my family when I'd reached my early thirties saying my little brother had killed himself. He had become an alco-holic because he didn't know how to deal with our past. Now he had taken his own life. I knew I'd better get counseling to deal with the emotions I was having, and asked my husband if I could get help. He told me it was in the past and to get over it! So I did the next best thing—I went to my hairdresser.

When I sat in her chair, she put her hands on my shoulders, and I could feel the love of God coming right out of her hands. She was a Christian, and she wanted to help me find healing. I was reluctant at first; I didn't think God wanted to help me. After all, I had made some wrong choices in my life. I did want to stop hurting, though, so I let her and another woman from her church pray with me to receive Jesus as my Lord and Savior.

Wow, I felt better! I had someone I could pray to, someone who would love me without wanting anything in return, except to love Him in return. I needed Him and had for a long time. I started going to church to be with other believers and feel closer to Jesus. I dragged Henry with me. He was still hard and angry.

Soon, I couldn't take the anger any longer that was coming from my husband. I wanted God in my home and he didn't. So I decided I would look for a godly man. I went on the Internet and found a man I thought was godly. He was going to leave his wife of thirty years and I was leaving my marriage of seventeen years to have a godly marriage together. The enemy can make wrong sound right!

I told Henry and our sons, who were twelve and fifteen years old at the time, that I was leaving. Our older son said he wasn't going to go to college because everything I'd taught him was a lie. Our younger son screamed, "NO FAIR!" The enemy was taking my family.

Henry went into the back room of his business the next morning, angry at life. He wanted to make his own plans now, with the help of the enemy, when something stopped him. He felt he was put into a trance, and he didn't know if he was alive or dead. He heard a voice say, "She's suffered enough!" It was the Lord speaking to him. The Lord spoke many things to Henry, and he came home to tell me.

I believed all Henry told me that day. He was a lot of things, but he wasn't a liar. I told him I was glad he'd found the Lord; he was going to need Him. I had hardened my heart, and when you block the bad out, you also block the good. I proceeded to say every bad thing I could think of to Henry to make him throw me out of the house. You see, I was leaving my beloved boys behind, and just couldn't bring myself to walk out on them. I wanted to be thrown out, and the Henry I knew would have no trouble doing that after all I was saying to him. But he didn't. He smiled at me and said if I wanted to come back someday, the door would be open.

Who was this man? I knew he was different, and I knew it was God who had done it. So I decided to stay. My heart was still struggling, because I still didn't feel love for Henry.

After three weeks, Henry called me from work and told me the Lord had something to tell to me. God had told Henry I was struggling in my spirit, that He was sending the love and I was blocking it, and that all love flows through Him. I started to cry. Only God would have known this about me. I had been very good at hiding pain, and only God knew it was still there.

I stood in my kitchen and said to the Lord, "I hate Henry, but I want You more than I want me." As soon as I said it, I felt release. I mean, a huge release! Sadness, unforgiveness, unworthiness, pain from my childhood—it was all gone. Henry came home, and I could feel love for him again. We remarried right there in the Spirit.

The Lord called us into inner healing and deliverance

prayer. We've been praying for people for nearly sixteen years now.

In Matthew 11:28, Jesus says, "Come to me, all you who are weary and burdened, and I'll give you rest." That's what He did for me. And restoration! Our older son went to college and became a clinical psychologist. Our younger son is studying to be a dentist. That's restoration! That is God. Jesus restored my childhood and youth. I am free. I am happy. And I am helping those who believe they have no hope for redemption.

Pam's story is just one of many.
All around us, people are suffering
terribly from deep inner wounds.
Perhaps you are suffering.
But healing is possible.

Pam's story continues:

I have to tell you, "Nothing is impossible with our God." You just need to surrender your life to Jesus. You need to stop listening to the lies of the enemy and start listening to God's voice. You need to believe and receive Jesus' healing touch to the deepest and the most hidden part of your heart. Jesus said, "All things are possible for those who believe." Today may be your day of emotional healing.

*The thief comes only
to steal and kill and destroy;*

I have come that they may have life,
and have it to the full.
JOHN 10:10

Receiving Is a Gift!

Receiving is a gift. The Holy Spirit whispered those words to my heart a few years ago. As simple as it sounds, I immediately felt the profound truth in that little sentence. Often we speak about *giving* as a gift. We always quote Jesus about how giving is better than receiving. However, receiving is a gift too, because it takes faith to receive something. It takes faith to believe that you will have something—especially something you have long needed. You need to look through the eyes of faith to be able to accept that gift, whatever it is. So even the ability to receive, in itself, is a gift.

And it is a gift God is making available to every one of us, anytime we will come to Him and believe Him.

Many struggle to receive. But if you can accept receiving as a gift, right now you can be free. You can have your emotional healing.

Let's Do A Little Surgery

When you ask, "Is it really that easy?" you are not at a place of receiving yet. Your questioning is the evidence that you are not ready to receive. You are in the process, but you are trying to analyze and solve it in your mind first.

Dear friend, let me be up front with you: you and your intellect are way too much in the way. The more you question, the more doubt and lack of faith will prevent you from receiving the healing you need.

Healing comes through a two-way communication link with a person at each end: a giver and a receiver. God and you. All you need to do is open yourself up to receive.

Doubt will prevent you from receiving.
You may need to get your intellect out of
the way!
Receiving is a gift.
All you need to do is open yourself up.

If you are finding this too hard to grasp right now, don't worry. In Part 2 of this book, we will deal with emotional healing, freedom and receiving, in greater depth.

For now, though, let's look at a foundational question. Does God *want* you to be emotionally healed?

Is It God's Will For You To Be Emotionally Healed?

What do you think? Is it God's will for you to be healed emotionally?

Just as many Christians don't realize that God really wants them to be free, many don't realize that His will is for them to be emotionally healed. We may think that being emotionally wounded is "bearing our cross" or "being holy." But this is a wrong idea. It is a lie of the enemy. To bear our cross for Jesus means to serve Him even when it is difficult or dangerous. It doesn't mean to continue to carry wounds He has healed us of on the cross!

So what does the Bible really say about this?

First, you need to understand that emotional healing means freedom. Emotional healing equals freedom. With that understood, let's ask the question again, but in a different way.

Is it God's will for you to be free?

Jesus came to set us free!
Free from death!
Free from eternal condemnation!
Free from the devil's dominion!
And more!

Yes and yes, a thousand times! We've already seen this clearly, earlier in the book. "It is for freedom that Christ has set us free" (Galatians 5:1).

I don't know what abuse and tragedy you have been through, but Jesus Christ knows, and He died on the cross for your freedom. You can have that freedom today. Jesus said He wanted us to experience His joy to the fullest (John 15:11). If you don't have freedom, you don't have joy. If you are not free, you are not enjoying your life. You are not living the abundant life He came to give (John 10:10).

Jesus Christ wants to heal you emotionally today. No chain is too big or too strong for God to break. Today may be your day, if you are willing to receive.

What Did The Thief Steal From You?

The thief who comes to steal, kill and destroy (John 10:10) is the enemy of our souls. The thief is the devil. He wants to steal every good thing God intended for us. He wants to steal our innocence. He wants to steal our joy. He wants to steal our sleep. He wants to steal our dreams and visions. He just wants to steal and destroy God's blessings in our lives.

I am well acquainted with this thief. The enemy stole my childhood dreams. He stole my childhood and youth. He stole my innocence when I was molested at age five. I never had a real childhood. I had to grow up quickly and become an adult while I was still a little girl. However, God gave a double portion of my childhood back to me after my thirties. He healed me emotionally and restored my broken past.

What is impossible to you?
What has happened to you
that you don't believe God can fix or restore?
You may need the supernatural touch of Jesus Christ
to be made whole again.
God can restore your joy, your youth,
your childhood and even your innocence,
if you believe and receive.
"Nothing is impossible with God."

Oftentimes, we cannot receive healing until we acknowledge our wounds. Be very intentional about asking what the thief has stolen from you. Make a list. Acknowledge the pain you have felt and still feel over the theft, killing and destruction that has come into your life.

Then, just as intentionally, confess that it is God's will for you to be healed from these losses. Jesus came to give you an abundant, joyful life. The Bible says that we are healed by His wounds and that He came to bind up the brokenhearted (Isaiah 53:5 and Isaiah 61:1).

Without question, it is God's will for you to be emotionally healed. Wherever your wounds come from, you can receive healing and freedom, even today. You simply need to believe God and open your heart.

Dear Lord Jesus,

I thank You that You want me to be free. I thank You for healing by Your own wounds. I thank You for giving me abundant life! Lord, the thief has stolen _____ from me [name the specific loss]. I have suffered destruction and soul murder in these areas of my life: _____ [name the areas]. I need to receive healing from You. I ask You to help me overcome my doubting thoughts and just receive. Thank you that it is a gift. In Jesus' name.

Amen.

If you are a rape victim, pray the following prayer:

Dear Lord Jesus,

I have been suffering since the time of the rape I went through. I need Your supernatural touch for me to be healed and restored. I believe You died on the cross for me and for the sins that were committed against me. I believe that through Your blood, Lord Jesus, You can make me whole again. Today I forgive those who have hurt me deeply. I ask You to cleanse me from all sexual demons and make me a new creation. In Your name I pray.

Amen

Chapter 5

What is Your Purpose?

God gave you a purpose!
Dream according to His will for your life!

"For I know the plans I have for you,"
declares the LORD,
"plans to prosper you and not to harm you,
plans to give you hope and a future.
Then you will call on me and come and pray
to me,
and I will listen to you.
You will seek me and find me
when you seek me with all your heart."
JEREMIAH 29:11–13

My Lovely Daughter,
You are Mine, and I am yours. I know you have many plans and dreams for your life. But I have better plans for you. My dreams for your life are better than your own dreams and visions. My will for your life is better than your own will.

Today I invite you to surrender your will, your plans and dreams, and take Mine instead. I promise you that you will not be disappointed. I will pour My blessings of abundance upon you if you truly give up your plans and trade them with Mine. I always seek your best interests. My plans are not burdensome or hurtful. I am not looking for an excuse to punish you or hurt you. I want to bless you beyond your imagination.

When you seek Me and My will with all your heart, you will find My treasures.

Dear Lord,

I seek Your face. I come to trade my will, my plans and dreams with Yours. I want what You want for my life. I want Your very best for me. With open heart I ask You to replace my dreams and visions with Yours. Please forgive me for seeking my will instead of Yours. I want nothing but Your will to be done in my life. In Jesus' name I pray.

Amen.

Seek first his kingdom and his righteousness,
and all these things will be given to you as well.
MATTHEW 6:33

The Good (But Sometimes Difficult) Plans of God

Once you know your identity in Christ, it is easy to find your purpose! As human beings, living with purpose is a huge part of living with true freedom. But it is not always easy to say *yes* to God.

When I became a follower of Christ, He started pouring into me His will and purpose for my life. In the first years of my walk with Him, I was sharing my testimony mostly in churches. Then I received an invitation to be on TV and preach the gospel to Muslims. I absolutely didn't want to preach to Muslims! I had a tragic past in an Islamic culture. I didn't want to face it and deal with the hostility of my own race.

My first pastor had taught me that if I was asked to do something I didn't want to do, I could say, "I will pray about it." That is exactly what I told the TV channel Kanal Hayat.

Two years passed. They didn't call to ask if I had prayed, and to tell you the truth, I didn't pray about it at all. I knew I didn't want to do it. I was like Jonah. I didn't want to go and share the good news with hardheaded Middle Easterners who would tell me the Bible was altered, that Allah had sent the last book, the Quran, which was perfect; and that calling Jesus the "Son of God" was and is blasphemy. I didn't want to deal with them. I didn't want to debate or argue. I was happy in my life.

God chased after me for almost two years. One morning, as I was having my devotional time with Jesus, God started dealing with my heart.

(Thank God for our private times with Him. Where would I be if I hadn't had that quiet time with my Lord?)

He started asking me, just like He asked Peter, "Do you love Me, Işık?"

I answered, "I love You, Lord."

Jesus asked me again, "Do you love Me, Işık?"

I answered again, "I love You, Lord. I love You with all of my heart, mind and soul."

Jesus asked me a third time, "Işık, do you love Me?"

I couldn't control my tears by that time. I answered, crying, "I love You, Lord. You know I love You. I love You so much that I would die for

You." That last bit was what a good Muslim would say. But I was not a Muslim anymore.

Jesus answered me, "I don't want you to die for Me. I want you to live for Me."

I knew immediately what Jesus wanted from me, but still didn't feel ready to go to the Muslim world.

I told the Lord, "I have no burden for them. If You want me to preach the gospel to them, You need to give me Your burden."

At that very moment, God gave me His burden. It was so strong that I couldn't carry it. I was filled with great anguish for Muslims, as Paul stated about his own people in Romans 9. I was on the floor on my face, weeping with uncontainable grief as I saw the faces of Muslim men and women. I begged the Lord to take the burden away from me. It almost felt like my heart had turned into wax and melted within me, as the psalmist once said. I was seeing the faces of Fatmas, Husseins, Abdallahs, Moham-meds, Aisas, and more.

Then Jesus said, "I will give you a burden that you can carry."

As soon as I was able to walk, I ran to my husband, who was praying in his closet. I interrupted his prayer and told him what had happened. I was still crying. I told him I needed his blessing to do what God had called me to do, as he was my covering.

My husband said, "Honey, I know you are called for your people. You have my blessing. How can I stand against the will of God?"

Then I went up to my daughter, who was about twelve years old at that time. I told her I was going to preach the gospel on TV to the Muslims and that there was a risk involved. I told her my face was going to be on TV and we were going to have many enemies.

My daughter answered, "Mom, you always taught me that fear could not stop us from doing what is right. You always do what is right. I trust Jesus in you."

As soon as I finished my talk with my daughter, the phone rang and it was the president of the TV channel. I was speechless at God's timing. We had not talked about the possibility in two years, and now they were calling only minutes after I had surrendered to God!

In a short period, we started taping programs that would change lives for eternity. Six years from that morning, as I look back, I see the divine purpose and plan of God in my life, and I am in awe.

Our Purpose In The Plan Of God

Back in chapter 2, we read Ephesians 1, about our identity in Christ. There, it says we were called and chosen for Christ.

In Ephesians 2:10, we are told even more about our purpose:

> *For we are God's masterpiece.*
> *He has created us anew in Christ Jesus,*
> *so we can do the good things*
> *he planned for us long ago.*
> EPHESIANS 2:10NLT

Every Christian has a purpose! Every princess in the kingdom is chosen by God for a specific task. Not every purpose is dramatic. Not every calling comes in a dramatic way. But God has something for each of us to do and be. And sometimes it is the "quiet" callings that end up making the biggest impact on the world around us.

I believe we instinctively know that we were born with purpose, even if we are not Christians. We all desire to be special. We all want to matter, to have significance. That is the cry of our hearts. It is why we dream.

In fact, many times our dreams can tell us a lot about God's purpose for us. The more we get out of our flesh and walk after the Spirit, the more true this becomes. That is why Psalm 37:4 says that if we delight ourselves in the Lord, God will give us the desires of our hearts.

Our Dreams Are Precious To God!

When I was a child in Turkey, I used to watch *Little House on the Prairie* all the time. In one episode, there was a wedding in a white little church in the country. I started shouting, "One day I will get married in a church just like this one!" My mother rebuked me, saying, "We don't get married in a church. Church is for infidels. Christians get married in a church."

I started crying. "I will get married in a church. I want to get married in a church."

Approximately twenty-five years later, I was about to walk down a church aisle as a Christian bride. Right before I started walking down the aisle to be married for the first time in Christ, my Muslim mother reminded me of my childhood prophecy. "Do you remember when you used to say, 'I will get married in a church'? Look at this."

I smiled at her and said, "Yes, Mom. Jesus ordained this day."

Many girls dream of becoming a princess one day! Their dream reveals God's truth about them. *What is your dream?*

It is nearly every little girl's dream to become a princess one day. Why? Probably because being a princess is like the ultimate declaration and endorsement of how special a girl can be. We girls grow up with princess tales, prince charmings, and happily-ever-afters. We all dream that one day we will fall in love with the man of our dreams. (Of course, that happened to me twice and ended in disaster! Thankfully God's dreams are better than ours sometimes.) Most of us dream of having the happiest and most meaningful life possible. The world gives us this dream. Even God gives us this dream.

I have some single girlfriends who are made to feel really uncomfortable by their loved ones just because they are single at a certain age. They are treated like handicaps by their families. I am a mother of a teenage daughter, and I hope she will marry the man of her dreams one day. She tells me she doesn't dream of a man, so she will not get disappointed! But as a mother, I pray for her future husband without ceasing.

The truth is, though, we are not really looking for a husband. We are looking for a purpose. *Significance* is the word. We all look for our significance. I had been looking for significance all my life, and once I embraced my identity in Christ, I didn't need to look for significance anymore.

I didn't need to look for people's applause to make me feel special. I was special regardless, because of who I was, and am, in Christ.

God does have good works for us to do. For some of us, that might mean getting married and having a family. For some it means working in the media or ministry, and for others, it might mean painting, working in an office, writing or selling shoes. We are all different. We all have different callings.

But for all of us, significance is ultimately found in our identity in Christ, not in what we do. What we do may change over our lifetimes. Some of our dreams may have to be released and replaced, but we will always have the love of God. We will always have His faith in us. We will always have the significance He bestows on us as His daughters, His princesses, His bride.

Ask the Lord to reveal your purpose to you. Ask Him to give you a vision for your life and the good works He has for you to do. But even more than that, ask Him to show you who you are and who He is in your life. Your relationship with Jesus is your ultimate purpose for living.

Dear Lord Jesus,

Today I embrace Your plans and purposes in my life instead of mine. I want Your will to be done. Your plans and dreams are much better than my own dreams. I ask You to reveal Your plans for my life and give me an obedient heart to yield to Your will. In Jesus' name I pray.

Amen.

part two

Set Free

Finding Real Freedom In Christ

Shattered Dreams

Something happened to our childhood dreams
Once they were white and powder pink
They were only dressed in silk
They smelled good like a blueberry muffin
Or chocolate chip cookies just out of the oven
Then something happened.
They were ripped apart and shaken
They got dirty, stained and shattered.
Their smells changed, their colors faded
The feelings saddened, our faces were darkened
And we forgot all about our dreams.
Our precious childhood dreams
Became the saddest stories of our lives,
Stories we never mention
Until we remember them and make peace
We all were in our own dungeons
We were all captured and imprisoned
The enemy held us hostage
We desperately needed to be ransomed
Until the Redeemer came into our lives
We were chained and lived under bondage

Chapter 6

You Have A NEW Name

*No longer will they call you Deserted
or name you Desolate, but you will be called
Hephzibah, and your land Beulah;
for the LORD will take delight in you,
and your land will be married.
As a young man marries a young woman,
so will your Builder marry you;
as a bridegroom rejoices over his bride,
so will your God rejoice over you.*

ISAIAH 62:4–5

My Sweet Princess, My Treasured Possession,

I love you with an everlasting love. I feel your pain. None of the injustice and abuse you have suffered was hidden from My eyes. When you cried, I cried with you. When you were hurt, I hurt with you. I carried you in My arms even though you felt all alone. Even though you felt no one cared, I cared and understood your pain. When everything you have suffered caused you anger, I understood you. I have been waiting patiently all this time for you to return to Me. Only I can cure your pain and give you a new destiny. Come to Me. Just come to Me and release your pain to Me. I will heal you and make you whole. I will remove your shame and crown you with joy.

Dear Lord,

You know everything about my life. You know my past. You know my pain. Today I give all of my pain and hurt to You. Lord my God, I receive Your healing and Your plans for my life. I will no longer live in despair and hopelessness as a desolate woman. I receive Your new name for me. I am Your bride. I receive Your love. Please forgive me for rejecting Your hand to rescue me from my desolate place. I thank You for seeking me out and wanting to help me. I love You, Lord Jesus. It is in Your mighty name I pray.

Amen.

One Of The Saddest Stories In The Bible

During my first twelve years of ministry, I used to state that there was not a single unfinished or incomplete story in the Bible. Well, I was wrong. One day I was reading about King David's life in 2 Samuel 13. There, I found an incomplete story—and a terribly sad one. It is the story of Tamar, the king's daughter.

Tamar was a young princess, the daughter of King David. She was beautiful, kind, and full of hopes and dreams just like every young girl. She was a virgin. She was saving herself for "the one." She had a romantic dream that one day she would marry a young man, most likely a prince or someone special who would sweep her off her feet and write her the most beautiful love letters. He would come to see her even if it meant a day's ride on horseback to see her face only for a single minute. He would bring her the most beautiful roses, picked by hand for her. He would serenade her by her window at night.

Tamar had her father's attributes and good qualities. She was delicate and sensitive to others' needs. She was a special girl. On top of that, Tamar had it all. She had been born into every girl's most wanted dream: she was a princess. She wore royal robes and always looked amazing. Her voice was sweet, as it reflected her tender heart.

But one day, the most feared tragedy that can happen to any girl happened to Tamar. Her dreams were shattered, and her heart was broken. Her destiny was changed and her royal robe was torn into pieces.

How did this happen? Her half-brother, Amnon, wickedly desired to have her in his arms. His lustful obsession consumed and controlled him. With his friend's advice, he started plotting a way to get her into his bed so he could satisfy his lower-than-animal instinct. He lost sleep over it until he hunted and devoured his prey. This time, the prey was a sister, and the vicious animal was a brother.

Amnon pretended to be sick and lied to his father, the king, requesting that his sister bring him some food and allow him to eat from her hand. His father didn't see the evil plan behind the pretense. Tamar, in all her innocence and compassion, brought the meal to her brother without knowing he was her worst enemy. Then she experienced the darkest moments of her life. The moments that would change her wonderful life and turn her youthful joy into an old maid's mourning. She was raped by her brother.

As if that was not enough torment, Amnon then threw her out of his presence. He hated her deeply after the deed was done. He threw her out like a piece of trash or a worthless napkin he had used to clean his hands.

Tamar had been doing nothing but good to her brother. She was young and full of hopes and dreams. Then suddenly, her dreams were shattered by a brutal tragedy. She was humiliated. She was denied justice. King David didn't do anything about it. Her rapist paid no consequences for his crime. Eventually, Amnon was murdered by another brother, Absalom, for his evildoing. But Tamar was never restored. She was ignored. Her pain was ignored. She was abandoned. Scripture says she lived like a desolate woman all of her life.

Tamar begged Amnon not to let her go after he raped her. Physically and emotionally hurt, violated and traumatized, she put every effort into surviving and pleaded with Amnon to marry her so she could at least keep her dignity. But Amnon denied her any reconciliation or comfort.

It's interesting that the story says Amnon hated her after the rape. Actually, without knowing it, he hated himself and the ugliness of the very sin in him. Men send me messages from the Muslim world who are abusers, woman beaters, and even murderers or rapists, and they hate themselves. As a result, they hate their victims for reminding them of who they really are.

Tamar tore her royal robe and ran in despair and pain. She left her father's palace and chose a destiny much different than what her Creator had planned for her. She went to another brother's house and lived all her life as a desolate woman—unmarried, barren, empty, without joy or happiness.

There is no victory in Tamar's story. There was no vindication or restoration for her. The revenge taken by Absalom only glorified the pain. There was no healing. There is only one sentence that explains all her grief and misery: "She lived as a desolate woman all her life" (2 Samuel 13:20).

Tamar lived as a victim, not a victor. She did not overcome the tragedy. The tragedy overcame her.

Tamar did not overcome tragedy. Tragedy overcame her.

Maybe today you are living like Tamar—desolate because of a horrific tragedy in your life years ago. Perhaps you are going through life chained up by past hurts. Or maybe you are wearing the chains of self-hatred that come from your own sins. You know in your head that you are forgiven by the blood of Jesus, but you are not really free.

I must tell you that the enemy comes to steal, kill and destroy, and he wants to use the tragedies and sins in our lives to steal our years. He wants us to waste our lives, stuck in the past or in incidents and memories that hurt us deeply. The devil knows that if he binds us to our painful past, we will be paralyzed and will fail to live to our full potential—to live the life God has intended for us.

There is healing for you. It only takes receiving. And receiving is a gift!

You may be going through something today that looks unfair and unjust. You may have been abused and abandoned brutally, just like Tamar. Perhaps the person who committed the crime against you has not paid any penalty or even shown any remorse or repentance. No one has asked your forgiveness or even acknowledged the wrongdoing that you had to suffer.

But God has a different plan and message for you. He is near to you and wanting to hold you in His arms if you will just receive His love and healing. Receiving is a gift. Many people don't know how easy it can be to receive God's love and healing. It only takes receiving.

In Part 1 of this book, we looked at the issues of freedom, identity, labeling, purpose and emotional healing. In Part 2, we're going to dig deeper into the specific chains that can bind us—and we're going to find the way to be truly free.

The words that summed up Tamar's life do not need to sum up yours. Instead of desolation, you will live a life of freedom, purpose, and joy.

> *"The nations will see your vindication,*
> *and kings all your glory;*
> *you will be called by a new name*
> *that the mouth of the LORD will bestow.*
> *You will be a crown of splendor in the LORD's*
> *hand,*
> *a royal diadem in the hand of your God."*
> ISAIAH 62:2–3

Freedom from Desolation (Encore)

I created you to be my princess
My heart leaped with joy
When I saw your face
I loved looking at your little hands
I hemmed you in the secret place
I gazed upon your eyes
And planned a future for you full of happiness
I picked the color of your hair
And selected your frame carefully
I created you to be my princess
When you fall and hurt
I will hold you, carry you, and heal you
I created you to be my princess
Always sweet and true
Always near to my heart
Forever with me, I created you to be
The special one:
My beautiful princess.

Chapter 7

No More Living in the Past

Forget the former things;
do not dwell on the past.
See, I am doing a new thing!
Now it springs up; do you not perceive it?
I am making a way in the wilderness
and streams in the wasteland.

Isaiah 43:18–19

My Precious Daughter,

I have prepared an incredible future for you with much joy, healing and restoration. I made a new path for you that has My blessings for you. I don't want you to stay chained in the past. I want you to go forward and enjoy each day with Me. I want you to look to the future with excitement instead of fear. If you make a decision today to stop thinking about and replaying the past, I will hold your hand, and we will go to the place I prepared for you together. I love you, and I want you to receive what I have in store for you.

Dear Lord,

I release my past to You today. I am asking You to remove any pain and any fear that is attached to me from my past. I will only speak about my past when I am giving my testimony to glorify Your name. I will only think about my past trials, abuse and tragedies to think of Your goodness and remind myself how far You have brought me. Please forgive me for fixing my eyes on my past. Forgive me for allowing the enemy to steal my days by staying chained to my past. From today on, I will fix my eyes on You and your goodness. In Jesus' name I pray.

Amen.

No eye has seen, no ear has heard, and no mind has imagined what God has prepared for those who love him.

1 CORINTHIANS 2:9NLT

Where Do You Live?

Coming from an abused background kept me in the past for a long time. I was chained to my past and didn't even know it. God spoke to me one day and said, "From now on, you are only going to talk about your past when you share your testimony, or to glorify and thank Me for how far I have brought you. Other than that, I don't want you to ever talk or think about your past. It has no power over you."

The more you speak or think about your past, the more you are chained to it, and the more it has power over you. God wants to set you free from the bondage

Many people live in the past. *I was one of them!*

of the past today. If you are chained to the past, you cannot live in your present or have hope for your future. The thief, who comes to steal, has purposed to steal your present and your joy by using your past. Only you, with your free will, can put an end to that.

What Tense Do You Speak In?

When I minister to people, one of the first things I notice is what tense they speak in. Most of them speak in past tense—*did, was, were,* etc. A lot of hurt people speak about what happened many years ago. It doesn't matter how old they are, they seem to not be able to overcome their past hurts and trials. I meet people in their seventies or even eighties who are still hurting over things from their childhood.

I recently held a Freedom Conference in the United States, and during the altar call, an eighty-four-year-old woman came and wept on my shoulders and told me about all the abuse and suffering she went through when she was a child. I prayed with her, and she felt a release for the very first time in her life. This is why I do the Freedom Conferences!

My mother lived all her life in the past, and she is still living in the past. Every time I see her, the entire content of our talks is about the events that took place many moons ago. When I brought this to her attention, she was in shock at acknowledging the truth. She couldn't believe this was something she had been doing nearly all her life! It is the same way with a lot of people. Especially when anyone says "the good old days," you can hear that they live in the past. It is a very sad statement, really.

Many people are living chained to a host of negative things from the past, and most of these are related to their childhood. This is the very reason the first thing any therapist or psychiatrist is interested to learn about is your childhood. According to the statistics, 90 percent of divorces take place because of a tragedy or abuse that occurred before the age of eleven.

Daughter of God, you cannot live in your past and hope to be a conqueror in your future. You cannot look back and walk forward without walking into something or stumbling and falling. I recently heard someone say, "The enemy doesn't know your future. This is why he wants to keep you in your past."

It is for freedom that Christ has set us free. Therefore, we must become free of the past.

I was chained to my past for many years. I would remember again and again (and talk about again and again) how my first husband beat me up, spit on me and kicked me on the floor. I used to remember all the time how my mother mistreated me, had nervous breakdowns, and verbally and physically abused me when she found out about my father's ongoing affairs with other women. My mind used to list and relist all the horrific events I had been through in my life. And I used to feel sorry for myself.

You might be thinking I had a right to feel that way. But let me tell you something, sister: replaying past events opens a huge door to the enemy, and opens it *wide*. And he loves to throw a pity party alongside your personal old movie reel.

Getting Free From Bondage

My past was a major area of bondage in my life. I have learned that I have to *want* to be free from it. It is a deliberate choice.

The first step to freedom from bondage of the past is to acknowledge the chain and receive God's freedom. (Remember, receiving is a gift. You don't have to work for it or try hard. You just open yourself to Him and allow Him to give it to you.) I prayed to be set free from my past. And I was set free by Jesus.

I would like to stop and underline a very important point here. When we are delivered from any bondage, it doesn't mean the enemy is not going to bring it back up to tempt us. After any deliverance, the person who has been delivered has an incredible responsibility and assignment to protect her freedom from the enemy. So when the enemy continuously brings up your past and throws scenes at you, you need to be aware of what he is trying to do and reject it. Being delivered and free doesn't mean the thief is going to stop trying to steal from you!

The freedom walk is a daily walk. It is a daily stand and a daily choice. This is why we need to abide in Jesus. "Abide in me, and I will abide in you" (John 15:4). In other words, "Stay with me, and I will stay with you. Be in continuous connection with me."

Need a New Start?

When we invite Jesus into our hearts and surrender our lives to Him, He gives us a new heart and a new life. But God doesn't erase our memories. We might wish He would erase all the painful, hurtful and wicked memories from our minds and put a new memory card inside our brains so we only remember what is good, innocent and noble, but it doesn't happen that way. The devil, the enemy of our souls, knows that. He knows which button to press to receive what reaction. Unfortunately, many people, including Christians, are toys in his hands.

The enemy will do his best to use your past to steal your future. He builds a huge, gloomy castle on the foundation of our painful past, then does his best to keep us trapped there. Many people cannot go any further in the Christian walk than where they are now. They are crippled and paralyzed just because they listen to the devil's lies instead of God's truth, and they live under bondage all their lives. Many speak and preach or teach on freedom in Christ while they are trying to function in their chains.

You've probably heard of functioning alcoholics or drug addicts. They drink and do drugs, yet can act decently and hold a job for awhile without anyone noticing their addictions. They don't even accept they have an addiction problem because they are functioning while there is a dysfunction in their lives.

In the same way, many Christians function in their dysfunction. They can carry bitterness and anger under a mask of religion. They can live, go to church, and sing praises while there are chains, addictive behaviors and unrighteousness in their lives. People quote "You shall find the truth and the truth will set you free" from John 8:32, yet often they do not live like free people. They get saved and redeemed by the truth, but do not lose their own free will to live in lies.

The good news is, a new start is available to all of us. The Bible says that when we receive Jesus, we are baptized into his death (Romans 6:3). Our past life goes into the grave, and it does not come out! We are resurrected with Christ to live a new life. That is why Paul says we are "new creations in Christ" (2 Corinthians 5:17). We are not the "old man" anymore; we are the new man! But we still have to choose to live in this new life. It is always available to us, but it is our choice to put off the old and put on the new.

> *That you put off, concerning your former*
> *conduct,*
> *the old man which grows corrupt*
> *according to the deceitful lusts,*
> *and be renewed in the spirit of your mind,*
> *and that you put on the new man*
> *which was created according to God,*
> *in true righteousness and holiness.*
> EPHESIANS 4:22–24NKJV

God says when we are in Jesus, we are "holy and beloved" (Colossians 3:12). That is a new way of life and a new identity! And it comes to us as a gift. We have to receive it. But it is a gift.

Freedom From The Past Is A Choice

If you are in Christ, you are the King's daughter, His princess. But the most important question is, are you living your life as the King's princess? Or do you have the title and the royal crown, but are still living your life like Tamar, who couldn't get past or overcome the hurts and tragedies of her life?

You have your own will to choose. You have a choice and a decision to make about your past. And then the next choice. And the next. You will continuously need to make the same choice again and again as the enemy comes and throws his fiery darts at you.

But there's no need to be afraid. God has called you to a glorious future. You only have to stand in what He has already done.

But one thing I do:
Forgetting what is behind
and straining toward what is ahead,
I press on toward the goal
to win the prize for which God has called me
heavenward in Christ Jesus.
PHILIPPIANS 3:13–14

Freedom From Your Past

I looked from the window
To the same view I have seen every day
Gray and dark clouds I saw
From the eyes of hurt
Without any hope, sparks, or glow
I looked within to my heart
Where I only found deep wounds and sorrow
I cried out for help and looked everywhere
Where to find hope I didn't know
When my heart's cry turned into a prayer
I felt a sudden breeze and a gentle blowing
Amazed I looked for my darkness
That was erased with light and snow
My scars were nowhere to be found
They were all gone with the Master's one breath

Chapter 8
The Power of Forgiveness

Forgiveness breaks the chains of your past!

*If you forgive other people when they sin
against you,
your heavenly Father will also forgive you.
But if you don't forgive others their sins,
your heavenly Father will not forgive your sins.*
MATTHEW 6:14–15

*Jesus said, "Father, forgive them, for they do not
know what they are doing."*
LUKE 23:34

My Beautiful Child,

I love you very much and hold you close to My heart. I want you to release the people who hurt you deeply and forgive them no matter how much they wounded you. I want you to forgive them not for My sake, but for your benefit. I want the poison of unforgiveness out of your system. It is hurting and damaging you more and more as it stays each day. You may not have the power to forgive the people who injured you or betrayed your trust. But I have that power. Ask for My miraculous power of forgiveness. When you pray for the ability to forgive, you are praying according to My will. It pleases Me for you to ask this, even if it means forgiving the unforgivable or forgiving someone who does not deserve your forgiveness. I love you so much that I want to set you free from this chain of bondage.

Dear Lord,

Please help me to forgive. I need Your help desperately to clean my heart from any bitterness and resentment toward people who have hurt me and wounded me deeply. I confess that I don't have the power to forgive them. I can only do it with Your help. Please bless those who wounded me and betrayed me. I don't want to seek revenge or wish any punishment for them. Please, You too forgive them and show them mercy. I ask You to fill my heart with love and compassion toward those who are mean, hateful and hurtful toward me. In Jesus' name I pray.

Amen.

"I hate my mother and I will never forgive her!" Laura shouted.

"I Will Never Forgive!"

During a Bible study I was leading, where we were studying the Scriptures on forgiveness, Laura shouted, "I hate my mother! And I will never forgive her!" At first we were all quiet. Then everyone's eyes were on me.

I knew what to tell her. But I didn't want to do it in the flesh. Do you know that we can tell the truth in the flesh? We can! And many times we fail in this way. At least, *I* have failed many times by telling the truth in the flesh and accomplishing nothing!

Laura had just begun attending our Bible studies. She was Jewish, and at the beginning she hated to hear the name of Jesus. But she kept coming. She said she liked how loving our little group was, and it attracted her to come. She was in her fifties. Just by looking at her, you could tell she'd had a rough life with many regrets. She looked a lot older than her age, but I saw a little girl in her who was hurting terribly.

Even though what she said about not forgiving her mother sounded terrible to all of us Christians (since we are convinced we know the right thing to do), I decided in my heart not to correct

Sometimes we need to keep our mouths shut!

her publicly. However, as in every fellowship, we had our own share of legalistic, dry and religious ladies. Carla was one of them. She jumped up and said to Laura, "You must forgive your mother, dear. The Bible says if you want to be forgiven, you must forgive. If you don't forgive your mother, God will not forgive you. It is as simple as that."

Laura shouted all the more, "I don't care! Don't you hear me? I will never forgive my mother! I don't care what you think. I don't even care what Jesus thinks. My mother is a horrible person. The things she did to me shouldn't be done to any girl. I hope she will burn in hell!"

At this, I stood up and hugged her. She broke down in tears and then started sobbing violently. I rocked with her for a long time.

At that point, we all knew the Bible study was over. I hugged her and cried with her. Her pain was so great that it was almost tangible to me. I prayed in my heart that the Lord would give me the right words to comfort her and minister to her. The Lord spoke to me gently and told me to keep hugging her and pouring love on her.

We stayed like that until everyone left. My husband walked each one to the door gently and wished them safe travels. Then he left us alone in the living room. He went to our bedroom. I knew he was praying for me to find the right words.

The Lord told me to keep hugging her and pouring love on her.

When Laura stopped sobbing, I released her from my arms. Her eyes were swollen. Mine were too. I made up my mind that I was not going to say a single word unless I knew for sure the Holy Spirit was leading me. I remained silent. I remembered words I had once heard from Chuck Swindoll: "Ministry is simply just being there." I just wanted to be there without trying to fix everything, which I had no power to do anyway.

Laura tried to say something, but couldn't. As soon as she tried to talk, she started weeping. After a long pause, she said, "No one knows what she did to me. I was nine years old, and she started selling me to men. She started taking me to an old man's house. He was in his sixties. He had a big belly. He was a big guy. She used to take me to his house. Then she used to wait in his living room for him to do what he had to do to me. She took me there for years. And then took me to others too. All she would tell me was, 'Now go and be a good girl. Do what he tells you to do.' This is why I hate people telling me to 'be a good girl.' I hate it. I hate it. I hate it. I hate my mother. I know she is in a nursing home now. I hope she will suffer terribly and go to hell for what she did to me."

She started sobbing uncontrollably again. I was weeping with her. My daughter was ten years old at that time. I was hurting with this woman who had a little wounded girl inside of her. I cried with Laura and just poured love on her. I didn't pray for her except in my heart, silently. I didn't lecture her about forgiveness. She didn't need a sermon. She didn't need someone hitting her on the head with the Bible. She needed a miracle—the miracle of forgiveness that could only come from Jesus.

Laura kept coming to our Bible studies after that night, and she started reading the Bible on her own. During our Sunday services, I saw her singing and worshiping Jesus. I watched her falling in love with Jesus every day. Religious and legalistic members of our fellowship pressured me to push Laura to forgive her mother. But I couldn't do it. When I asked the Lord about it, He told me, "Remain silent and wait on Me."

Despite all the pressure, I stood my ground and didn't open my mouth. I had to trust the Lord to do His work. I decided not to play the Holy Spirit.

One day, Laura called me and asked if she could come meet me privately. She said this was very important and couldn't wait. I told her to come immediately.

As soon as she came into our home, Laura fell on her knees and cried out loud, "I know Jesus wants me to forgive my mother. I cannot resist Him. I cannot reject His voice. Please pray for me now—that I can forgive her. I need a miracle in my heart."

I prayed for her, and then she prayed. I have to be honest here: even though she wanted to forgive her mother, it didn't happen right away. After three months of praying, she finally felt peace in her heart. She called me and told me she had forgiven her.

After another few months, Laura decided to visit her mother at the nursing home for the first time in many years. She told her mother that she had invited Jesus into her heart as her Lord and Savior and that He had healed her heart and given her miracles of forgiveness even toward her. Her mother marveled at the change of heart in her daughter. She gave her life to Christ as well. Soon after surrendering to Jesus, Laura's mother passed away. Laura didn't grieve. Instead, she celebrated her mother's making it to heaven.

Unless you forgive those who hurt you deeply, you are not free!

Forgiveness Frees!

Sometimes it can seem unfair of God to ask us to forgive those who have truly wronged us. But the fact is, in a very real, tangible way, forgiveness sets us free. In many cases, it even brings physical healing. Many times it also has the power to heal relationships. Unconditional love entails unconditional forgiveness. You cannot say, "I love you unconditionally, but I cannot forgive this and that." We have to follow God's example.

One day, a Muslim man wrote to me saying, "You always speak about the abuse you went through. You always speak about how you were brutally beaten by a man. I am that kind of man. I am a woman beater. Is there any hope for me?"

I broke down in tears as I read his words. God brought much forgiveness to my heart that day toward all men and reminded me of a very important thing:

Everyone needs redemption: the abuser as well as the abused!

Everyone needs redemption. The abused and the abuser, all need the redemption of Jesus Christ! For all of us, forgiveness is the key to receiving and giving freedom.

Lifestyle Forgiveness

Many of us have a significant event in our past that we need to forgive, or a person who continually hurt us whom we need to release. But forgiveness is not just a one-time event. God wants us to live a lifestyle of forgiveness.

Doing so sets us free in many unexpected ways. For one, people who have difficulty forgiving others are also hard on themselves! When we judge others severely, we also tend to be harsh toward our own mistakes. When we live a lifestyle of grace and forgiveness, we take the pressure off ourselves as well.

"I am so stupid. I am so stupid," Leila would say repeatedly. I noticed that every time she made a very small mistake, she would call herself degrading names. She was one of the secretaries of the company I was managing. One day, I invited Leila to have lunch with me. During our conversation, I asked her why she was so hard on herself every time she made a small mistake. I pointed out that she always called herself stupid.

Leila said, "Good point. Thank you for telling me that. I didn't know it was that noticeable." I found the freedom to ask her who had called her "stupid" when she was a child. She answered without a pause, "My dad and my brother. Both of them always called me stupid, and even idiot. My father was very hard on me. Nothing I did to please him was ever good enough."

Leila's father was living far away, but the words he had spoken echoed in her heart and ears over the years. She took her father's example and became very hard, even harsh, toward herself. Because she had not forgiven him, she was bound even more tightly to that attitude of criticism and harshness.

When I helped her see where her attitude of being hard on herself was rooted, she cried. I prayed with her that day, and she broke the agreement she had made with her father's words . . . and she forgave her father. She also repented from believing in lies.

Today, God wants to set you free from being hard on yourself. He loves you with all your imperfections and weaknesses. Don't worry that you won't grow in holiness if you aren't hard on yourself! You will be corrected and perfected through the work of the Holy Spirit as you seek Him and spend time with Him and in His Word. We just get frustrated and exhausted when we try to change others and ourselves with our own strength!

Now, loosen up and give all your needs to the Master. The Potter will mold you, shape you, and use you as you stay soft and keep yourself teachable. *He* is the potter; you are the clay (read Jeremiah 18).

Forgiving Yourself

When we talk about forgiveness, many times the most natural focus is on forgiving others—but we don't realize that we also have to forgive ourselves. Another way to put this is that we have to agree with God's forgiveness of us. The enemy loves to bring shame, guilt and condemnation. Even though we know technically we are forgiven when we ask forgiveness from Jesus, sometimes we have a hard time forgiving ourselves.

From time to time, someone will ask my forgiveness over and over again. This is a sign that the enemy is overly burdening them. One "I am sorry" should be good enough. If we truly repent from a sin or a mistake, once we ask God's forgiveness sincerely, we need to believe that He immediately forgives us.

We need to believe in and agree with God's forgiveness of us. It is an offense to God that we don't believe He truly forgives us when we truly repent!

Believe me when I say that I don't speak to this issue without knowing what I am talking about! Even though God had forgiven me, for a long time I couldn't forgive myself for the many wrongdoings I had committed. I murdered my two unborn babies through abortion, and our family pictures will always be missing them. At that time I was already a young mother, one who was in deep depression and didn't know the true God. But no excuse can justify murder, especially a mother killing her babies in her womb.

The sadness and regret I have carried over the years took my joy and peace away. Despite my repentance, I continuously condemned and judged myself. One day, Jesus spoke to me gently and said, "Don't you know I died on the cross for all the sins of the world, including murder?

Your over-grieving is not from Me but from the one who wants to steal your joy and peace."

Jesus ministered to me that morning in such a special way that I found myself in tears as I received His love and comfort. It is an offense to God that we don't believe He truly forgives us when we truly repent!

Forgive, and you will be forgiven.
LUKE 6:39

But to you who are listening I say:
Love your enemies, do good to those who hate you.
LUKE 6:27

Bless those who curse you,
pray for those who mistreat you.
LUKE 6:28

Then Peter came to Jesus and asked,
"Lord, how many times shall I forgive
my brother or sister who sins against me?
Up to seven times?"
Jesus answered, "I tell you, not seven times,
but seventy-seven times."
MATTHEW 18:21–22

Return To Me

I waited patiently as a man waits for his only love
Every day and every moment
I looked from my window of clouds afar
I just longed for you to return to me
Fall came and leaves burned with passion
My heart ached with each new season
I looked at your ways, your going and coming
Desire filled my heart to have you in my arms
Wondering if you were ever knowing
I waited for you through the snow and spring
When the sun rose for thousands of times
And the stars were singing
Felt like you were going farther from my arms
Still waiting for you to return to me
I asked, "Does she know my love and passion?"
I waited whispering your name
With an unending invitation
While each of my tears sang for years
Echoed in eternity, calling your name
Return to me, oh my love
Please return to me

Chapter 9

No More Pretenses!

What has happened to your joy?
Are you truly happy or just pretending?
It is your turn to be happy!

The joy of the LORD is your strength.
NEHEMIAH 8:10

My Beloved,

Are you missing My joy in your life? If you are, then you are out of strength to go on. I want you to be filled with My joy every day in order to live your daily life. My joy is part of the fruit of the Spirit. The more you are filled with My Spirit, the more you will be filled with joy. The more you try to do it with your own strength instead of Mine, the less energy and happiness you will have to go on.

Today I invite you to come to My arms to find rest and joy in My presence. The more you come to Me and ask Me to fill you, the more I will pour My love and joy over you. Then you will have more strength and power to do the things I call you to do.

Dear Lord,

I need Your strength that comes from the joy You have promised. Please fill me with Your Holy Spirit continuously so that I will have the fruit of joy in my heart and life. I have been lacking joy for awhile because of so many things, and from time to time I feel tired and too dry to go on. I am sorry that I have been seeking to find joy in other places, such as my friends, entertainment, eating or shopping, rather than receiving it from You. Please forgive me for that. I acknowledge that the earthly things will only leave me dry. Today I come to You, asking You to fill me with Your joy in the midst of my trials and tribulations and in the midst of the routines of my daily life. I receive Your joy right now. I find my strength in You. In Jesus' name.

Amen.

*Restore to me the joy of your salvation
and grant me a willing spirit, to sustain me."*
PSALM 51:12

Joy Out of Misery

"After all the abuse and the tragedies you have been through, how can you be so joyful?" the interviewer asked

"How can you be so joyful?" the interviewer asked.

me. "I see you always smiling and happy." A Christian minister on TV, she was interviewing me about my testimony—but she looked very sad. The deep lines around her mouth were strong and told her sad story. I could tell she was in depression, and she was not aware of it.

I answered, "Joy is a true miracle of God. He restored my childhood too."

"So how do you get this joy?" she asked. "Some people might say it is easier said than done." She looked angry—upset at me for having joy!

I answered, "It is really simple. We just need to receive it from Jesus. It is His miracle. We must believe and receive it."

The interview went on, but this lady just got more and more upset each time I talked about the joy of the Lord. I prayed for her in my heart. She was not ready or open to receive a word from me or anyone.

Unfortunately, many live a miserable life. They look unhappy like this lady did and cannot hide their misery anymore. But they don't admit their problem or seek help. It's like I say: "The problem is not the problem. Denial of the problem is the problem!"

I have seen many women in depression, and most of them deny that they are. You think you hide it, but your countenance tells a story. It tells about your chains!

But I will sing of your strength,
in the morning I will sing of your love;
for you are my fortress,
my refuge in times of trouble.

PSALM 59:16

I meet a lot of people from different backgrounds and cultures, and they all have this in common: their countenance and the lines on their face tell their story. I feel how desperately they need the freedom of Christ in their lives. I see their invisible chains, and I am deeply burdened for them. Some of them even minister in the name of Jesus, but they are still in chains.

I know their pain. I have been there—where one smile takes all of your energy, where every breath gets heavier as time goes on. If you are in that place, I am praying for you. I am praying for your hurting heart. You are loved. More than you know, you are cherished by the Father who made you. You are His treasured possession.

You can be free!

And because God loves you—because you are His princess—and because He has died to make you free, you *can be free.* Your depression can be displaced by joy.

The Trap of Self-Pity

I stopped feeling sorry for myself a long time ago. God spoke to me and said, "Self-pity is idol worship. When are you going to quit feeling sorry for yourself?" I responded right away and repented. I used to feel sorry for being used and abused. I used to feel sorry about my parents and how awful they were. Oh, there were so many things I felt sorry about, and they were all related to me. But you know that you know when you hear the voice of God! I quit feeling sorry, and what a surprise—there was so much freedom in quitting pity parties!

I quit having pity parties a long time ago! Now it is your turn!

Move on, and don't look back anymore or feel sorry for yourself. You are loved unconditionally!

The Lies That Steal Our Joy

When I was a grown woman, I told my mother that I had been sexually molested by a relative as a child—abuse that went on for two years. Her response was, "I knew that."

In shock, I asked, "You knew about it, and you didn't do anything to stop it?"

She smiled in a sick way and said, "I thought you liked it."

Perplexed, I repeated after her, "I *liked* it? Did I have any say about it or any power to stop it?" I was five years old when it happened!

After my mother told me that, I started believing a lie that somehow I had deserved the abuse and that I must have done something to invite it. Years later, I was sitting with two Christian counselors who were telling me that I was listening to the voice of the enemy. What I believed was a lie. The enemy didn't stop when he took my innocence. He also wanted to torment me for the rest of my life by telling me I had invited sexual abuse at age five.

In that counseling session, I confessed and repented of my sin of believing in the devil's lies that were spoken to me by my mother. She was the mouthpiece of the enemy in that situation. I wept, prayed, and received my freedom from shame, guilt, condemnation and self-hatred. I repented from believing in the devil's lies. At the end, I was free. My chains were broken. The memory of the incident had no power over me anymore.

Usually people who are abused, raped or molested suffer with guilt, condemnation and shame. If you were abused, you need to know it was NOT your fault. Nothing can justify abuse. No one deserves to be mistreated or made to endure violence of any kind.

Other lies can steal our joy as well. Sometimes the devil tells us we were just born a certain way—worthless or messed up in some specific area. Sometimes he claims our past sins were too terrible to be forgiven. Sometimes he tells us that our worries and fears are just too serious to be let go of—that we need to take them seriously. All of these lies steal our joy.

You are loved by God unconditionally.

Tonight, I am praying for you to be healed and made whole completely. I am praying that you will be set free from any shame or guilt. You are loved by God unconditionally. He cares for you. You are not alone. You are special. And if you were the only person on the face of this earth, Jesus would have come and died on the cross for you.

Who has been the mouthpiece of the enemy in your life? What are the lies about yourself that you have believed? Today it is time for you to acknowledge those lies and break the agreement you made with them just by believing in them. Pray a simple prayer of rejecting them and ask God to restore His truth in you.

"Only easy and bad women would laugh out loud," my father said.

Restored!

My father hated for my mother and me to laugh. I was restricted at a young age to smiling, never laughing. "Only an easy and bad woman would laugh out loud," my dad would say. Laughing was a crime in our home. My father would insult my mother and me if we found something funny—which was very rare anyway!

In this and other ways, I was denied happiness at a young age. I was denied laughter. But no story with Jesus Christ in it is ultimately a sad story! My story is a story of restoration in abundance. God has restored His joy in me abundantly.

One day while attending my church, I overheard a lady minister say of me, "She is very spoiled. She keeps giggling and laughing all the time." As soon as she turned, we came face-to-face, and she had no place to run. Out loud, she had just criticized the joy God had given me without knowing my story. I didn't say anything to her about it; we just acted as if nothing had happened and exchanged plastic smiles, as many do in church.

Not long afterward, my pastor asked if I could share my testimony the following Sunday. This was my new church, so I accepted gladly. Each time I testified for Jesus, I felt myself becoming more free.

When the time came for me to go to the pulpit to share my testimony, I saw the minister who didn't like my joy, sitting in the front pew. The pastor announced my testimony as "a surprise treat" for the congregation. I prayed in my heart as I saw her disapproving countenance and her mocking half-smile. I was very insecure back then, and I went to the pulpit with much fear.

Then, as usual, God took over. I am so very grateful for Him helping me each time! As I shared my testimony, I tried not to look at her face so as not to lose my courage. (Actually, what courage? I was a wimp! God made me a warrior later. But I was a wimp at that time.)

At the end, I invited people to the altar to pray if they wanted emotional healing and God's joy to be restored in their lives. The minister lady was the first to throw herself to the altar, weeping uncontrollably. Many people rushed to the altar and went on their knees. I didn't know if I should go and pray over her. I still didn't know if she could receive it from me. I heard the Holy Spirit gently whisper into my ear, "Go to her. Do not be afraid. Just hug her and pour love on her."

I went up to that woman and hugged her. She wept more and more in my arms. She was hardly able to say, "Please pray for me." I prayed for her and held her in my arms.

That day, God restored His joy in her and healed her from many things. Her scars were gone, and she was made whole. For the first time in thirty-five years of her Christian walk, as she told me later, she experienced freedom and joy.

Joy is a fruit of the Spirit and a supernatural gift of the Lord. No matter what we have been going through, when we come to God and open ourselves to receive, we can receive. It is a part of our freedom and a gift freely given.

Dear Lord:

It has been awhile, and I haven't had true joy in my heart. I have been very serious, as I have been fighting many battles in my life. I miss laughing and enjoying life. I come to You, asking You to restore the joy of Your salvation. Fill me with laughter. I need Your joy to have strength in my life. I come against the voice of the enemy that wants to steal my joy with fear, worry, anxiety and with his lies. In the midst of my trials, please give me Your supernatural joy. In Jesus' name I pray.

Amen.

To bestow on them a crown of beauty instead of
ashes,
the oil of joy instead of mourning,
and a garment of praise instead of a spirit of
despair.
They will be called oaks of righteousness,
a planting of the Lord for the display of his
splendor.
ISAIAH 61:3

A cheerful heart is good medicine,
but a crushed spirit dries up the bones.
PROVERBS 17:22

Our mouths were filled with laughter,
our tongues with songs of joy.
Then it was said among the nations,
'The LORD has done great things for them.'
PSALM 126:2

He will yet fill your mouth with laughter,
and your lips with shouting.
JOB 8:21

Chapter 9

Are You Really Free? Getting Free from Lies

If you believe in lies, you are not free. If lies and deception are still in your life, you are under bondage, and you need Christ's freedom. It is time to stop the denial.

*You will know the truth
and the truth will set you free.*
JOHN 8:32

My Lovely Daughter,

You are beautiful in every way in My sight. I created you to be free and happy. I love to see you dance and rejoice in life. I love to see you free like a butterfly. The enemy put shackles on you, and he wants to keep you under bondage. But I want to set you free. I want you to live in truth. My Spirit is called the Spirit of Truth. Lies and deception will only bring you down and chain you. But when My truth comes, it sets you free. Today I am offering you My truth and the freedom that comes from the truth that can only be found in Me.

> *Dear Lord,*
>
> *Please fill me with Your Holy Spirit, which is the Spirit of Truth. I want no lies in my life or in my heart. Please cleanse me and set me free from all the lies of the enemy. I only want the truth. Please forgive me for believing the lies of the devil about me, about my family, and about my future. Today, by the power of the blood of Jesus Christ, I cancel the agreement I have made with the lies of the devil just by believing in them and receiving them. In Jesus' name I pray.*
>
> *Amen.*

Jesus said, "I am the way, the truth and the life. No one comes to the Father except through me."

JOHN 14:6

What Do You Believe?

As a young woman in my twenties, I weighed 115–120 pounds and wore a dress size one when I started dating a young man who told me I was fat and needed to lose at least twenty pounds to be perfect. He tormented me with his negative criticism about my appearance. He would speak nonstop negative words about how I looked. His words weren't really anything new—I already came from a family that spoke down to me at every opportunity. My father thought putting others down and insulting them increased his self-worth and made him superior to them. I was constantly told I was ugly and stupid, and I believed it! If they said I was dumb and ugly, then I was dumb and ugly. I believed in the devil's lies, and agreed with him.

As a result, I had a very poor self-image. I always felt there was nothing attractive about my appearance. I didn't like it, but thought it was the truth.

The ironic thing, of course, was that lots of other people told me I was attractive, but I didn't believe them! It didn't matter how many millions of people told me I was beautiful or pretty, I wouldn't receive it. I had believed and settled in my heart that I was not beautiful.

This settlement followed me even after I invited Jesus into my heart. I remember the day I turned forty-two. I felt like my youth had passed me by and that I had missed it due to my life's struggles. I felt like I'd missed it all without enjoying it. But our God is a God of restoration! Our God loves to give us a double portion of what was stolen from us.

One day, suddenly, the Holy Spirit spoke to my heart and said, "You are pretty. You are young. You didn't miss anything. In fact, today I am multiplying your youth and giving it back to you."

I feel pretty after forty!

I can't explain what happened in my heart at that moment—it was truly a miracle! I jumped to my feet and started singing the song from *West Side Story,* "I feel pretty. I am so pretty and pretty and happy."

(And no, I'm sorry to burst your bubble if you're a fan, but I don't like *West Side Story,* because of its sad ending. Plus, I don't like musicals. I am sorry to disappoint you. But I always tried to be someone else in the past, so I am telling you this with God's freedom!)

Anyway, I started singing this song at my workplace, and all the ladies joined me as if we were redoing the movie. The freedom and joy I felt were overwhelming. That day I was truly set free from the lies of the enemy and filled with a new level of joy that is indescribable.

When you receive such a miracle of joy and freedom, many people won't understand it. A lot of girlfriends joined me in the ministry after that day, floating around like beautiful butterflies and singing "I feel pretty." I can't describe the new level of joy! Some brought tiaras and furs to work, and we were like little girls. Of course, with every miracle of Jesus, there will be cynicism and criticism. There were some religious folks who raised their eyebrows. We can only pray for their freedom.

As it turned out, God wanted to do more than just set *me* free that day.

The "I Feel Pretty" Women's Freedom Conference

In the following months, the "I Feel Pretty After 40" motto spread like wildfire among my friends and other women. Soon after, I was invited to hold a Freedom Conference at a church. At one of the sessions of the conference, I shared my journey of restoration and how Jesus gave me a miracle of joy and freedom.

As I began sharing with the ladies how that now I saw myself for the first time truly through the eyes of Jesus, and realized how beautiful I looked to Him, I saw chains being broken across the room. Then I closed the message with a secular song. Yes, you heard me right, religious people. I made an altar call with the background song "I Feel Pretty." (And I still don't like *West Side Story.)*

I said, "Maybe until today, you too had a poor self-image. Maybe you feel too fat, too short, too tall, too old, too skinny, too this and too that. But today, Jesus is telling you, you are beautiful. You are pretty. You are His princess. You are the apple of His eye. And He wants you to be free."

As the song started playing, I started dancing, and hundreds of women joined me in dancing and singing. Then I made an altar call. "This is not a vanity message. This is not a 'let's all get gorgeous to match the Hollywood standard' kind of message. This is a message of restoration, freedom, joy and truly feeling like God's princesses—what we are created to be as women of God. So I invite you to come to the altar to receive your identity in Christ as God's daughters. Reject the devil's lies that have been spoken over you. Pray and break the agreement you have made with the devil's lies and receive the truth from your Father in heaven."

Many women came forward. They were crying and releasing their pain to the Lord. Many young girls came forth in tears. Many teenagers confessed that they believed in lies and that they were struggling with anorexia and bulimia. I prayed with each young girl who was struggling with her appearance or wrestling with an eating disorder. The deep pain of being chained to the struggle of food is unbelievable.

That day, many were set free and filled with God's joy as they embraced freedom.

"I am free from the bondage of anorexia," she told me.

A year after that conference, I was invited to do another one. At the end of that second conference, a mother and daughter approached and stopped me while I was leaving. The mother was in tears, and she could hardly speak as the tears were choking in her throat.

She managed to say, "From a mother to a mother, I just want to thank you for saving my daughter's life last year. She was anorexic. We tried everything to help her, but it was no use. Finally we decided to bring her to your meeting. Last year at this time, she was set free from anorexia when you made an altar call with 'I Feel Pretty.' Thank you."

Her teenage daughter was in tears too. She said, "I am free from that bondage. Thank you."

As always, I knew who should receive that thank-you! Thank you, dear Jesus, for Your healing, restoration and freedom! As you have worked these things in my life, they can spread to others. You are an amazing God!

"I am sixty-four years old. For the first time, today I feel pretty."

After the altar call at the same conference, a lady came to me. She didn't look well-kept. She had long, greasy gray hair that had not been washed for a long time. Her dress was not very clean, and she truly looked like she had given up on life. Usually these are signs of intense depression.

She said, "My name is Sarah. I am sixty-four years old. I want you to know that for the first time in my life, today I feel pretty. And I have invited Jesus into my heart today. I want to have a personal relationship with Him."

I saw the spark and the joy in Sarah's eyes. I hugged her and whispered, "And my precious friend, today is the end of your depression. It is gone."

She wept on my shoulder and said, "Yes, my depression is gone. These are happy tears. I am happy. I am so very happy. I had almost forgotten feeling happy."

Faith comes through hearing, period. Many of us have great faith in our lies!

The Root Of Our Bondage

Many of us are not free—not *really* free—because we believe in lies. We have heard them; we speak them; we are committed to them. In fact, we have incredible faith in them!

The apostle Paul said, "Faith comes through hearing, hearing the word of God." But today I am telling you that FAITH COMES THROUGH HEARING. PERIOD!

Watch what you hear and what you tell yourself! Like Leila, whose story I told earlier, many people say, "I am so stupid. I can't believe I am so stupid." They might say "I'm so fat," or "I never get anything right. Nothing good ever happens to me." Their words have power!

There is no truth in him. When the devil lies,
he speaks his native language, for he is a liar
and the father of lies.
JOHN 8:44

Lies I Believed

With every fight my parents had, my mother made sure to tell me that men were pigs and none of them were good. She shouted at me, "All men are evil. Don't you believe in fairy tales!" *I believed her.*

When I was a little girl, I was told I was ugly and stupid.
I believed it.
I was told God was impersonal, angry and mean.
I believed it.
I was told no one could love me unconditionally.
I believed it.
I was told I was good for nothing.
I believed it.
I was told the Bible had been corrupted and Islam was the last and perfect religion.
I believed it.
I was told Jesus did not die on the cross, but instead, Judas died in his place.
I believed it.
I was told two women were equal to one man.
I believed it.
I was told women were inferior to men.
I believed it.
I was told it was okay to lie and cheat to serve a higher purpose.
I believed it.
I was told men would get seventy-two virgins when they went to paradise, but there was no equal reward for women.
I believed it.
I was told it was okay to beat up a woman if necessary (in my case that was every other day).
I believed it.

I was told men could have more than one wife, and that was fine with God.

I believed it.

I believed many, many lies before You, Jesus! On the day I was going to commit suicide, I believed life was not worth living. Then You came into my life and revealed Yourself to me, and the Spirit of Truth started living inside of me. And I believed!

I believe You are the Son of God, Jesus, as difficult as it may be for many people to understand. But I believe. And I believe that I am fearfully and wonderfully made. You died on the cross for my sins, and You conquered death so I can have eternal life. It is a free gift of God to all who believe. *I believe.*

Why Do People Lie?

Before Christ, I was a lying machine.

Before I accepted Jesus as my Lord and Savior, I was a lying machine. In my culture, people often tell white lies, and lying for a great purpose is permitted in Islam. My parents are still lying machines. As of today, when my mother is telling me something, I have to ask her, "Are you lying to me right now or telling me the truth?" She is always amazed that I can tell immediately when she is lying.

I grew up like this. My parents trained me to be a liar. Here is the dangerous part of it: when you are so trained to lie, and when the culture and religion you are part of promotes lying—and you are, after all, part of a deception and false religion—a lying spirit blends in with your DNA. It took me years to be set free from the lying spirit after I became a Christian. Even though I wouldn't make up a lie on purpose, I would believe something that was not true about myself, or others, or even God. During my years in the ministry, I have worked with many Muslim-background believers for whom lying is still part of their lives, and they live in much pretense. Yes, I can hear you say, "That is very serious and dangerous." That's true—it is.

Many of us are captive to lies—and in many cases, those are lies *we tell*. We're not just captives to a few lies told to us by the devil, but to a general dishonesty in our lifestyle and thinking. We need to deal with the root of the problem. So why do people lie?

People in general lie for several reasons:
1. To manipulate and control a situation;
2. To be liked or respected, impress others or to look better;
3. To benefit themselves—in other words, to gain something by lying;
4. To protect themselves from a situation, or to either cover up a mistake or transfer it onto someone else.

There are layers under the layers. But underneath them all are two main reasons: power and control.

The devil, or Satan, is called the father of all lies. He tempts people to lie, and with our fallen nature, we are prone to lying more than to honesty. We believe that lying gives us power and control, and so we find it very hard to let go of.

Living In A World Of Lies

"All I did was cheat on my wife . . . why is everybody making a big deal about it?" asked Osman. His wife was in tears, sitting next to him while he talked about the night of his affair. He could not accept that the lies he told himself were not true—that his actions really were a big deal, and that he was not the victim in this situation.

When I first met Osman, he was applying for a job to work for me.

However, he had a pretty ugly track record. He said he had given his life to Jesus about ten years ago. Some said, "Don't hire him. He will bring nothing but grief to you." Others said, "This guy is a pathological liar. Don't hire him." Some (mostly Americans, who are usually very naïve about people from our culture) said, "Our God is a God of grace. Everyone deserves a chance." I followed my emotions and hoped that the love of Christ I would show him would make a change. Well, I was as naïve as my Western friends!

Osman started out great. He appreciated the job and became a valuable worker in a short period of time. After six months, he started becoming high maintenance with his prima donna attitude, and brought much stress to the ministry with his lies and strife. According to him, everyone was jealous of him and hated him. He was living in a world of lies. He believed he was the victim, and everyone was trying to take advantage of him. I have never met anyone professing to be a Christian who was living so deeply in a world of lies, and he spoke and treated his wife as much like a slave as any radical Muslim. My ministry was the only one he left on good terms, as my team and I put every effort into keeping love and peace between us. From one ministry to another, one country to another, he became a wanderer, dragging his poor family with him as he ran from place to place. He didn't know the person he was truly running from was himself.

Osman is not the only person who lives in a lie-based world. Many women I have met live in lies and deception. They believe many things about themselves that are not true. Unless a woman finds her identity in Christ, she lives in a world of lies. This is bondage. Truth sets us free.

Manipulation and exaggeration are natural gifts for women. Yes, of course men can be very manipulative too, but I believe manipulation is a woman's natural gift. Ladies, please don't get mad at me, but it started with Eve, and it runs all through the Bible. Look at what happened with Sarah, who took her maidservant and gave her into her husband's arms. Rachel hid her father's gods underneath her and pretended she was on her period so she wouldn't have to stand up. Let's get real here. I know many women who manipulate their shopping in every way possible and hide money from their husbands here and there. I *was* one of those women! As mothers, we are also very crafty in justifying our children's bad behaviors. We may be good at this and even successful at it, but the main point is it doesn't please God. It's a lie-based way of living that creates a lie-based world.

Manipulation comes from the desire to control. When we try to control, we lack trust in God, and it is an offense to Him.

Let me tell you something, sisters: manipulation, exaggeration, and white lies *are all lies,* and they come from Satan, the father of all lies.

"In a few minutes you will die and will open your eyes in hell."

The Truth Will Set You Free

My husband I were sitting by the deathbed of my husband's aunt. Her doctor said she had a few minutes more to live. The first concern we had was her salvation. Where was she going to spend eternity? All her life she had been into New Age teachings, horoscopes, tarot cards and all kinds of witchcraft. Every time we tried to talk to her about the saving power of Jesus Christ, she would shut us up and get upset at us. But what about now? What about at the very moment she was about to leave this life?

Truth hurts and offends!
But it also saves and sets free!

My husband and I were by her side, and I said to her, "Aunt Natalie, Jesus died on the cross for your sins and rose from the dead so you can have eternal life. If you accept Him as your Lord and Savior today, you will be with Him as soon as you leave this world. Death will not have any power over you."

She snapped at me as she always did and said, "I know God, okay? I don't need a stupid prayer to go to heaven." At that moment, I felt something like electricity running all over my body, and I was filled with anger and grief. I said, "Listen, Aunt Natalie, you lived all of your life for you and what you thought was right and what suited you. But you are dying now, and if you die in this stubbornness of rejecting Christ Jesus, you will open your eyes in hell. God is giving you a chance to humble yourself to accept His Son Jesus for your eternal freedom."

As much as I hate Christians forcing people to salvation and hitting people over the head with the Bible, something truly divine happened to me at that moment. As soon as I finished speaking, she started crying. The reality of being at the end of her life hit her hard. The truth hurt her—and it set her free. Right then and there, she repented and gave her life to Christ Jesus. A few minutes later, she closed her eyes to be with Him for eternity.

There is a time for everything. There is a time to be sweet and soft. There is a time to be firm and strong. Truth hurts and offends. But the truth also saves and sets free.

"I skydive every weekend!"

Lying For Significance

I used to tell people that I skydived every weekend. I even made up stories of accidents that I had been through. Many of my friends considered me a hero or something. I wanted to look different, special and brave. I would lie about going places I hadn't really gone and tell stories like the skydiving because it gave me a false significance.

Then one day, my girlfriends and I went to a restaurant. They saw a friend who was sitting at the bar and ran up to him to say hello, dragging me along with them. "Oh, you've got to meet this guy!" one of my girlfriends said. "You and he have so much in common!"

I looked at him curiously. He looked like an old fellow in his late sixties. I was about twenty-six at the time. I wondered what we could possibly have in common. When my friend introduced me to him, she said, "Tell him. Tell him what do you do during the weekends."

I said calmly and with pride, "I skydive." (Yes, now it feels ridiculous, but at that time it was serving its purpose.) He was very impressed and interested. "Every weekend?" he asked.

"Yes, almost," I told him.

He asked, "How high do you jump?"

I immediately and foolishly answered, "About thirty thousand feet."

"Wow," he said, "I have been a pilot of different aircraft for thirty-five years, and I have never heard of anyone jumping from that high." I blushed and justified the height I'd given to a confusion of feet and meter differences in Europe and America—which backfired on me more, since thirty thousand meters is a whole lot of feet! That was the end of my skydiving tales.

The Sermon That Changed Me Forever

After I became a Christian, I didn't hear much teaching about lies or lying. I believe many preachers assume that every Christian knows not to lie! However, that is not the case. New believers need biblical teachings on simple and basic subjects like this one.

One day at a church service, a preacher gave a message on lying and how we become Satan's mouthpiece when we lie. Before he made an altar call, I threw myself to the altar and wept. I confessed and repented of my habit of lying.

After that day of sanctification and cleansing through repentance, I stopped the purposeful lies and fabricated stories for popularity. However, it took me years to be set free during Christian counseling from the lies I believed about myself and my identity.

The Spirit started asking me to share things that made me look bad.

One of the lies I believed was that I was inferior to men. I believed in that lie for nearly the first fourteen years of my Christian walk.

As I became hungry and thirsty for God's righteousness, the Holy Spirit led me to become more transparent and honest than ever. God started asking me to share things from the pulpit that made me look bad, weak and imperfect. That level of honesty was beyond my natural understanding and ability. I just had to obey Him. I just knew I had no other option than to obey Him and be brutally honest.

During my TV programs, I share about my family life, my recent struggles and failures, and how God works in my life through my short-comings. This approach has attracted large audiences to my programs in the Middle East.

A few years ago, a female evangelist who has been in the ministry for many more years than I have, asked me what I believe are some of the reasons for the fast growth of my TV ministry. My answer was simple. It is first and foremost the anointing of God and the moving of the Holy Spirit—as Paul said, the kingdom of God is not a matter of talk, but power. *But the second reason is being transparent and honest.* I will share things in front of the camera that make me look bad, but that show the goodness of God. And that truth is helping to set people free.

People don't want to see another perfect preacher, but someone like them. Someone who is human. They want to hear a person who has a testimony of having failed and yet gained victory.

I asked the minister lady if she would be willing to share her testimony on my TV program. She told me she didn't share her testimony anywhere. And she has been in the ministry for decades! That puzzled me, because without a testimony, there is no ministry. Over the years I have met others who have been working in different ministry capacities for many years and have never once shared their testimony. I believe this is a sign of chains. It is a sign of bondage.

Daughters of God, your Father wants you to be free!

Let's tell the world how bad we were,
so they will know how good our God is.
ANONYMOUS

If I must boast, I will boast of the things that
show my weakness.
2 CORINTHIANS 11:30

No More Pretense

A lot of women live in a world of pretense. They put on a happy mask and act like everything is going perfectly. They pretend they have the perfect marriage and the perfect children. It is a very sad place to be. I know, because I have been there!

I believe many women pretend just because they don't trust people. Some chronic pretenders have even told me they feel that people are their enemies and are waiting for their failure, or that people are just curious about their private business so they can use it as a gossip tool. I have to admit there are many inappropriately curious people out there who are just bored and have nothing better to do with their lives except talk about other people, but that's not a good reason to hide ourselves away behind a fake wall. If we can't always trust people, we *can* always trust God. And that means living with greater honesty.

In the past I've had to confront a couple of girlfriends for their pretenses. There are layers of reasons for pretense. The belief that the outside world is an enemy who is expecting a failure is a big one. In the eyes of those who can't trust anyone, pretense protects them from the world. They don't want to be subject to anyone's opinion, advice or criticism. Of course, pride is one of the main reasons we want to hide under an excuse of "privacy." Pride holds us back from truth—and freedom.

> *But Jesus said to me, "My grace is sufficient for you,*
> *for my power is made perfect in weakness."*
> *Therefore I will boast all the more gladly about my weak-*
> *nesses, so that Christ's power may rest on me.*
> *That is why, for Christ's sake, I delight in weaknesses,*
> *in insults, in hardships, in persecutions, in difficulties.*
> *For when I am weak, then I am strong.*
> 2 CORINTHIANS 12:9–10

During my first marriage, I wanted to prove to the world that my marriage was the best. I had to pretend to my family and friends that my husband and I were from the storybooks. All that time, behind closed doors I was going through torment and torture. I have met several couples over the years whose marriages were falling apart, but because of the wife's pretense, the breakdown seemed very sudden to the husband. One day, she decided she just could not pretend anymore.

I notice pretense when one of the spouses, and in many cases it is the woman, overly advertises the other, whether through just praising them in conversation or on social media such as Facebook or Twitter. The sadness and hurt is so very deep that women feel they have to compensate for their misery somehow by pretending they have the perfect marriage. It is plastic. It is fake, but they need a hiding place from the world.

On the other hand, nothing is so sudden for a woman as it appears to be to a man. A doctor friend once told me, "When there is a sickness, there are always symptoms and signs. If anything internal is going wrong, sooner or later it reflects on the outside." This applies to our emotional condition as well as our physical bodies. Even while we're trying to hide it, we women somehow articulate our disappointments, hurt and pain. Sometimes we even use sarcasm and jokes to camouflage the pain and hurt. But it takes a good listener to hear it before it is too late. Many men lose their marriages by choosing to stay in their comfort zones and disregard their wife's emotional pain. Everybody has a limit to pain endurance. I don't care how spiritual you are, you have a limit. Everyone has a limit, even the prophets. Elijah had a limit. David had a limit. Naomi had a limit.

When you build your life on a lie, there is always a day when living in the world of lies ends, whether at the end of your life, through a nervous breakdown, a divorce, or some other tragedy. Sooner or later, what has been hiding inside for many years grows too big and becomes a monster that you cannot hide anymore.

It is time for the pretenses to end. It is time to reject lies and embrace the truth. Today, if you are feeling cornered and stuck, I suggest that you start speaking to God and ask Him to guide you through the Holy Spirit to find the right counsel. Ask Him to comfort you and give you peace. If you feel like you are reaching your limit and you cannot go on anymore, I pray you will choose to hear God's voice and truth instead of the enemy's lies. I assure you that God will make a way when it seems there is no way. Be still and know that He is God.

Dear Lord Jesus,

Please forgive me for being manipulative and trying to control circumstances instead of trusting them to You. I repent from manipulating, exaggerating or stretching the truth, and from all forms of lies that come from my mouth and actions. I reject the lying spirit in my life, and ask the Spirit of Truth, the Holy Spirit, to reign in me. I ask You to be completely in charge of my life. I surrender my will and my ways to You. Yours is the power and the control. I want to please You. I plead the blood of Jesus over my heart in this area and ask you to set me free from lies in Jesus' name.

Amen.

The worst lie is the one with some truth in it.

ANONYMOUS

Chapter 11

Do You Feel Pretty on the Inside?

Create in me a pure heart, O God,
and renew a steadfast spirit within me.
PSALM 51:10

My Dear Daughter,

I know everything about you. I know your heart. I know the secrets of your heart. I know the hurts, pain and anger. The condition of your heart matters to Me. I can only dwell in a pure and clean heart. If you want your heart to be a home for Me, seek Me to purify it from all that contaminates it. Come to Me and ask Me to cleanse your heart. It is My will for you to have a pure heart.

Dear Lord,

I want You to be pleased with me. I want to make my heart Your home. You are a holy God, and for You to dwell in my heart, it has to be pure. Please purify my heart. Please cleanse my heart from any filth. Create within me a pure heart. I pray that the meditation of my heart will be pleasing to You. Please forgive me if there is any offensive way in my heart to You, Lord. If there is any unforgiveness, please forgive me and reveal it to me so I can pray for it to be removed.

Amen.

Blessed are the pure in heart,
for they will see God.
MATTHEW 5:8

Other People's Garbage

I'll never forget when Carry, the wife of our missions pastor, told me, "My husband told me that if you are friends with Pastor Neil's wife, I cannot be your friend." She gave me an ultimatum that I couldn't even sit in the church with the other pastor's wife. After she told me that, I went home and wept for days—my heart was so wounded to see the division and the power struggle between these pastors and their wives. I told my husband about it, and he said we should pray.

(By the way, I am so glad I had a personal encounter with Jesus Christ at the beginning of my Christian life! My faith in Him is not based on book knowledge but on a personal experience. Otherwise, seeing this kind of garbage in the church would shake my faith. Many people have claimed they mentored me to steal the credit and glory from God. When I look at my walk with Christ, I see only one mentor who has to be mentioned: the Holy Spirit.)

Well, we prayed for a year. At the time, I was under the spiritual authority of a very manipulative and controlling person. Because I grew up under a mother who was very controlling and manipulative, I didn't recognize it easily. It was normal for me. I was submissive. But I was submissive to the wrong person. I listened to her, and her garbage became garbage in my heart. I took her offenses. I took her words to heart and judged others through her eyes.

One Sunday morning, my husband and I were having a devotional before the church service when God spoke to us and told us to leave the church. We left that fellowship wounded. We left hurt, and it took us a couple of years to recover from the bad taste of what I now know was the influence of a Jezebel spirit. However, God also used that experience to make us alert to the spirit of Jezebel at work in many places. The spirit of Jezebel, named after Jezebel in the Bible, is a spirit of manipulation and control that seeks to work through religious people and institutions. It comes against God's people and tries to destroy them and make them ineffective.

If today you are having bad thoughts against the church or God's people because of a bad experience, open your heart to Him and ask Jesus to purify your heart. Forgive those people who claimed to be godly but acted wickedly. Do not let others' example of wrongdoing become a stain in your heart. Don't let other people's garbage become your garbage.

People aren't born with prejudice. They learn it!

Impurity of Heart

"My granddaughter is dating a black guy. Can you believe it?" Kathy was crying and sobbing uncontrollably. It was 5:00 a.m. when she called me. At first I couldn't understand what she was saying, as she was weeping so violently. I thought something very bad had happened to her—I thought maybe a sudden death. She started almost choking when she said, "My granddaughter, Brook," and I thought something tragic must have happened to her granddaughter.

Kathy had been attending our church services with her husband for awhile. She had been a Christian for almost thirty years. As it became clearer what she was saying, I started to feel confused. What was the problem here?

When she said, "She met this black guy at college. Now she is in love. Can you believe it?"

I said, "Yes, of course I can believe it! What is wrong with that, Ms. Kathy?"

"What is wrong with that?" she answered, getting angry. "What do you think their children would look like?"

I answered kindly, trying not to show my disappointment in her, "Their children would look just like Jesus."

I was more shocked than ever at her response. "But all the generations of our family are white and blonde. We have been proud of that. And look, now we will have dark babies in our family."

At this, I couldn't hold it back. I burst out, "You have got to be kidding me, Ms. Kathy! Right? Please stop here and think whether what you are saying lines up with Jesus. Please don't continue before you check with the Holy Spirit. I have no doubt you are grieving the heart of God. And how many years have you claimed to know Christ? This is pure racism, and you need to repent from it!"

If you can't tell, I was really very angry by that time. I thought, *I've had enough of this!* I had no tolerance for her to go on even one more second.

She answered, "This is not racism. I am not racist. I just grew up in segregation. We are not used to this blending."

I answered firmly, "You may not call this racism, but I do. It is nothing but racism. You have been a professing Christian all these years while thinking that you and your white and blonde family are superior to blacks. I am sorry, I don't have any tolerance for your nonsense. I think our conversation is over. I will be praying for you."

That was not only the end of our conversation, but also our friendship. In the next little while things escalated, and our friendship ended. Did I react too strongly? Yes, I believe I did. Was I harsh? Probably I was. But even today, I grieve at the words she said on the phone to me. And this was a woman of prayer.

"Why are my prayers never answered?" she wondered.

But here is the interesting thing: Ms. Kathy was a woman of prayer, but she often wondered why her prayers were never answered. Over the years, I have heard similar comments from different people. They were deeply prejudiced, and even though they would pray, their families were always in strife and turmoil. Ms. Kathy later on confessed that she never knew what true peace was.

When your heart is not pure and in line with the heart of God, peace in your heart and family will be a stranger to you. How can you have a pure heart with prejudice inside?

No one is born with prejudice! It is taught, whether by family, other people, culture, or some kind of experience. When someone comes under the bondage of prejudice, it takes a specific decision to break that bondage and overcome it.

If you feel prejudice in your heart in any way or form, confess it and ask God's forgiveness. Repent from your pride. Prejudice is connected to pride in our hearts, because in some way we feel we are superior or better than someone else.

Prejudice doesn't only come with skin color, ethnic group, or racial differences. Many people are also prejudiced toward the poor or uneducated. For that matter, some are prejudiced against the wealthy and educated! As God hates pride, he also hates prejudice. Without repentance and a pure heart in this area, you can bring hindrance to yourself and your family.

Freedom From Impurity

Prejudice, division, pride, envy, greed, bitterness—impurity of heart can bring great bondage in our lives. But freedom is possible, even for the worst offenders in all these areas!

I grew up in a household where racism was a deep problem. "My grandparents burned fifteen Armenians, and they received a gold medal," my father always bragged. That hurt me deeply. I cannot explain the sadness that pierced my heart when he would say that. I had to repent on behalf of my family after I invited Jesus Christ into my heart as my Lord. I prayed to be free from the generational curse that my forefathers brought upon me and my family through being a part of the genocide that the Turks committed against the Armenians. According to my dad, the Armenians deserved it. "They were rebellious and caused much trouble to the country. Our family fought to keep peace and burned them."

I was nine years old when I first heard this, and I started crying uncontrollably. "You are weak. This is not good. You cry at everything," my father said. Compassion was weakness to him.

My mother pulled me aside. "Don't listen to him," she said. "We are all equal in the sight of God. What his family did was barbaric. That is what he is. He is a barbarian." My mother hated my dad and his prejudice.

Unlike many Muslims, my father liked Jewish people. We lived in a Jewish neighborhood. When my father was young and poor, a wealthy Jewish man mentored him in business and taught him everything he knew. My father didn't forget his kindness. But toward the Armenians he was always hostile. He hated the Kurds as well. When we talked about someone, the first thing he would say was, "He is a Kurd" or "He is an Armenian." My mother used to say, "So? They are created by God too."

God can break even the bondage of the worst racism. "It is an Armenian church. You cannot go with me," I found myself telling my father one day. I was going to speak at an Armenian church in Istanbul. I loved Pastor Kirkor and his wife, and knowing how hostile my father was toward the Armenians, I didn't want him to go to their church with me.

My father responded in anger, "It is not enough that they are living in our land and eating our bread, and now they have a church too in our Muslim land?"

My heart ached, just like it had when I was a child. I wanted to cry. I wanted to scream. I couldn't. I felt like choking at his hatred.

I tried to be calm and loving. I answered, "Yes, Dad, they have a church too. This is their land too, you know. This is why I don't want you to come. You are full of hatred and hostility."

Well, he wasn't going to listen to me. "I am coming to protect you from them," he insisted. "They may harm you knowing that you are a Turk."

I was angry this time. I responded, "The only people who would harm me are the Muslims like you, not Armenians! Now I share the same faith with them."

He became sarcastic. "So you became an Armenian, huh? Is that true? You are an Armenian. You are a traitor. You betrayed your own country, your own religion, and became one of them."

I couldn't take this anymore, I thought. But I still had to demonstrate love. He was my own father, but I needed God's help to love this man! I responded, "I am not an Armenian. But I am one with them in faith and love in Christ. This is why I don't want you to come with me. You are so messed up, Dad."

He didn't want their love.
He didn't want their kindness.

He didn't accept my words. "I am coming with you. I have to protect you."

So we went to the church. My father was in shock as he saw the amount of love people were pouring on me. They were so very loving toward him too. He didn't want their love. He didn't want their kindness. I could tell.

Then the pastor started preaching. I looked at my father. He had such a hardened heart that it was visible on his countenance. Each time the pastor made a statement about our faith or the Scriptures, my father sarcastically said, "Yeah, right!" He was loud enough to be heard. In the front pew, a father was sitting with his handicapped daughter, and I saw my father staring at them. My heart was hurting for my dad because of the intensity and thickness of the hatred in his heart. I prayed silently to the Lord, telling him that I could do nothing about it. This was something only the Holy Spirit could fix.

At some point during his sermon, Pastor Kirkor spoke about how it felt to face racism and be treated as a second-class citizen just because of his name. He spoke about how employment doors were closed to him and his father for being Armenians. He talked about how much the condition of our hearts matters to God and shared that he had to forgive and seek the Lord to keep his heart pure.

I was so engaged with his message that I didn't look at my father for awhile. When I did look at him, he was quiet. I looked away quickly, as I didn't want to upset him.

After the service, there was a Bible study. My father told me to feel free to attend the meeting; he wanted to stay outside to wait and get fresh air. He was still awfully quiet, I thought. After the Bible study, I found him outside the church talking to the man who had been sitting in front of us with his handicapped daughter. I saw my father giving him money and hugging him. I tried to control my tears.

The entire time we were driving back home, my father was quiet, which was very rare. He was usually talkative, opinionated and arrogant in his views. He would only really quiet down when he was sick. I didn't try to hold a conversation—I thought maybe the Holy Spirit was working, and I wanted to give him room. When we arrived home, my mother noticed right away that something was off. With sign language, she asked me what was wrong, but I couldn't say anything in front of my father. Later on, he told us that he was afraid he would burst into sobs the moment he opened his mouth.

After a short while of quiet that felt like eternity, he knelt in front of my mother, who was sitting on a chair. He started weeping. "I am sorry. I am sorry for everything." This was the most shocking thing I had ever seen in my life! The strong man I'd known all my life, the man who hated Armenians and Kurds, was in tears. The man who hated crying, and considered people who cried easily to be emotionally sick and weak, was crying like a baby. He just wept. I was weeping too. My mother was crying as well.

Then he came up to me and sobbed, "I am sorry. I am sorry. I love you." He couldn't stop crying. Every time he opened his mouth to speak, he choked into tears. Finally he was able to say, "Those people are very precious. They were so nice and loving. They are poor. I feel so bad." He couldn't continue anymore. He just wept and wept.

In the following weeks, my father and mother brought some baked goods and clothing to the Armenian church. My father wouldn't let anyone speak against Armenians after his heart change. He came to another service where I was speaking at the same church. When I made an altar call to receive Christ Jesus, he buried his head in his hands and wept bitterly. Since then, I have seen a great change in him. He never talked about it afterward or confessed openly that he had become a Christian. There was much garbage that God had to cleanse from him and his heart. But since that day, I have seen a lot of good changes in him, only possible by the power of the Holy Spirit.

Getting A Heart Change

The heart is deceitful above all things
and beyond cure.
Who can understand it?
JEREMIAH 17:9

Jeremiah's words are very strong. The dictionary says that *deceitful* means misleading, false, insincere, two-faced, cunning, calculating, crafty, sly, treacherous, sneaky, foxy, crooked, fraudulent, not trustworthy. According to Jeremiah 17:9, this is our heart's condition.

David prayed, "Create in me a pure heart, O God, and renew a steadfast spirit within me. Restore to me the joy of your salvation and grant me a willing spirit, to sustain me." (Psalm 51:10,13). We too need a steadfast heart that is unchanging and pure. Thankfully, God makes this available to us! Not only does He make us new creations when we first come to Jesus, but He offers us an ongoing heart change as we surrender our impurities to Him and seek a clean heart.

Let's break down the words in David's Scripture to see what God promises to do for our impure hearts:

- **Steadfast:** Loyal, faithful, dedicated, dependable, reliable, solid, firmly fixed in a place, immoveable, unshakeable, firm in believing, determined.
- **Renew:** New, fresh or strong start, to make a promise, restore, to do it again, to begin again.
- **Restore:** Bring back to original condition. Bring back to existence, reestablish.
- **Sustain:** Give strength, to be encouraged, keep going, bear the burden.

David wrote Psalm 51 after the prophet Nathan confronted and rebuked him following his affair with Bathsheba, an affair which led him to murder her husband, a righteous and innocent man. This psalm is also called a psalm of repentance.

When we sin, until we repent, there is no true joy residing in us. Even though we laugh and may seem happy, it is not God's joy. It is a counterfeit joy. David committed many sins through his affair with Bathsheba, and his joy was gone. You may be able to take pleasure in something, but it doesn't mean you have joy. You may have pleasure in shopping, but it does not bring God's joy. Our hearts can't really be joyful or full of God until we receive his forgiveness and walk in purity again.

After sin, we need restoration. Sin damages our relationship with God. Sin separates us from God. Then we need to be restored.

We continuously need to pray for a pure heart that is also steadfast. You may need to pray today for an unchanging heart and devotion for Christ Jesus. No matter how much you fail in your walk with God, remember that He is waiting for you with His arms wide open. Go to Him with confidence that it is His will for you to ask Him to purify you from all your sins.

Dear Jesus,

I confess that my heart has not been pure before You. I have had a heart filled with _____ [name it—racism, pride, bitterness, envy, division, etc.]. I desperately need You to cleanse me. Create a clean heart in me. Renew me and give me a willing, stead-fast spirit. Give me the joy of Your salvation. I want to live a pure life from the inside out. In Jesus' name. Amen.

·····ᏩᏏᎣ·····

Man can fail many times,
but he is not a failure until he gives up.
ANONYMOUS

Chapter 12

Absolutely Fearless

You have a new name: Fearless!
God will make you brave today!

Perfect love casts out fear.
1 JOHN 4:18 NKJV

My Sweet Daughter,

I love you unconditionally. My love is perfect. It has no flaws or short-comings. I love you with an undying love. No one has ever loved you or ever *will* love you the way I love you. There is no match, no equal for My love for you. When you truly understand and receive My love, you will not live your life in fear. You will know that I am and always will be there for you. I will never leave you nor forsake you.

My Perfect Father,

I have lived most of my life in fear, not trusting in You. I surrender all my fears and worries to You right now. Please give me more faith so that I will be unshakable. The enemy has bullied and intimidated me in the past by using people. They hurt me and abused me. I started fearing people and the future, as if something bad was always going to happen to me or to my loved ones. Now I cast all my fears on You, Lord. I receive Your perfect love, and in Your perfect love I will be secure. Please forgive me for the times I have failed to trust You. Please forgive me for being filled with fear. Dear Jesus, set me free from all of my fears. Make me fearless. In Jesus' name I pray.
Amen.

Fear of People

The LORD himself will go before you
and will be with you;
He will never leave you nor forsake you.
Do not be afraid; do not be discouraged.

DEUTERONOMY 31:8

"You think you are funny, but you are stupid. You are an idiot!" shouted Hasan in front of all my classmates. Everyone agreed with him. I looked down. I wanted to cry, but I couldn't. I just wanted to be invisible. I wanted to disappear. Once again someone else had confirmed my parents' hurtful comments: I was stupid, and now everyone knew it.

As a young student, I was afraid of Hasan. He was a chubby boy, arrogant and outspoken, from a wealthy family. I tried never to open my mouth when he was present. He could easily say the meanest things. Previously I had been beaten up in front of the classroom by my elementary school teacher. Then I met others like Hasan who injured me deeply, and the scars started bleeding internally.

Over the years, my fear of people turned into deep insecurity. I didn't know I was afraid of people until God revealed it to me one day.

Many of us live our lives with this kind of stuff without knowing it. We just try to survive life without acknowledging past hurts.

Wounded and fearful people are all around us.

Being verbally and physically abused at home fed my fear of people more and more. Over the years, I became paralyzed when I first met people. I was always afraid of them, believing that one day eventually they would hurt me. I carried this fear over the years. And I wasn't alone. Wounded and fearful people are all around us.

As a result of my insecurity, I tended to choose controlling and manipulative friends in my young adult years. They liked me to be codependent on them and their opinions. I was seeking love, affection and approval all the time. This emotional disability caused me to become a people-pleaser more and more. Every friendship depended on what I could give to the other person instead of being a mutual and equal relationship. However, when the controlling and pushiness became intense, I would run away instead of communicating my feelings, issues or disappointments.

Insecure people try to control!

Insecure people are controlling people. Controlling others makes them feel important and powerful. It feeds their ego. They find their worth and value in telling others what to do with their lives. They feel good about themselves if they manage someone else's life, as though they are accomplishing something. Now I run away if I come near a controlling individual. And believe me, many people try to control me! That's a common thing when you're in ministry or a public position. However, I have boundaries, and I only depend on Jesus. I only need His approval. Living like this is true freedom.

There may be many reasons we choose to live with insecurity, codependency, and other problems. But one thing lies at the root of all these things: *fear.*

The Bondage of Fear

If you have a hard time saying *no*, you have fear! Fear of losing people causes many insecure people to say *yes* to everything. If others, including your children, are the center of your life, you have several serious issues, such as idol worship, fear of losing your loved ones, and fear of losing control.

There is freedom in not trying to prove yourself to anyone. For a long time I tried to prove myself to my father and seek his acceptance. Each time I tried, I failed. I felt that I was never going to be good enough for him. After I invited Jesus Christ into my heart, I met my heavenly Father, who accepted me and loved me just the way I was. And He set me free from seeking man's approval. God showed me that people's opinions and approval mattered to me more than His opinion and approval, and He helped me become free.

I remember when my friend Becky told me about her grown-up children, "I am tired of doing everything for them." We had been friends for a long time, and she allowed me to speak into her life. Two of her children were boys who were in their late twenties, and one was a girl who had just turned twenty. Becky was cleaning, cooking and doing many things for her children even though they were adults. I had been hearing her complaints over the years and remaining quiet. I guess I was afraid to hurt her feelings. (You see, we all let fear enter from time to time!) Even so, I had to wait for God's timing to tell her what the Holy Spirit had revealed to me. I also wanted to be face-to-face with her, holding her hands and looking into her eyes. Texting, e-mailing, and even talking on the phone can't do justice to an important conversation most of the time.

One day we were together and again she was sharing how difficult it was to take care of three children. I listened to her carefully and patiently. Then I offered to pray for this situation. After we prayed together, I held her hand and looked into her eyes and said, "You need to let them go, Becky. You need to let them become adults. You are not doing them any good, my sweet friend."

Becky started crying. She admitted that she was afraid to let them go and that she had made them dependent on her by taking care of their every need. Even though it might have looked like a sacrifice and a won-derful, motherly expression of love, she was doing it out of selfishness. Without realizing it, she wanted them to be codependent on her, and was disabling them.

Of course, there was a reason beneath the reason she was doing that.

She had a fear of them going away and not needing her, and ultimately, a fear of dying alone. You would be amazed to learn how many of people's behaviors are driven by fear.

People who are not right with God live in fear too.

Fear of Tomorrow

When you have trust issues, and especially issues trusting God, it is normal to fear tomorrow. We might fear accidents, sickness or losing our jobs. We might fear being abandoned or getting hurt. If you have faith in a mean, brutal and sadistic God who is always looking for an excuse to punish you, get you, and discipline you, then the fear of tomorrow is very natural!

I struggled with the fear of tomorrow until Jesus set me free. I feared I might lose my job and be unable to pay the bills. I feared I would get sick and be unable to go to work. I feared I might get into a car accident. I feared that my daughter might be kidnapped and molested. My life was completely and utterly controlled by fear.

If you have been living your life like this, now is the time for you to repent for not fully trusting God. Ask God's forgiveness. Then receive His perfect love that casts out all fear.

Make a list of things you fear and surrender them to Jesus. He will fill you with his peace, because if you are living in fear, you have no peace in your life. If you are living in fear, as I always say, you are restless and you need a vacation! Enter into God's rest and thank Him for His goodness, kindness and protection.

I know a young girl who was only interested in married men in a wicked way. She lived her life in fear. She had a seductive spirit and caused some marriages great harm. She was fearful that her secret would come to light one day.

"Two hundred thousand people signed up to curse you, Sister Işık."

Supernatural Freedom

When we repent of a lack of trust in God, supernatural freedom from fear is available to us.

You can only imagine how far God has brought me in order to be able to do what I do today! I was someone who had a very fearful personality and was paralyzed by many fears from childhood. But today, fanatical Muslims from the Middle East write me with all kinds of insults and threats, and my heart doesn't even move a bit with fear.

A fanatical Muslim man named Lotus wrote to me and said, "We created a sign-up sheet on a private website just for you, for Muslims to log in and enter their names to commit to curse you and your family every day, every hour. So far two hundred thousand people have signed up to curse you."

> *Though an army besiege me, my heart will not fear;*
> *though war break out against me, even then I*
> *will be confident.*
> PSALM 27:3

If this had happened three or four years ago, I would have cried and wept and crawled into my corner and asked God to take this task from me. But instead, I praise God that I was found worthy to be persecuted for His name's sake.

I wrote back to that Muslim man and said, "You say two hundred thousand people signed up to curse me daily. I am committed to bless them every day." He got more upset. My heart was not even moved a bit with fear. If this is not the supernatural power of Jesus Christ, I want to ask you, what is?

Do not be afraid of those who kill the body
but cannot kill the soul.
Rather, be afraid of the One
who can destroy both soul and body in hell.
Are not two sparrows sold for a penny?
Yet not one of them will fall to the ground
outside your Father's care.
And even the very hairs of your head are all
numbered.
So don't be afraid;
you are worth more than many sparrows.
MATTHEW 10:28–31

Fear is a paralyzing feeling. It is the opposite of faith and trust. When we have fear, we cannot reach our full potential. Fear keeps us crippled.

The Gateway To The Devil

When Celina reached me, she had already tried every possible option. She was seeing snakes everywhere. Snakes were crawling on her chest. They were in her room, slithering all over everything. They were real to her. Doctors were giving her morphine to calm her down and put her to sleep. They didn't know what to do with her. She was tormented by fear. She didn't want to live anymore and tried to kill herself several times. Her husband and children had all lost hope.

One day she saw one of my programs on TV, and for the first time, in her own words, she thought there might be hope for her. She wrote to me and told me she believed I was the only person who could help her.

"I see snakes everywhere! Please help me!"

Now, we all know who the only person who could help Celina is. His name is Jesus. And he uses ordinary people like me and you to do his extraordinary work.

I called Celina on my Turkish live show. She was so very happy to hear my voice. I asked her if she was seeing the snakes in the room. She said they were still all over her room, but she had faith that I was able to get rid of them. That was a problem—her faith was depending on my faith instead of hers. But I didn't realize at the time how much of a problem it would become.

As we talked, she gave her heart to Jesus on the air, telling everyone that she had tried to kill herself, but Jesus had appeared to her and saved her life. After she invited Jesus into her heart as her Lord and Savior, I prayed and cast 104 demons out of her! The main demon that controlled all of them was a demon called Python. He was the chief of the demons in her, and he fed and multiplied through fear.

I called her the next day to see how she was doing. She said she hadn't seen the snakes for twenty-four hours, and it was the first time in years. I called her every day for a week and prayed with her. I gave her Scriptures to read and study. She did it all, and for one week she didn't see any snakes.

Then I wanted to see how she would do without me, so I decided not to call her for a week. But on the third day that I didn't call, she sent me an urgent message that the snakes were back and she needed me to call her and pray. Now I knew the problem. She was cleansed of the demons, but she still had much fear, and her fear was acting as the gateway to the demonic forces to come and invade her temple.

I called her immediately. I prayed on the phone with her. I taught her how the devil was operating in her mind and life by fear. I told her that fear was an open door, an invitation to the enemy. I told her she had to get strong in the Word of God. And I gave her more Bible studies over the phone.

She believed everything I said—but that also represents a problem! When someone just easily believes in you, she will believe in the enemy's voice just as easily. For this very reason, I had to direct her to Christ Jesus, not to myself. I taught her to seek God, ask God, and knock on God's door. I taught her how to pray against fear and against the demonic attack.

After three weeks, I was sure that Celina was cleansed of all the demons. I also taught her that if she didn't seek God, and allowed fear to enter in, they could come back. But she learned that she had a choice. She learned that she had to abide in Jesus continuously.

It has been more than a year, and Celina hasn't seen any snakes. She hasn't been on any medications or morphine. She has called my live program several times and thanked me on air. She has testified on air about the goodness and delivering power of Jesus Christ.

> *But now, this is what the LORD says—*
> *he who created you, Jacob, he who formed you,*
> *Israel:*
> *"Do not fear, for I have redeemed you;*
> *I have summoned you by name; you are mine.*
> *When you pass through the waters, I will be*
> *with you;*

and when you pass through the rivers,
they will not sweep over you.
When you walk through the fire,
you will not be burned;
the flames will not set you ablaze."
ISAIAH 43:1–2

Fear Is Your Enemy!

Fear opens doors to the enemy to bully you and torment you. Fear is the opposite of faith. You can only make fear disappear with more faith.

Faith comes through hearing and hearing the Word of God. The more you dig deep in the Word of God and His Word becomes engraved in your heart and mind, the less fear you are going to have.

Faith is your spiritual immune system! Fear is a disease that brings your immune system down!

When you have fear, you are hearing the voice of the enemy. When you have faith, you are hearing the voice of God. The only fear we should have is a healthy fear of God that causes us to please Him and submit to Him. No other fear is good for us, no matter what the enemy says!

To strengthen your spiritual immune system, you need to immerse yourself in the Word of God. When your faith is weak, your spiritual immune system is down. Then the enemy can inject many of his diseases of disbelief, doubt, fear and insecurity, and you will be ruled by them.

The more you spend time with God and discipline yourself to read the Scriptures, the more spiritually healthy you will become.

> *"No weapon forged against you will prevail,*
> *and you will refute every tongue that accuses you.*
> *This is the heritage of the servants of the* LORD,
> *and this is their vindication from me,"*
> declares the Lord.
> ISAIAH 54:17

Identifying Your Fears

Fear comes in many shapes and forms. To become free from it, we need to repent of our lack of trust in God, our desire to control, our idolatry of people, and our belief in the enemy's voice. Then we simply need to turn our eyes on God, commit to trust Him, and ask for His peace in place of our fear.

Check or Circle the Fears You Have:
- Fear of death
- Fear of being embarrassed
- Fear of poverty
- Fear of sickness
- Fear of evil
- Fear of loneliness
- Fear of rejection
- Fear of terror
- Fear of tight or closed places
- Fear of people
- Fear of an accident
- Fear of dying alone

- Fear of failure
- Fear of the dark
- Fear of disaster
- Fear of abandonment
- Fear of losing control
- Fear of losing a loved one
- Other types of fears

If you have any of the above fears or one that is not listed above, write it down in your own words. Then pray and repent for not trusting God with your fears. Ask Jesus to fill your heart with faith and peace.

A thousand may fall at your side, ten thousand
at your right hand,
but it will not come near you.

PSALM 91:7

Chapter 13

No More Boring! No More Dry!

I will make them and the places surrounding
my hill a blessing.
I will send down showers in season; there will be
showers of blessing.
Ezekiel 34:26

My Precious Child,

I love you limitlessly and abundantly, and I want to shower you with My love and blessings. I want to see you always full of joy and always seeking My presence. As you seek Me and spend more time with Me, your cup will be overflowing. The more you seek Me, the more you will find the spiritual treasures I have prepared for you. Even though you walk in the midst of a famine or drought, you will have rain and you will have oil. Empty yourself so that you can be filled with My Spirit continuously. It is not a one-time filling that I will give you. It is a continuous communion.

Dear Lord,

I want You more than anything. I don't want to live one minute apart from You. I don't want a dry season or day in my life. I never want be disconnected from You. I want to hear and follow Your voice. I want to continuously abide in You. I make up my mind that I will seek You every day and every hour. I empty myself and want to be filled with Your Holy Spirit every day. I never want to say, "I've had enough." Please keep me always hungry and thirsty for You. Amen.

You, God, are my God,
earnestly I seek you;
I thirst for you,
my whole being longs for you,
in a dry and parched land
where there is no water.

PSALM 63:1

A Dry Season?

Lisa's Bible was always open on her desk. She could quote the Scriptures remarkably. She was a mother of three grown children and was working in the ministry. She was even teaching a Sunday school every other week.

She was almost ashamed to tell me she was going through a dry season. Looking embarrassed, she asked me to pray for her.

Pray for me. I am going through a dry season.

It is not easy for God's people to admit they are going through a dry season. But what is "a dry season?" We hear this expression a lot in the Christian world. Let's look closely into it so we can understand how to prevent it or help someone get out of it.

> *Dry: dull; uninteresting: a dry subject, plain; bald; thirsty; causing thirst; dry work; free from tears: dry eyes; drained or evaporated away: a dry river; having or characterized by no rain; the dry season; characterized by absence, deficiency, or failure of natural or ordinary moisture. (Dictionary.com)*

What is a dry season? It is a season in a Christian's life that is boring, monotone, routine, and always the same. You're not growing. You're not hearing from God. You don't even care that much. It's a season where God seems distant and faith is uninteresting. Where you once were passionate about Him, now you're just content to go on like always.

> *As the deer pants for streams of water,*
> *so my soul pants for you, my God.*
> *My soul thirsts for God, for the living God.*
> *When can I go and meet with God?*
> Psalm 42:1–2

Full of Yourself or Full of God?

When people are full of themselves, they cannot be full of God. Dry seasons often take place when what you think, believe, and say is more

important to you than what God says or thinks. This is a very dangerous place to be. Especially after many years of serving and working in
the ministry, many people have a tendency to know "how to run the
ministry" without God. Very few people realize they are getting into this.
It is a sneaky and silent destruction.

When we come to that "arrived" place, pride sneaks in. We don't say
it. We don't articulate it. But without even knowing it, we are in that dangerous valley of dryness. We start trying to run on the fuel we previously
received, but the tank is empty and we're running on fumes. We are in a
very dry place.

And the enemy watches closely and waits. He knows that soon we
will run out of fuel entirely.

Most of the time the enemy doesn't attack you while you're still
running on your own strength. He attacks when you are out of fuel,
when you have nothing in you to bounce back and fight with. At that
point he will bring all kinds of temptations and seductions into your life.
This is why, unfortunately, you see many ministers fall, give up, or leave
the ministry burned out. Some of their families are destroyed, and their
children end up in terrible situations.

During my short years in the ministry, I have seen many people who
want to advise me on how to run a ministry and also how to manage my
life, yet they don't hear from God. They are out of fuel themselves, and
many are going through a dry season. The Bible says there is wisdom in
a multitude of counselors (Proverbs 15:22). However, I watch where my
counsel is coming from. I have to follow the counsel of people who are
counseled by God—who follow the voice of the Holy Spirit.

Unfortunately, there are not many godly people who can give you
Holy Spirit–led counseling. I am an observer. I watch and listen. I watch
how people live their lives and learn their history or "trail marks," so to

speak. I listen to people, but I don't want to follow their advice if it comes from a carnal mind, or in other words, if they are full of themselves instead of full of God. My advice to you is this: If you don't trust or respect a person, do not listen to them, especially when you have to make a critical decision. Unfortunately, you cannot respect and trust everyone you love.

Pastor Tim was talking nonstop without breathing. He was telling me how everything works in the Middle East. Even though I was born and raised in the Middle East and spent the first twenty-five years of my life there, I was quiet and listening. I felt stuck. I didn't have anywhere to run or hide. I was in a church and had to wait for the next two hours for someone to take me to the airport. At one point I thought I just wanted the torture to be over!

Tim had been working in the ministry for about thirty-five years. He was more than knowledgeable about missionary work in the world. But his speech was so dry and long, and I was just plain tired. We were not holding a conversation. He was speaking, and I was praying in my heart that God would have mercy on me.

After a long while, I started praying that God would give me more grace and patience for him, because I was getting angry in my heart at his dry talk. Since I came to Christ, I've had no patience for boring and dry. I had it plenty when I was a Muslim. Nevertheless, I started praying silently that God would change the attitude of my heart. Moreover, I prayed that God would give me compassion for Tim.

Well, God answered my prayer. If we pray earnestly and according to God's will, He answers! As Tim continued to talk, I started filling with such compassion for him. I saw through the Spirit that he was going through a lot.

After awhile, he stopped, saying, "Anyway, this is all God wanted me to share with you." I tried not to get my flesh in the way because he'd brought God into his God-less speech. I asked for God's grace once again. I am telling you all the details and being vulnerable here so you can see and understand what a continuous walk we need to walk, hand in hand with God!

Revelation of God is the presence of God.

After Tim paused, I asked him, "Is there anything I can pray for you? While you were speaking, God showed me that your heart is heavy for your children, especially one who is going through a divorce."

God gives compassion!

At this, tears started running down his cheeks. He was speechless for the first time that day. This time I was very patient, because God was there. You see, when the presence of God is there, you can stay in that place forever. It is not dry. It is not boring. It doesn't even require patience. One of my professors said, "Revelation is the presence of God." In that moment, Jesus was there, and this poor man who had served in the ministry most of his life was hurting in the midst of his dry season.

"How do you know my son is going through a divorce?" he finally said. That might sound surprising for a minister to say—"How do you know?" But it is not surprising for someone who has been going through a dry season to say that. God's voice becomes the voice of a stranger if you are trying to live your life without the Hoy Spirit's fuel. This is why we all need to "remain in Him, and He will remain in us" (John 15:4). If we remain in Him, there is no dryness or boredom.

At that point, Pastor Tim broke down. "Please pray for me," he said. "I don't feel God anymore."

At that moment, God filled my heart with greater compassion, to the point I was ashamed of being impatient with this poor man's talk. As I bowed my head, I prayed in my heart that the Holy Spirit would help me pray. I know by now that whenever I submit to the leading of the Holy Spirit (which should be always!), I need to be slow to say the words and take my time in prayer. That doesn't mean I have to pray a long prayer. I just need to wait on the Lord patiently instead of saying many clichéd words and articulating a perfect, but empty prayer.

As I followed the leading of the Holy Spirit, with every word that came out of my mouth, Pastor Tim seemed more and more broken and crying. He took his handkerchief and cleaned his face and nose. With a shaky voice he said, "I miss this. I miss what you just did. I used to do that. I used to pray in the Spirit like that."

What Relationship Stage Are You In?

At the beginning of the book *The Five Love Languages,* Gary Chapman shares a very valuable observation. He says, "When you enter into a restaurant, you can tell just by looking at the couples which ones are at the dating stage, which ones are on a honeymoon or newlyweds, and which ones have been married for many years."

In the same way, when you meet a Christian, you can tell after a few minutes of conversation if she is still in her honeymoon stage with God or if she's in a routine—in other words, on autopilot, living in the dry and monotonous. Thankfully, those aren't the only two options! I know couples who have made it forty or fifty years in marriage and are still in love. For them, the honeymoon continues. However, I know many married couples who have been married for over forty years, and I can tell just by spending time with them that they don't like each other. They are annoyed by each other. They don't have a good marriage. This is sad. What relationship stage are you in with God?

I met two couples who have been married for forty-six and forty-eight years, and I asked them, "What made your marriage so very successful?" These are the answers these two precious couples gave me:

"Like everything, marriage needs maintenance. It is a continuous commitment. You need to spend quality time with each other. Being a good listener helps the marriage. It tells the other person, 'You are important. I value your thoughts and feelings. I care for you.' Consider others better than yourself. Selfish and prideful people make miserable marriages."

For our "marriage" with God to be healthy in the long-term, that advice applies! Our relationship with God has to be maintained in a continuous commitment. We need to spend quality time with Him and listen attentively to His voice. We need to show God that we value Him, and be loving and humble. When this is always the attitude of our hearts toward Jesus, we will not fall into dry and bored and irritated and miserable!

Dry Seasons and Depression

If you are going through a dry season, your doors are wide open to depression. During a dry season, people are disconnected from the Holy Spirit. They are out of oil. This is why it is called *dry!* They go on in their own strength, intellect and wisdom. They may be serving in the church. They may be preaching and serving in the ministry. They may even be attending Bible studies and studying theology. But without the constant fueling of the Holy Spirit, they are dry. They may have the religion, but they don't have the relationship.

Depression is real and starts with a dry season!

I once heard a preacher say, "Depression is being disconnected from God even though you may do your religious duties, such as praying, reading your Bible, and going to church." I agree. We can have religion. We can automatically do what we are supposed to do and yet might very well be in depression.

I just want you to know, I am not talking like an outsider—I have been there. I was in depression for twenty-five years of my life. My mother is seventy years old today. She has been in depression all her life. That is not an exaggeration. I know what it is like to be lifeless, to not want to get out of bed or take a shower. Depression is the absence of joy. It is an almost numb state of mind and body. It is doing things over and over again on autopilot. It is real, it is crippling, and it can be very serious—leading to nervous breakdowns, suicidal thoughts and substance addictions.

People go into depression for many different reasons, and dry seasons are one of them. If you are in a dry season with God, it's time to get out! It's time to come back to God, to ask Him to fill you, to leave the routine of dull and boring and get back to newness and love. When we let ourselves run out of fuel and burn out, we put ourselves and others in danger.

Since I became a believer, I have never been in a dry season. Not even for a full day. Maybe for several hours I felt I was in the flesh or dry, but

Even Christians get annoyed when I say this. But it is true.

not for days or more. Asking me if I have ever disconnected from God is like asking, "Have you ever stopped breathing?" Our walk with God is a constant walk, like breathing. The moment I am disconnected, things start going wrong. My behavior or the attitude of my heart doesn't line up with the leading of the Holy Spirit when I am not seeking God, and I know something is wrong with me. It's not always instantly, but soon, the Holy Spirit prompts me that I am acting or thinking in the flesh. That brings a healthy fear to my heart.

Fear of God is missing in the church. In Islam everything is motivated by fear of Allah. But in Christianity, many times people take God's goodness, grace and mercies for granted. They take him lightly. They don't have a healthy fear of God.

I am writing this part of the book in a hotel room right now. I am at a Christian networking conference, and I am hiding in my room. Today after two meetings, I thought, *I cannot endure another one.* It is all about everyone selling their ministry, or in other words, giving sales pitches to raise funds. At some point I couldn't breathe, and I ran into my room. I thought, *I need you, God. I cannot do this.* I came to my hotel room and put on worship music and immersed myself in the Word. Then I felt like the weight lifted off my shoulders.

Out there in the conference, it felt dry. It felt like everyone was trying to impress others with their agendas and curriculums to save the world. I felt the Holy Spirit was grieving, and I started grieving too. Our ministry is doing great. We have incredible responses. Our statistics are off the charts—and it really is a work of God. But after sharing with several ministry leaders, everything looked cheap. Even when I said "Praise

God!" or "All glory to Jesus," the words felt fake and plastic. It felt like we were bragging. It felt like we were trying to show off. I couldn't stay in the meeting room one more minute, so I ran out. I came to my room and prayed, "Lord, please forgive me. I am nothing without You. You can save the world. I can't save anyone."

How Long Would You Like To Stay In Your Desert?

Whoever runs away from the truth will stay in the same place facing the same problems over and over again. Many stiff-necked Christians are in the desert way too long! Some blame God, and some blame others. But those who are mature take responsibility, change, and go to the next level. Unfortunately, many stay in the same place for forty years, playing the victim, just like the grumbling Israelites in the wilderness.

But I'm here to tell you: you don't have to stay in the desert. Life does not have to be dry. The same God who called you is waiting to fill you up again. In Jesus, there does not have to be a single boring day!

Some people watch action movies to bring some excitement and adventure into their lives. Instead, I walk in the supernatural every day. I have never had a single boring day since I gave my life to Christ. Every day is an amazing journey for the one who is holding hands with God. How can you have a boring day if you are walking in the supernatural? It is better than any action movie you could ever watch!

Today, I invite you to start seeking Jesus to bring you into a new place in your spiritual life. Seek Him to walk in the supernatural. Seek Him to live far away from the dry places. It is His will for you. Pray that God will show you His purpose for your life and that you will get excited for Jesus Christ.

I have a couple of friends, a husband and wife team, who are traveling evangelists. They told me, "It is sad to see that there are not too many Christians excited for Christ. Every town where we go, we ask the local people, 'Do you know any excited church around here?' Even unbelievers say, 'I think I know what you are looking for.' Once we asked a store clerk if he knew any church in the neighborhood that was excited for God. His answer was, 'You sure don't want to come to my church. It is death.' Then we asked, 'Why are you going there then?' His response was remarkable: 'God called me to be in that church to pray for them.' "

Maybe your spiritual life is like death. Maybe you haven't been excited for God in a long time. Well, I am praying for you! It is time for you to come out of this desert and get new oil from the Holy Spirit. The first step is to confess where you are. Don't deny it anymore! Then just receive refreshment from the Lord.

> *Dear Lord Jesus,*
>
> *I am done with being in a dry season! It has been too long since I really felt Your presence or felt connected to You. It has been too long since I've heard Your voice or felt excitement to be with You. Lord, I confess that I have been content with this state for too long. Please come and renew me. Refresh me. Anoint me with fresh oil from your Holy Spirit. And let me never come to this place of dryness and boredom again! In Jesus' name.*
>
> *Amen.*

If you are in depression, pray this prayer:

Dear Lord Jesus,

I know You love me, Lord. But I cannot feel Your love. It has been awhile since I lost Your joy in my life. I am basically just living and breathing. You know where this depression is coming from. Today I am asking You to break the chains of depression and cover and cleanse me with Your blood. I ask you, Jesus, to restore me to my emotional and physical health. Lord, I seek You and Your help in this situation as your child. I receive Your healing power to my mind, heart and soul. I command depression to never come back to me again. I command the devil and all the evil spirits to leave me and my household in Jesus' name. I have a purpose to live as a child of God. I embrace the delivering, healing and cleansing power of Your blood, Lord Jesus. I praise You, God, and thank You for answering my prayer. In Your name I pray.

Amen.

Chapter 14

Pride is Unattractive!

Pride is the sin of Lucifer. It is one of the most dangerous bondages in the Christian life. But you can be free!

If cats have nine lives, pride has nine hundred.
ARTHUR BURT

*Pride goes before destruction,
a haughty spirit before a fall.*
PROVERBS 16:18

My Dear Daughter, My Joy,

I love you with an everlasting and unfailing love. Your humility attracts My favor and victories in your life. I want you to crucify your pride in every way. When somehow it sneaks in, My Spirit will convict you. You just need to seek Me and My righteousness to be aware of the pride in you. Each time you seek Me, you actually humble yourself, telling Me that you need Me in every area of your life. When you humble yourself, I will exalt you and show you the depths of the heavenly riches and treasures.

Dear Lord,

I love You, and I need You every moment of my life. Please cleanse my heart from any pride. I don't want pride in my life. I want to humble myself before You. I want to do so on my own, because when You have to humble me, it is painful. Please show me, Holy Spirit, in which areas I have pride in my heart. I want to be holy, and with pride in my heart, there cannot be any holiness. Please forgive me for any pride in my heart. I want to walk with you in humility. I pray in Jesus' name.

Amen.

Confronting Pride

Now Moses was a very humble man, more humble than anyone else on the face of the earth.
NUMBERS 12:3

When pride comes, then comes disgrace, but with humility comes wisdom.
PROVERBS 11:2

I will break down your stubborn pride.
LEVITICUS 26:19

Ellen came for prayer. She said her marriage was falling apart and she hated her husband. She said they had too many issues—so many that she didn't know if there was hope for their marriage. However, through the entire talk, all I was noticing was one single problem: pride.

"Why am I the one who needs to apologize?" asked Ellen.

Out of all the sins, pride is the most difficult to confront for three reasons:

1. Pride is a blinding sin. It is the most deceiving sin. It is a barrier against anyone being able to see, hear and receive the truth.

2. Pride rejects and despises confrontation and hates to acknowledge, confess or apologize. It is the craftiest sin, as crafty as its original owner, Lucifer.

3. Pride usually blends into the rest of the human character and heart so well that it can be very difficult to recognize and point out.

What Is Pride?

The pride of your heart has deceived you.
OBADIAH 1:3

Pride is blended secretly into the depths of a person's thoughts and heart. Most of the time, it is hidden. It is the belief that you are better than others, and that you are better because of some innate quality of your own. Pride believes it is wiser or smarter than others, regardless of what the facts might be. Pride comes with superiority, entitlement and selfishness. Pride does not really believe it needs God's help or forgiveness or transforming power. Pride doesn't see that anything is wrong with it. This is why pride is the most dangerous sin of all sins, because it opens up doors to other sins.

In his pride the wicked man does not seek him;
in all his thoughts there is no room for God.
PSALM 10:4

The "I Am a Humble Person" Deception

I find it funny when I hear people say, "I am a very humble person." The moment you think you are humble, you almost certainly have pride!

I have confronted pride in myself as well as others. I find it truly funny when I get compliments from people for being humble. I recognize my pride, and I crucify it whenever I recognize it. Purposefully, I take a stand against pride by deliberately humbling myself in words and actions.

For the sins of their mouths,
for the words of their lips,
let them be caught in their pride.
PSALM 59:12

When I say that, I am not talking about false humility. A lot of Christians know how to act humbly without truly humbling themselves at all. It is the easiest thing for anyone to say, "Oh, it is not me. It is the Lord," when someone compliments us. Our mouths are on autopilot to say that, whether it is from the heart or not. It doesn't prove or demonstrate any humility for someone to say, "It is not about me. It is the Lord. All glory and honor due to Him." This means absolutely nothing, and as a matter of fact, it is rubbish! Of course glory and honor are due to the Lord. But He is choosing to use you, and that is fine to gratefully acknowledge. This comment, instead of a simple "thank you," is usually a way to cover up a heart that is actually responding pridefully.

It also isn't real humility to wallow in a poor self-image or constantly call attention to how downtrodden and worm-like we are, and how we're not worthy and people shouldn't love us or pay any attention to us. That is just buying into a lot of lies about ourselves, and sometimes it's pride masquerading as humility, because *we* are still the most important one in all of that!

Instead, we glorify God and humble ourselves with actions. I believe you are humble when you can take correction without getting offended and angry. You are humble when you take the end of the line in a restaurant and give your place to someone else. You are humble when you can quickly agree that someone else is right and take their side, even if you disagreed at first. You are humble when you honor other people without jealousy or competition. You are humble when you know how dependent you are on God, and constantly turn to Him throughout the day. These are only a few very simple examples out of hundreds.

The Fruit of Pride

Pride bears a lot of bad fruit in our lives. It might look different, but it all stinks! If these attitudes and mind-sets are in your life, it's a sign that you need to give up your pride to God:

Entitlement.

Through my travels I come in contact with a lot of ministers and Christians who don't care to show any kindness or appreciation to waiters or anyone else in the service business, whether through tips or words. It just amazes me that we want to go to the ends of the earth to save the world somewhere far away, yet we are careless about what is right in front of us! The entitled "I deserve it" attitude comes from pride.

Controlling or pushy personality.

It amazes me how many people seem to know how to run my life and manage me. Over the years, I have met with a lot of people who have wanted to be my friend. I have to seek God's wisdom in that. People who often want to control and fix others have serious pride issues. They might not be aware of their own beliefs about this, but they think God is not doing a good job and they have to take control. I come across people like this in my own life regularly. I believe it gives people some kind of power to be in charge of someone else.

Inappropriately curious people are controlling people. They want to know everything. I stay away from people like this. I've had to end several relationships just because my business was theirs. Being curious in this way is not caring. Those are two different things! Inappropriately curious people just have to *know.* The information they possess gives them some sort of power and feeds their pride. They feel somehow significant for knowing it. There is a judgmental spirit behind their curiosity.

Many times, I've had to put distance, or in other words boundaries, in place because of people who had to be in the middle of my daily life to the point where I felt like I couldn't breathe. I had friends who had to know where I was, when I was, and bragged about being closer to me than others just by obtaining some piece of information. Information gives power, and people seek that, even curious Christians.

Controlling = Not trusting God = Pride

When you think that no one will do the job right without you being in charge or in control, you have pride issues. You have a hard time letting go of tasks that don't belong on your shoulders.

Pride only breeds quarrels,
but wisdom is found in those who take advice.
PROVERBS 13:10

A Know-It-All Attitude.

"Are you here to teach me something?" asked William.

I responded calmly, "I was expecting the Holy Spirit would do the job. But you are one of the most unteachable men I have ever met in my life."

"So what are we doing here then?"

"I don't know; you asked to meet me!"

As we argued like this, his wife, Rita, was quiet the entire time. This was supposed to be a counseling session for their marriage, but William was already busy showing that he wasn't interested in counsel.

"I thought you would convince my wife to stay and tell her that she should try harder to be a better wife and mother."

I thought this man had some nerve. "I cannot convince your wife to stay in the marriage," I told him. "She has her own will. She is an adult. And she tells me that you are physically and verbally abusive. I can see you are even trying to bully me."

"I know it all" attitude =
Unteachable =
Pride

He went red and screamed, "The Bible says she must stay in the marriage! Right? And did you ask me why I hit her? Do you know the things she does to provoke me?"

I stood up and said, "Listen to me, Mister. The next time you touch her, you will be in prison. You can give your excuses to the judge."

He stormed out of my office, where I had two security guards waiting in front of my door. Rita stayed with me. She was shaking. We found a home for her and her children. She got a protective order and went through Christian counseling for many years. After a year, I learned that William had been arrested for physical violence, injuring someone in his neighborhood. I was not surprised. His pride made him unteachable.

> *There is no wisdom, no insight, no plan*
> *that can succeed against the LORD.*
> *The horse is made ready for the day of battle,*
> *but victory rests with the LORD.*
> PROVERBS 21:30–31

The Masks of Pride

In some cases, pride is very obvious. But remember that we said pride is the most deceptive of sins. It can wear many masks. People are sometimes shocked to discover that what they thought was their humility is actually a form of pride in disguise!

Self-Pity = Pride.

You wouldn't guess this one, would you? Let's do a little surgery to self-pity. I promise you, if you take this to heart, you will never pity yourself again.

- What is the first word of self-pity? SELF
- Who is in the center of self-pity? ME
- Who do I worship when I indulge in self-pity? ME
- What is self-pity? It is idol worship. You worship *you*. You think of you and worship you when you have self-pity. It is pride.

> *Pride goes before destruction,*
> *a haughty spirit before a fall.*
> PROVERBS 16:18

Victim Mentality = Pride.

Self-pity and a victim mentality go together. They are best friends. Both of them have "me" in the center. A person who has self-pity and a victim mentality is an idol worshipper, worshiping the self. This is one of the most common and manipulative types of pride. When you hear people speak with a "poor me" attitude, you certainly don't think they have pride. On the contrary, it seems the world owes them something! They have suffered so much that someone has to compensate them. Then entitlement comes and finds its root blended with pride.

> *Pride brings a person low,*
> *but the lowly in spirit gain honor.*
> PROVERBS 29:23

> *The end of a matter is better than its beginning,*
> *and patience is better than pride.*
> ECCLESIASTES 7:8

Impatience = Entitlement = Pride.

When we don't want to wait and we are impatient, pride starts rising up within us and telling us secretly that we deserve better and faster service and treatment. We think we have a right to be angry with others for not treating us the way we deserve. This is nothing but pride!

> *The eyes of the arrogant man will be humbled*
> *and the pride of men brought low;*
> *the LORD alone will be exalted in that day.*
> ISAIAH 2:11

The List Is Long

Pride is a blinding sin. When we have pride, we don't see our other sins.

We think we have a right to them. We have a right to be angry, or contemptuous, or impatient, or self-pitying, or harsh, or even fearful. It is very tricky. Prideful people are unteachable. Prideful people are unrepentant. To repent, one has to have humility. Pride opposes repentance.

The list is long.

If you get offended easily: PRIDE.

If you get defensive when someone corrects you: PRIDE.

If you judge and criticize others: PRIDE.

If you have a hard time receiving and asking for help: PRIDE.

If you can't admit your mistakes: PRIDE.

If you cannot submit: PRIDE.

If you talk a lot about yourself: PRIDE.

If you don't listen to others: PRIDE.

If you don't respect other people's requests or feelings: PRIDE.

If you are not a good team player: PRIDE.

If you are overly independent: PRIDE.

If you are a perfectionist: PRIDE.

If you are sarcastic: PRIDE.

If you are intolerant: PRIDE.

If you have an "I-know-it-all" attitude: PRIDE.

If you have an "I-am-right" attitude: PRIDE.

If you get angry when people will not take your advice: PRIDE.

If you insult others: PRIDE.

If you have a hard time saying I'm sorry or asking forgiveness: PRIDE.

If you have a problem forgiving people: PRIDE.

If you think you are entitled to anything: PRIDE.

If you expect others to call you first: PRIDE.

If you have too much confidence in yourself rather than God:
PRIDE.

If you don't like to be told what to do: PRIDE.

If you like to be always in charge: PRIDE.

If you are not open to other people's opinions: PRIDE.

If you are a complainer: PRIDE.

If you are a faultfinder: PRIDE.

If you always speak "I think . . . I, I, I": PRIDE

Pride will leave you lonely and miserable.

Pride can't make many friends, and it loses friends easily.

Pride quits easily if there is a conflict or correction. A prideful person will throw in the towel if she is questioned or confronted. Pride comes in many shapes and forms. Sometimes a very humble-looking person can be full of pride.

Pride is like a snake. It is sneaky and poisonous.

Pride is like a snake. It sneaks in uninvited and secretly. Friendships, marriages, businesses, ministries and even countries can be damaged and destroyed because of pride. Also, be careful: pride recognizes pride. It easily recognizes and reacts against pride in other people. If you are hypersensitive and always thinking other people are so proud, it may be a sign of the pride in your own heart!

A prideful person wants to be recognized, respected, complimented and acknowledged. A prideful person thinks she is better than others, and any problem or mistake is always other people's fault. Pride doesn't take responsibility for any failure or mistake.

Pride does not want others to discover its weaknesses and does not like to confess. The most dangerous part is, pride is a hindrance to repentance. And without repentance, there is no salvation and no transformation.

Finding the Way to Humility

The first step to genuine humility is accepting that to some degree and at some times, you are proud. We all have pride, and we must crucify it by doing the opposite of our flesh.

Second, we must take no confidence in the flesh! Self-confidence will get you stuck and lead you nowhere in life and in ministry. I know many very confident people who are not used by God to the fullest because their confidence is in themselves or their natural gifts, talents and intellects. Some people may even look super-spiritual, or call it "the authority of the believer" and still be operating under a fleshly confidence—spiritual pride, which will result in nothing for the kingdom.

The authority of the believer is real, and it's given to all of us. God wants us to operate in it. But there is nothing good in "self." Selfishness, self-centeredness, self-pity, self-confidence, self-seeking and all that is linked to the word "self" comes from our carnal nature. In biblical terms, *self* represents our flesh and needs to be crucified. There is a difference between speaking with self-confidence and speaking with a spiritual authority that comes from God. Self-confidence comes from pride, and it will not bear good fruit, while authority in Christ comes from humility, acknowledging that the one and only source of our strength and wisdom is God. Spiritual authority in Christ is powerful and bears much fruit.

I have disciplined and trained my mind that I must have zero confidence in me before I go in front of the cameras to preach the gospel message to millions. I have to deny myself to depend on God's power.

I can't do anything by myself!
If I can, it will be a disaster or a failure.
I can do all things THROUGH CHRIST
who gives me the ability to do the things
HE has called me to do!
Jesus said, "Apart from me you can do nothing."

When we come to humility, we are in a truly healthy place. John the Baptist, the forerunner for Christ, summed up the secret of his high position in a lowly state: "I must decrease. He must increase" (John 3:30). Humility means we see ourselves accurately and we see Jesus accurately. We are able to look at the world through lenses of truth and love. We are able to stay connected to our Father in heaven, who is the source of our life. And because of that, God can exalt us!

For it is we who are the circumcision,
we who serve God by his Spirit,
who boast in Christ Jesus, and who put no confidence
in the flesh—
though I myself have reasons for such confidence.
If someone else thinks they have reasons to put confidence
in the flesh, I have more: circumcised on the eighth day,
of the people of Israel, of the tribe of Benjamin, a Hebrew
of Hebrews; in regard to the law, a Pharisee; as for zeal,
persecuting the church; as for righteousness
based on the law, faultless.

But whatever were gains to me I now consider loss
for the sake of Christ.
What is more, I consider everything a loss
because of the surpassing worth of knowing
Christ Jesus my Lord,
for whose sake I have lost all things.
I consider them garbage,
that I may gain Christ and be found in him,
not having a righteousness of my own
that comes from the law,
but that which is through faith in Christ—
the righteousness that comes from God on the basis of faith.
I want to know Christ—
yes, to know the power of his resurrection
and participation in his sufferings,
becoming like him in his death,
and so, somehow, attaining to the resurrection from the
dead.
PHILIPPIANS 3:3–11 *emphasis mine*

Humility & Insecurity

Many times, people confuse insecurity with being humble. Insecure people are thought to be humble people. This is far from the truth. Insecurity comes from the enemy. Humility comes from the Holy Spirit. Insecurity focuses on self and says, "I can't. I can't." A humble person focuses on God and says, "I can, only through God's help."

Because insecure people are "I can't" people, they are often perceived as humble. On the contrary, they are not humble. They are prideful. They try to figure things out with their own wisdom instead of God's. They look at the source of strength and ability in themselves.

If you want to know the difference between an insecure person and a humble person, correct them. Immediately the insecure person will get offended, while the humble person will get on her knees and ask your forgiveness.

Humble people are easy to be around. Insecure people are high maintenance. No encouragement is enough for them. You can't pat them on the shoulder enough. Their identity depends on other people's opinions and comments about them. You walk on eggshells around an insecure person. Insecure people are supersensitive. Insecure people don't trust people. They don't trust God. Everything feels shaky with them. Their happiness depends on other people's behaviors and treatment of them.

It requires so much energy and patience to be around insecure people! It is heavy labor to be with them. It may rob your time and energy. You talk with a humble person and walk away feeling edified and humbled. You talk with an insecure person, and you may walk away drained, angry and frustrated.

I was a very insecure person, and I believed I was humble.

For many years, I was a very insecure person and believed I was humble. It was far from the truth. I was going in front of cameras to preach the gospel, and I was insecure. I was going behind a pulpit to speak, and I was insecure. It was torment! What other people thought of me was very important. I was supersensitive and self-conscious.

One day, God spoke to me and told me He was not pleased with my insecurities and that I couldn't continue like this in the ministry He had ordained for me. Jesus told me He wanted to set me free from my insecurities. I only had to trust Him and receive it. I had to repent from my disbelief and from looking at others as my source of strength and encouragement instead of God. I had to repent from always expecting a pat on the shoulder. I had to be satisfied to receive my reward not on earth, but in heaven. I had to change my perspective and see everything through the eyes of Christ.

Insecurity Is Dangerous

Put two insecure people in a marriage, and it will be a disaster. Insecurity is dangerous. I see it all the time. Take an insecure man and marry him to a successful woman, and he will despise her and resent her after awhile. The wife cannot compliment him enough for him to feel secure in his manhood. If you marry a successful and emotionally healthy man to an insecure woman, it is double shift work for the man. He has to work harder and harder for his wife to feel loved and secure, as her insecurities suck up his love, affection and exhortation like a vacuum. When both parties in a marriage are insecure, it causes more damage than you can imagine. Two insecure people become friends, and their friendship will not last too long. At the beginning they will be best friends through flattery. After awhile, it gets too tiring to keep up the hard work.

The truth is, insecure people listen to the enemy's voice, not God's. Many people who were abused and abandoned by their parents became insecure. The enemy often repeats and whispers to them what their parents or other unkind or cruel people told them in the past. Their parents' voices echo in their ears, and they believe in the devil's lies. They will also spread them.

If you feel you fit into the "insecure" category rather than the "humble" category, I invite you to pray the following prayer. God wants to set you free from all your insecurities. There are deep hurts beneath your insecurities that God wants to heal and set you free from today. After you are free, you will see a big difference in your relationships. But before you pray this prayer, I suggest you sit in God's presence and quietly ask Him to reveal to you where the root of your insecurity is. It is mostly people who were verbally or physically abused or bullied who become insecure. Ask Jesus to reveal to you the very origin of your insecurities. God doesn't want you to be insecure anymore. He wants you to be humble, but confident in His power to move in your life.

> *Dear Lord Jesus,*
>
> *I come to you, Lord, asking you to deliver me from my insecurities. You know where my insecurities are coming from. I ask you to please reveal it to me and remove it from me. I repent from listening to the voice of the enemy instead of Yours. I ask Your forgiveness for not trusting in You and for trying to look to myself or to others for my security. Please wash me with Your precious blood and cleanse me from any offensive ways in me. I want to be a humble servant for You. I can only do what You called me to do with Your help. Please restore my identity, which You gave to me from my birth. In Jesus' name I pray. Amen.*

If you have realized that you have a pride prob-
lem in your life, please pray this prayer:

Dear Lord Jesus,

Please forgive me! I realize that I have been proud.

I have considered myself superior to others. I have

been entitled. I have not recognized my need for You

or humbled myself before You. Lord, in this moment

I repent, and I confess that I need You desperately.

I can't even take a breath without You. I need You

to meet all of my needs, and I have many. I repent

of my behavior toward You and others. I commit to

fight against pride in my life every day. I humble

myself in Your sight. Thank you for Your acceptance

and Your love. In Jesus' name.

Amen.

Healing from the Wounds of Rejection

If you just knew I accepted you
And it all matters,
Then you wouldn't care and hurt
For the one that shutters your life to hide
If you just knew my arms are always open wide
Available for you to run, rest, and abide
Come without any fear or reservation
Know that I am here to accept you
you will not suffer my rejection.

Chapter 15

Freedom from Rejection

Rejection is very painful. But the Lord can and will set you free from this hurt.

The Lord your God goes with you;
he will never leave you nor forsake you.
DEUTERONOMY 31:6

My Dear Child, My Beautiful Daughter,
I always accept you and welcome you with open arms. My love is unfailing and unconditional. You cannot do anything that causes Me to love you less. You also cannot do anything to cause Me to love you more. I love you with a perfect and incredible love that no one else can give to you.

I know that in the past you were rejected and hurt. There are and always will be people who reject you. But today, I invite you to receive My love and acceptance. In My arms, you will always be safe. You will be always embraced by Me. I will never, ever leave you nor abandon you. Come to Me today, and do not let the devil emphasize people's rejection to hurt you more. I am going to heal your heart if you allow Me. You are Mine, and I am yours forever and ever.

Dear Lord Jesus,

I come to You, Lord. I embrace Your love and healing to my hurting heart, of the pain caused by rejection. I ask You, Lord, to completely deliver me from the fear and pain of rejection. I plead the precious and powerful blood of Jesus over my heart, mind and soul. I receive Your love. I receive Your embrace. I will not focus on people who rejected me. I will reject the voice of the enemy and ask You, Lord, to make my heart whole and healthy. In Jesus' name I pray. Amen.

The Deep Wounds of Rejection

Though my father and mother forsake me,
the Lord will receive me.
PSALM 27:10

At one of my conferences on freedom and inner healing, a young girl came to receive prayer. Her grief and anguish were so heavy that she could not open her mouth to tell me the reason she came to the altar. She would burst into a loud cry if she opened her mouth to say a single word.

The moment I said the word "rejection" to her, she started crying violently. Then I said, "Dear Lord, please heal this precious girl's heart from rejection today."

I couldn't pray anymore after that point. She started sobbing and wailing out loud until she had no strength and fell on the floor. She had been rejected by her mother all her life. Every time she made any little mistake her mother punished her by not speaking to her for days. Then finally, one day, her mother sent her to live with her father. She was never given a reason. And this young, precious girl thought something was very wrong with her that she received such treatment from her own mother.

Rejection wounds us deeply because it directly attacks our self-worth.

Sadly, her story is not the only one. Every child who is adopted goes through rejection. Every child whose parents—one or both—are not pursuing a relationship with her goes through rejection. Every child who has a parent commit suicide deals with rejection. Rejection can also find us in adulthood. Every divorcee knows the pain of rejection. Every mother whose children no longer speak to her goes through rejection. Everyone who has had a good friend turn on them or just drop out of their life has experienced rejection.

Rejection is a poisonous and deadly weapon that can devastate, damage and mess up anyone for life, if not taken care of through prayer for inner healing.

Again, receiving is the key. You must receive it. Many people pray for healing many times or get prayers for it, but never truly receive it. *Receiving is a gift.* You don't have to work for it. You don't have to beg. You are not an orphan. You have a perfect Father in heaven. He is kind. He is patient and gentle. May He give you the gift of receiving Him as a Father and receiving His perfect and unconditional love! My prayer for you is that you do not harden your heart. Instead, open your heart to Him and receive from His hands.

Unhealed Wounds

I know a minister's wife whose mother was an alcoholic and left her and her father when she was very young. She was just a little girl, and after her mother left, she used to go in front of a mirror and tell herself she was ugly and stupid. This is what rejection does. When we are rejected, we interpret that rejection onto our self-image. Rejection directly attacks our identity and self-worth. Hurt that comes from rejection is very deep.

When I told this minister's wife that I could no longer be part of their fellowship because I had started going to another meeting, it took her two years to forgive me. I didn't even know it! After two years she wanted to meet me for the first time for a cup of coffee. And she told me that for two years she was angry at me for leaving their group, and now, finally, she was able to forgive me.

When we have been hurt deeply with rejection, we react to events and circumstances irrationally. Many people don't know why they get so upset if they are not invited to a certain event. Every little disappointment can cause a giant effect on a person who has not been healed of rejection. Today we see many children growing up without a father. There are a lot of single mothers out there trying to raise their children with minimal or no support from the fathers. It is creating an epidemic of rejection in our culture.

DANGER!

I want to take a moment to speak to young girls who don't have a good father, or who have been rejected by their fathers. Please know that you are more vulnerable than others in the area of needing to receive male love, and this is a potential danger for you. Because of your need to be

Many young girls who are rejected by their fathers are in desperate need of a man's love.

loved by a man, you are easy prey for the enemy to bring you the wrong person. I pray that you will get free from hurt and the fear of rejection before you enter into any relationship.

I have counseled several women who were abandoned and then divorced by their husbands. Abandonment and divorce also cause a deep scar of rejection. Parents need to know they are not the only ones who go through divorce. Their children go through divorce too.

I am very saddened to see that many parents think only *they* are the ones going through this difficult thing. On the contrary, divorce has its silent, voiceless victims. My daughter was one of them. When I was going through a divorce from her father, I thought I was the one going through it, but she suffered as much and even more than me. She experienced the pain of rejection as my former husband punished me by not seeing her. However, by the power of God, she has received her freedom and healing from rejection.

The new generation coming up is angry and hurting. There are many insecure, angry and hurt young people out there who are hurting others. Deep down, many of them are carrying the bruises and scars of rejection. And of course, let's not forget the voice of the enemy! The devil has no desire to stop whispering those words and memories of rejection over and over again, making the pain new every day.

I know personally the pain of rejection. I was deeply wounded when my parents rejected me as a way of punishment. I was rejected by my mother and denied her love until I was in my early thirties. I was never hugged or kissed by her until then. Most of the time she treated me with contempt, and that created much anger within me. Later on, I was rejected by the kids at school. I was not a good runner or player in the games. I was never invited to play anything, and felt behind and inadequate many times. This is why I have deep compassion and love for the outcast, unloved and rejected.

After I became a follower of Jesus Christ, I didn't even know I had a problem with rejection. But I used to get very angry if someone didn't return my call or say hello to me. When I got married to a Christian man, after two divorces from my Muslim past, I thought everything was going to be perfect. We were both strong believers, and plus, ministers! Perfection, right? But that was not the case. He had his own wounds from his past. When we had any disagreement, he wouldn't talk to me for awhile, and I received it as rejection. It was very painful for me to go through any arguments with him, because most of the time it would result in the silent treatment. I knew physical abuse from my previous marriages. This was nothing close to that, but it was just as painful. I didn't know I already had deep scars caused by rejection.

Later on, when I sought deliverance and counseling, and faced my past, I acknowledged that I had serious rejection issues. I started recognizing the voice of the enemy. And he was right there, whispering all the things wrong about me and my offenders as a reason for the rejection I had been through.

After a prayer of deliverance, I was completely free from the pain of rejection. My husband received the same healing and deliverance. God brought us through much and gave us His sweet love as we had never experienced before.

I will tell you this, though: this freedom is something I continuously need to exercise. As I preach the gospel message to the nations, I experience intense rejection daily. I am often rejected, condemned, insulted and threatened. I don't know how I could handle it if I hadn't been set free from the pain of rejection.

Pray to God to reveal the root of the pain of rejection so that you can be healed and set free.

The Fruit of Rejection

We experience rejection in many ways: abandonment (this includes children who are put up for adoption); neglect by parents; divorce; betrayal; breakups; being outcast, unloved, or unwelcomed by any group, fellowship, or society; getting a cold shoulder or silent treatment; being unnoticed or left alone, etc. Rejection is painful, and in most circumstances leads to other emotions that can hurt us further. Self-pity and anger are only a couple of them. Rejection bears a lot of fruit in our lives, and most of it hurts.

Rejection results in anger. People who are carrying the scars of rejection get angry easily. They get offended easily. They are supersensitive. We can meet them at the workplace as well as in the church. As gentle and loving as you try to be in correcting a person, she will be devastated and hurt if she is carrying the wounds of rejection. Rejected people are high maintenance, and you feel like you are walking on eggshells around them.

Stop trying to prove yourself to be accepted! You don't need to prove yourself to anyone!

Often, rejected people respond this way because they are still trying to prove themselves in order to be accepted. If you ever have to correct them for anything, they feel like they have failed and are being rejected again. There is freedom in not trying to prove yourself to anyone! As I already shared, for a long time I tried to prove myself to my father, and continually sought his acceptance. Each time I tried, I failed and felt that I was never going to be good enough for him. Thank God that when I met my heavenly Father, He accepted and loved me unconditionally, just how I was. He set me free from needing and seeking after man's approval.

People who have rejection issues become people-pleasers in order to be accepted. I was one of them! My mother rejected me so much that I would do anything or become anyone to be accepted and to make as many friends as possible. (You remember the skydiving, right?) There was a void in my heart that caused me to seek people's approval and acceptance. I could never make enough friends. I would like the color blue with the ones who liked blue and would like red with the ones who liked red. I would like ice cream when I truly don't like ice cream much. It took me years to admit that I don't like musicals and museums. What a freedom to be able to be yourself and not have to win anyone's approval and acceptance! After I received my freedom, I was not afraid of sharing my likes or dislikes with people anymore.

Rejection results in a needy and codependent personality. Rejection creates a needy and codependent personality. I suffered with this kind of personality for so many years. I was codependent on men. The rejection I received from my parents caused me to be needy for a man, and I was willing to settle for men who abused me. Many women, without meaning to, end up with the wrong guys just because they were so rejected in their past that the first man who accepts them becomes the one for them.

Many girls who never had their fathers around while they were growing up, give themselves to men who are abusive and controlling. I have been there and done that.

Rejection is degrading, and causes a poor self-image and false identity. Many times I have heard women who were divorced by their husbands saying, "What is wrong with me? Something must be wrong with me that he left me." Again, the first place the enemy uses rejection to hit us is our self-worth and identity. Despite his lies and condemnation, we need to seek God's Word and our identity in Christ and then believe in the truth.

Rejected people reject people! I remember when I was a young girl and dating a boy my age. When we started dating, the very first thing in my mind was, *Before he breaks up with me, I must break up with him.* That in itself can tell you how messed up I was! People who have been hurt by rejection also know how to reject others. This becomes their defense, their protection, or their offensive mechanism. Since they know rejection hurts, they use it to hurt others.

I have met many people whose parents, in their old, supposedly mature years, refused to see them or have anything to do with them. For a minute, I must stop and tell you that if you are a parent, it is your responsibility to build and maintain a relationship, pursue a relationship, and protect a relationship with your children. It is the parents' responsibility. I know many parents who stop talking to their children because of an offense. If you are a parent, you cannot let the enemy steal your children! It is your duty to be a good steward of God's gift of your children and go after them as the more mature party. Take the first step. Keep in touch. I am sorry, but what kind of garbage is this that mothers and fathers are not seeing their children for years?

As a perfect parent, God the Father always pursues us. He loved us even though we were still sinners (Romans 5:8). He never gave up on us. Then how can we give up on our children and stop talking to them? Especially if you claim to know God and have a personal relationship with Him! If you are one of those parents who hasn't seen or spoken to your children for years because you are trying to punish them, or because you are acting out of a deep hurt or offense, it is time to be a grown-up, pick up the phone, and set an example of forgiveness and unconditional love.

If you are the child who was rejected, if you can salvage your relationship with your parent, go ahead and seek peace and reconciliation. But if you are rejected again and again, you need to surrender it to the Lord and seek healing for the rejection you have suffered. God can heal your heart and give you perfect peace about your circumstance.

I have also seen cases where children have cut off their parents because of offenses, or because they are too busy or too enlightened or even too spiritual to continue honoring and visiting their parents. If this is you, you need to do business with God about it. Believe me, I understand having difficult parents! But it is my responsibility to love and honor them as God calls me to do.

Rejected Children of the Bible

Throughout the Bible, we see many rejected children and the negative results of it. Absalom was rejected by his father, King David. Later on, he fought against his father to take the kingdom from him. Esau was angry when he was rejected from receiving his father's blessings. Ishmael was another child who was rejected. Abraham had to send him and his mother, Hagar, away. As of today, we still see the seed of Ishmael full of turmoil, war and hostility. I was a seed of Ishmael. But through my faith in Christ Jesus, I became an adopted daughter of the Living God and a seed of Isaac.

The Secret of Healing from Rejection

Daughter of God, there are several things you need to know that will help with rejection in your life.

1. *Everyone experiences rejection!* Everyone experiences rejection at one time or another. You are not the only one. You can't find a person who is loved by everyone. Even though it may seem that way, it is not the truth. There will be always someone who will reject or dislike you, and that is true for everyone.

2. *Jesus was rejected too!* Jesus was rejected by many. And still today, there are billions of people who are rejecting God. Jesus was abandoned, betrayed and rejected. He knows your pain. He understands. If you are suffering because of rejection, know that you are partaking in His suffering. And what was Jesus' attitude toward the people who rejected him? He forgave them.

- Forgiveness is the key for you to move on from any emotional pain. It may not come naturally. If it does not, then you need Jesus' supernatural touch to be able to forgive.

3. *Rejection is very common in the Bible.* There are so many people in the Bible who experienced rejection! Think of the woman who was bleeding for twelve years. She was considered unclean in that society. The people with leprosy experienced rejection as outcasts. They experienced the pain and hurt of not being accepted into society. The Bible recognizes the common nature and pain of rejection. But it also shows God taking up the rejected, healing them, and choosing them for Himself.

4. *Stop asking "why me."* There will be a time in your life, if you are seeking freedom from the pain of rejection, when you need to stop asking "Why me? Why am I being rejected?" That question always

leads you to the enemy's voice, which will tell you that something is wrong with you and that is why you are rejected. Ultimately, it will only make things worse.

Finally, here is the secret to receiving healing for the scars of rejection: no matter who rejects us, we can truly put our trust in God, become adopted sons and daughters and receive His love and acceptance. That truth is powerful enough to heal all of our wounds and allow us to live truly free in His love.

Let's start going to our Lord Jesus Christ right now, asking for His healing and freedom in the area of rejection. I invite you to pray the following prayer for your healing from the wounds of rejection:

Dear Lord,

You know my heart and everything in my heart that has been hurting and crippling me. Today I ask Your help and healing for the wounds of rejection. I need Your touch. I was rejected, neglected, abandoned, and hurt deeply by _____ [name the person or people]. That created much anger and bitterness in my heart. Please heal my heart. And also forgive me for believing the lies of the enemy. After I was rejected, I believed that I was not good enough or I was ugly, or stupid, or unworthy, or _____ [list the things that rejection caused]. Now I realize that I believed the enemy's lies and made an agreement with him by accepting his lies about me. I repent from this and ask You to forgive me. I reject his lies in Jesus' name. I receive Your truth that I am wonderfully and fearfully made and that I am loved and accepted by You as my perfect heavenly Father. I forgive the person or persons who rejected me and hurt me very much. I ask You to set me free from fear of rejection. I ask You, Lord Jesus, to forgive me for hurting others through rejection as well. Please also forgive me for trying to please people so that I may be accepted. There is only one person I have to please and deeply care about, and that is You. I am Your child and very grateful for Your unconditional love. In Jesus' name I pray.

Amen.

For the Lord will not reject his people;
he will never forsake his inheritance.
PSALM 94:14

Can a mother forget the baby at her breast and
have no compassion on the child she has borne?
Though she may forget, I will not forget you!
ISAIAH 49:15

*The Lord your God goes with you; he will never
leave you nor forsake you.*

DEUTERONOMY 31:6

Chapter 16
Freedom from Generational Curses

I confess the sins we Israelites,
including myself and my father's family,
have committed against you.
We have acted very wickedly toward you.
We have not obeyed the commands, decrees
and laws you gave your servant Moses.
NEHEMIAH 1:6–7

My Dear Daughter,

I care for you deeply, and want you to have complete freedom in every area of your life. I want you to be free from the chains of your past sins and even from the past sins of your parents and grandparents. I want to restore to you the blessings I have planned for you for many generations. You are loved and favored. As you seek My face, pray to Me, and walk in obedience, I will shower you with My freedom, love and heavenly treasures. I am your portion and your inheritance.

Dear Lord,

Thank You for Your unfailing and perfect love. I embrace Your freedom in Jesus' name. I ask You to set me and my offspring free from any generational curses due to disobedience to You in previous generations. I ask Your forgiveness for myself and on behalf of my ancestors. I put a bloodline of Jesus Christ between me and past generations of my family. Thank you for covering me and my family with Your precious blood, Lord Jesus. In Your name I pray. Amen.

God maintains his love to thousands, and
forgives wickedness, rebellion and sin.
Yet he does not leave the guilty unpunished;
he punishes the children and their children for
the sin of the parents to the third and fourth
generation.
EXODUS 34:7

Generational Curses: The Best-Kept Secret in the Christian World

Generational cursing is something that is taught very little about in the Christian world. Why don't we talk more about this important subject?

Here's what I believe is the reason: we all want to believe that once we are in Christ, we don't have to worry about any generational curses, and we don't have to do anything about them. However, I have seen in my own personal life that there were things from my family line that were attached to me even though I was a newborn believer, and I had to go through full acknowledgement and renouncement in order to separate myself from my father's and mother's sins.

> **One person's sins can ruin his entire family for generations.**

I believe the main reason we have to do this is to be aware of what the old self can carry into the new self that will pop up from time to time. My father's family was racist toward Armenians. As I've already shared, he was one of the most racist men I have ever known. He would be proud to openly speak about the evil his family had done during the Armenian genocide. There was great hostility in my family for generations, and I inherited it. This was, of course, the seed of Ishmael at work. The hostility of Ishmael was in my roots.

The Bible says that the penalty of the sins of the fathers can fall upon several generations.

> *Our sins and the iniquities of our ancestors*
> *have made Jerusalem and your people*
> *an object of scorn to all those around us.*
> DANIEL 9:16

I have seen children and even grandchildren paying the penalty of their parents' and grandparents' sins. During one of my meetings, a mother in tears brought me a little girl about five years old, who was limping. The mother asked me to pray for her. At that very moment, God revealed to me that this little girl was paying the penalty of her grandfather. Her grandfather's lust and adulterous relationships had caused this little girl much suffering. I asked the mother if this was the case. She confirmed it. We prayed in agreement to break the generational curse.

Right after the prayer, the countenance of the little girl changed remarkably. Her cheeks got rosy. She kept looking at me and smiling. She started walking better. I have learned that by the next day, she was walking perfectly.

Now I want to be careful to point out that not in every case is a disability caused by a generational curse. As Jesus stated, some illnesses have a purpose for God to be glorified (John 9:3). However, it is important to recognize when a generational curse, specifically, is at work.

After King David's moral failure of coveting someone else's wife, committing adultery, then murdering an innocent man by purposely sending him to the front line during a war, the consequences of his sin infected his entire family. When the prophet Nathan visited King David and confronted him, he prophesied over him that even though David's sin was forgiven, he and his family would have to pay the penalty. We are seeing a generational curse here. At the very moment sin enters in, the same moment a curse enters into our lives instead of a blessing.

We see this in many places in the Bible, starting with Adam and Eve. They sinned, and the first rotten fruit of their sin was that one of their sons killed the other. What a tragedy! The curse they brought into the world has extended far beyond their time, all the way down to our day. Because of their disobedience, we all inherit two things: a sinful nature and the reality of living in a cursed world.

We Live in a Cursed World!

When we hear all the evil on the news, why does it surprise or shock us?

As soon as we are born, we inherit the curse that comes upon us from the disobedience of the first man and woman. A curse comes from disobedience. Sin brings a curse. We also inherit the curses of our parents, grandparents, and great-grandparents. In the book of Exodus, chapter 20 verse 4, God tells us He is a jealous God and will punish the children for the sin of their fathers, up to the third and even the fourth generation of those who hate Him. The prophet Nathan used the same word "hate," asking David, "Why did you hate God's Word?" He was telling David, "You knew better."

My father had a sex addiction, and his sins brought much grief into our lives. His speech was perverse, his eyes made me uncomfortable, and his actions came out of wickedness and perversity. My mother's closest friends would come over, and he would flirt with them and look at them, checking them out. I knew the evil sparks in his eyes when he saw a certain type of woman. Even as young as five or six years old, I was able to notice this. Before he saw a woman, I would worry in my heart that he would like her. I hated his happy expression when he saw an attractive woman. He would act differently. After asking for Jesus' cleansing and removal of the generational curses that came through my father's sin, now I can easily recognize the spirit of lust on men.

You give the devil an inch, he will take a mile.

If you give the devil an inch, before you know it he will take a mile and more. The good news, however, is that God will turn what the enemy has tried to do into good when you get free from curses!

When I minister, I leave it to the male ministers to pray over men who come to the altar for a prayer after I speak. Recently I was in Florida, ministering through one of my Freedom Conferences. Many came to the altar to receive prayer to be set free from bondages. Most of them were Christians. Two men came forward, and they both had a spirit of lust all over them. They didn't say a word. But I told each of them privately—to their shock—and directed them to get prayer from the pastor of the church.

The enemy is very crafty, so we have to be very careful as ministers as to how we minister to and interact with the opposite sex, especially when the subject is lust. In this way, God started using something very devastating in my life to bring freedom to others.

Family Contamination

Generational curses can take different forms. Sometimes they mean that the children will be prone to falling into the same sins as their parents. Sometimes they mean that health problems or mental problems will be passed down. Sometimes they mean that circumstances will always seem to fight against the children who are under a curse, bringing poverty, tragedy, addictions, or patterns of loss and failure. Curses can open your life to demonic influences.

I was not more than nine when I found pornographic materials in my father's closet. As I skimmed through them, I was defiled with those images. They influenced my thoughts about myself and others for many years. *Once the spirit of perversion sneaks into your household, it is difficult to get it out.* Not impossible, but difficult. Difficult because it is familiar. Your home becomes a regular residency of sexual demons. When the sexual demons are out, once you have cleansed your house, your heart and your life, you need to be disciplined to continue in purity. I have seen people cleansed from sexual promiscuity get too relaxed and comfortable, as if they don't need God's help anymore, and that "arrived" feeling opens the doors to demons seven times worse (Luke 11:26).

During my Christian walk and ministry, I have met many people who inherited generational curses from their parents, grandparents, or great-grandparents. I have seen many cases of married people who flirt with other married people of the opposite sex in the church because of the spirit of adultery. I know people whose parents were Masons or members of the KKK or other demonic clubs and who are suffering with terrible illnesses and demonic attacks. I know many disabled people who are struggling with certain health conditions as a result of one or both of their parents' or grandparents' sins.

Again, not all diseases and disabilities are a result of generational curses, but as a minister, I have come across cases that were. I have seen firsthand that once family curses are removed, healing takes place.

Personally, I inherited a spirit of lust, hostility and deception from my parents. I had to come to a place where I would repent and renounce these and ask Jesus to wash me and cleanse me with His

I inherited a spirit of lust from my parents.

precious blood. A repentant heart is absolutely necessary for anyone who needs cleansing from such generational curses. Maybe today you too have a spirit of lust that you need to repent of. Maybe you need to ask Jesus to remove all the sexual demons from you and your family. The spirit of lust is almost everywhere you go in the world, and unfortunately, it is also very present in the body of Christ. Maybe you need to repent of other generational curses, such as substance abuse, anger or deception.

As a new believer, I had no idea about living a holy life. I am not proud of the way I lived in the beginning of my walk with Christ! There is no doubt there was a drastic change in my heart and life, but it was not enough for me to live a godly life automatically. I was not under good biblical teaching at that time, and now I look back and realize how very worldly I was. I really had no clue about holy living. I loved the Lord. I was on fire for Jesus (I still am). I was even sharing my testimony in many churches, but was not rooted deeply in the Word, and my church didn't teach about holy living. Now I look back and say, "How did I do that? What was I thinking?"

I had a minister lady friend who one day pointed out to me the man she slept with in the church. She was my mentor at that time! I was attending her classes. My mentor and I both loved the Lord, but we had no clue about Christian living. Then I said to myself, *There must be more than this. I am not happy living my life like this. I want more of Jesus. I want more truth.*

The Bible says in John 16:24, "Ask and you will receive." And I asked. I wanted to come out of my comfort zone. I told the Lord that I wanted to live a holy life. I wanted to keep my heart pure and be devoted to Him. The more I surrendered and walked in obedience, the more God opened ministry doors and trusted me with His vision for the lost.

Whether you struggle with things inherited from your parents and grandparents or with sins that began in your own life, all you need to be free is to make the same decision. It is time to cut off the chains of the past and walk in holiness and purity. You are God's princess. Lust, hostility, lies, and all the rest have no place in your life!

God Can Set You Free!

When I was last in Sweden, I made an altar call for people who had suicides in their families. Many people flooded to the altars. A lot of young people who were suicidal came to the altar to receive prayer. They had suicide in every generation of their families for five to six generations. I had to pray with them to break that curse. I also prayed for many who had, for many generations in their families, patterns of accidental death, death at a very young age, and even murder.

One young man came forward crying. Two friends accompanied him, as he was shaking and weeping. He told me there was suicide in his family for five generations and that he was himself suicidal that day. He had wanted to take his life on the very day I was speaking. My words on suicide pierced his heart. I prayed for him, and then he prayed to break the curse of suicide. He wrote to me after a year and told me that since the day we prayed together at the altar, thoughts of suicide had never come back to him. He said for the first time in his life he felt free and was filled with joy. He shared that God had started using him to reach out to people who were suicidal.

In recent years, I have been primarily focusing on suicide and rape during my altar calls, and the responses have been incredible. Many people have been set free by Jesus, and God has filled them with joy for the first time in their lives. Our God is a living Redeemer, and He is the Restorer. No matter what sins or curses run in your family, today may be your turn.

If you have suicide in your family or are having suicidal thoughts, I invite you to pray the prayer at the end of this chapter.

God is not human, that he should lie,
not a human being, that he
should change his mind.
Does he speak and then not act?
Does he promise and not fulfill?
I have received a command to bless;
he has blessed, and I cannot change it.

NUMBERS 23:19–20

Dear Lord,

I recognize that generational curses are at work in my life. I acknowledge the sins of my fathers and grandfathers. [Name those sins.] I confess that I have followed in their footsteps in the areas of _____ [name the specific areas]. I ask You to forgive me and cleanse me from my sins, and ask You to break the power of generational curses in Jesus' name. I put a bloodline between me and the sins of my ancestors in Jesus' mighty name. I declare that I am a new creation and delivered from the power of the enemy. I ask You to bring healing and cleansing into my life from all these things. In Jesus' name.

Amen.

If you are struggling with thoughts of suicide, I invite you to pray this prayer:

Dear Lord,

I acknowledge that You are the Resurrection and the Life. I ask You to please remove any generational curses of suicide from me and my family. I pray you will also take away any suicidal thoughts. I come against the voice of the enemy in Jesus' name. I am a child of God. I and my family are under the blood covering of Jesus Christ. I pray from this day on that Christ's life-giving power will fill me and my family. I come against the spirit of death in Jesus Christ's name. I put a bloodline of Jesus Christ between me and the enemy. Please forgive me, Jesus, for my suicidal thoughts. I repent from them today, and I receive Your deliverance. Thank You for saving my life, not only in this life, but in the life to come. Thank You for Your free gift of eternal life. In Jesus' name I pray.

Amen.

The LORD bless you and keep you;
the LORD make his face shine on you
and be gracious to you;
the LORD turn his face toward you
and give you peace.
So they will put my name on the Israelites,
and I will bless them.

NUMBERS 6:24–27

Give ear, our God, and hear;
open your eyes and see the desolation
of the city that bears your Name.
We do not make requests of you
because we are righteous,
but because of your great mercy.
Lord, listen! Lord, forgive!
Lord, hear and act!
For your sake, my God, do not delay,
because your city and your people
bear your Name.

DANIEL 9:18–19

Chapter 17
Freedom from Shame & Guilt!

*Instead of your shame
you will receive a double portion,
and instead of disgrace
you will rejoice in your inheritance.
And so you will inherit a double portion
in your land,
and everlasting joy will be yours.*

ISAIAH 61:7

My Beautiful Daughter,

I love you. My love is different from the love of the world. It is liberating. It is selfless and caring. I came to set you free from shame and guilt. I want to set you free from condemnation. I am for you, not against you. The enemy of your soul has been trying to put guilt and shame on you. But if you allow Me, I will destroy his plans to keep your head down. You are My daughter. You are the King's daughter. Today if you ask Me, I will remove your shame and double your portion. You will be blessed because of Me.

My King and My Lord,

I am Your daughter. I am adopted into Your kingdom. Thank You for giving me the privilege to be called a daughter of God. This is an amazing gift! I want to be free. Please set me free from the shame, guilt and condemnation I have been carrying in my heart and countenance. I receive Your freedom. Please forgive me for my sins. I repent from all of them. I ask You, dear Lord Jesus, please wash me clean with Your powerful blood that you shed at Calvary. I thank You for dying on the cross for my sins and rising from the dead to give me an eternal life. I embrace Your freedom. From this day on, I will be walking as a King's daughter. You are the King of kings and the Lord of lords. I pray in Jesus' name.

Amen.

The Heavy Load of Shame

Therefore, there is now no condemnation
for those who are in Christ Jesus,
because through Christ Jesus

the law of the Spirit who gives life
has set you free
from the law of sin and death.
ROMANS 8:1-2

"I cannot carry this shame and guilt anymore. It is too heavy," said Fatima. We were talking during a meeting I was conducting in the Middle East.

I said, "You don't have to carry it anymore. You can release it to God with a prayer, and you can be free today."

"Is it that easy?" she asked. Nothing had ever been easy for Fatima. A Muslim woman for forty years, she had been divorced four times. She was married for the first time as a little kid. She never had a childhood, and as a teenager, became a mother of three. Her husband sold her to other men, and her shame was unbearable. She wished to kill herself, but wanted to raise her three children first.

"Yes," I told her. "My dear, it is that easy. Jesus died on the cross to remove your shame and guilt."

"What do I need to do to be free?"

"You just need to believe. Do you believe Jesus died on the cross for your sins and that He rose from the dead the third day to give you eternal life?"

"Yes, I do. I do believe," said Fatima.

"Do you believe Jesus Christ is the Son of God and the only way for salvation? That Jesus is the only way to God the Father? Do you believe?"

"I believe. I believe. I believe." She was on her knees on the floor, weeping. "Please Lord Jesus, set me free!"

Fatima was set free that day. She kept kissing my hands. I took her hands into mine and kissed them back. "Now you are the King's daughter. No more shame. No more guilt. You are made new. You are born again."

"Born again," she repeated. "I love it. I am born again!"

Fatima's shame was taken away. Everything was made new. She was free, redeemed and filled with joy. Only Jesus can do this. Only Jesus. Only Jesus Christ of Nazareth, who is the same yesterday, today and forever.

"Come now, let us settle the matter,"
says the LORD.
"Though your sins are like scarlet,
they shall be as white as snow;
though they are red as crimson,
they shall be like wool."
ISAIAH 1:18

I too carried shame and guilt for many years. These things defined much of my life until age forty, many years after I became a Christian. Then one day, I found myself sitting in front of two counselors, confessing my sin of believing in the devil's lies and carrying shame and guilt. At the end I was free. My chains were broken. The memory of many incidents had no power over me anymore.

"My daughter committed suicide," he said on the air.

Recently a man called during one of my live programs in the Turkish language. I wear a little earpiece during my live programs, and the control room tells me who is calling. This time they said a Muslim man was calling to ask for prayer for his daughter, who had recently committed suicide.

I was teaching when the call came in, but I couldn't stop thinking of him and his pain as a parent. The problem was, I had no clue what to tell him. But God told me to take the call, so I said, "Hello, we have a caller. How can I help you? What would you like to share?"

The man answered, "Well." You could feel in his voice the shame and guilt and condemnation as a parent. He said, "My thirteen-year-old daughter committed suicide. We just buried her."

At that moment, I couldn't control my tears. I just started crying. As a parent, I didn't even want to think of the pain of losing a child. This man was tormented with shame, thinking over and over, *What could I have done to prevent this? Why did this happen?*

As I listened, the Lord gave me the answer in my heart. Now, you need to be very careful when speaking to people whose shoes you have never been in. It's important to respect their pain, to respect their story.

God told me, "Take the call."

So I said, "I am terribly sorry for your loss. Nobody can understand, so I am not going to tell you I understand. But I feel your pain. In my faith, God is the God of the living. So we do not pray over the dead. But I can tell you this—God's grace is faster than a bullet. And I believe with all my heart that in her last breath, Jesus was in every way trying to reach out to her. That is all I can tell you."

I paused and continued, "However, you are tormented, and you are living in great misery. And I have to tell you: if you do not surrender your life today, that misery will continue in the life to come after this life. But if you surrender your life today, if you give your heart to Jesus Christ today, He will remove the shame. He will remove the guilt and the condemnation. And He will change your heart. I can promise you that. It may take time. I know, because I have Christian friends who have lost their children, and it may take time. It may take a lot of suffering and questioning. But I can tell you this, if you surrender your heart to Jesus Christ, He will comfort you, and He will change your destiny."

The man answered, "Yes, please, I want to give my heart to Jesus." We prayed together, and he gave his heart to Jesus.

The program was over, but the entire week I thought of him. I just couldn't get him and his voice out of my mind. I prayed for him. I wondered if his prayer was real. Did he really surrender his life? Did he really understand? I was so filled with compassion for this man, I knew it was the Lord in me.

The following week, another live show started, and during the program, this man called again. They told me, "This is the same man from last week." I quickly took the call, and he said, "I just want you to know since last week, this is real! I called to testify that Jesus Christ is real, because this joy that I have, this freedom that I have, is supernatural. I have never had this before in my life. I have so much joy, I cannot describe it!"

While I was rejoicing to hear this, he said, "I am a poor man. I have nothing to give to Jesus, but I thought and prayed, what can I give to Jesus? And I figured out something. I want to donate my kidney. I am announcing on air that I want to donate my kidney to Jesus."

When I speak at Western churches I say, "There is nothing better than seeing a Muslim receive Christ. There's no better investment for the kingdom than getting Muslims saved! In the Western world, pastors tell me they have a hard time getting tithes in their church. When Muslims give their hearts to Jesus Christ, they want to donate their kidneys." The following week, another man said, "I received Jesus Christ through your program, and I want to donate my kidney too." And I said, "What is this program? A kidney donation drive?" Everybody calls to donate their kidneys!

That man was filled with so much joy and freedom. Freedom from condemnation. Freedom from shame. Freedom from all the stuff the devil was putting on him. He was free, and he had the joy of the Lord.

Where Does Shame Come From?

Shame can come from many places. Shame is not guilt, which tells us we have done something wrong. Shame tells us that *we* are wrong. It tells us that something about us is just inherently worthless, broken or stupid. Shame is crippling. Genuine guilt can lead to repentance, but shame can never lead to repentance, because it usually comes from the sins of others against us, not from our own wrong actions. Others sin against us, and we take on the identity of that. It is one of the most damaging things we can have in our lives.

During the last twelve years of my ministry, I have met many men and women who were carrying the shame, guilt and condemnation of sexual abuse. They felt dirty. They felt like they deserved the abuse or they must have done something very wrong to invite it. The enemy loved to keep them under bondage with his lies. As I prayed with individuals who truly wanted freedom, I saw their chains broken loose just like mine. I saw them filled with sudden joy. I saw the change in their countenance and God's light shining through them.

It was obvious from her countenance that she had been intensely abused.

But getting freedom from shame is not easy for everyone. Recently I met a beautiful eighteen-year-old girl who came to the altar after one of my freedom talks. She was very pretty. However, it was obvious to me from her countenance that she had been intensely abused. Before she told me anything, the Holy Spirit led me to pray for her, giving me the gift of knowledge. She started crying hysterically as I prayed. She confirmed that she was sexually abused by her own father for many years.

When she grew up a little more, she moved in with a relative who offered her a safe and loving shelter. But she was not able to pass through her past abuse to enter a place of freedom. This is very common and normal. Many people think if they change their location and the abuse stops, they will be fine. Of course, changing the abusive environment and finding a safe place is always the first step! But it is not the end of the problem. Changing your location doesn't provide emotional healing. So this sweet, beautiful girl was tormented even though she was living in a better environment.

A couple of years after she moved away from her father, she surrendered her life to Jesus. Surrendering your life to Jesus is wonderful. But again, the emotional healing may not take place immediately. Most of the time you need to seek emotional healing. Awareness of your need for it is vital.

After receiving Jesus into her heart and changing her location failed to give this young girl the help she needed, she acknowledged that she had to forgive her father. She prayed for him and prayed for her heart to change toward him so she could truly forgive. There was a time she felt complete forgiveness in her heart toward her father. At that time, she decided she would go and tell him that she had forgiven him and that he needed God in his life. She met her father and told him that she forgave him for the sexual and verbal abuse.

His response completely shattered her. He said he didn't need her forgiveness. What happened was not his fault—she had asked for it and had seduced him from the age of seven to sixteen years old, and he couldn't resist her seduction. That's what he told her.

As she told me this, she fell apart. I hugged her for a long while and allowed her to weep in my arms. She needed to do that. I had hundreds of people waiting to receive prayer, but I was not going to rush her! My ministry prayer team was praying over many while I was holding her in my arms like a loving mother.

Freedom From Shame

Romans 10:11 says, "Anyone who believes in Him will never be put to shame." Today I want to talk to you about freedom from shame and guilt—your *freedom*. God wants to set us free from all paralyzing diseases of the heart. They are unseen, but they cripple us. They paralyze us. As God's daughters, we can be free from them all: from fear, from darkness, from the curse, from many things that cling to us because of false religions and false beliefs.

God wants to set us free from the paralyzing diseases of the heart!

Guilt, shame and condemnation weigh us down. Friends, when you have guilt in your life and you only operate through guilt, you live in bondage. For decades, I always lived with guilt. No matter what, I always had a guilty conscience. I remember when I was a new baby in Christ, one day my pastor said, "May I speak with you for a minute?" And the first reaction I gave him was, "Did I do something wrong?" He said, "No, I just want to talk to you about something I'm going to ask you to do. Can you speak at one of our events?" But that was always my reaction if someone asked if they could speak with me. I just lived like that all the time, with fear and guilt.

When I was a child and would leave for school, if I'd done something displeasing to my mom, she would say, "Oh, you disobeyed me and you're going out? See what is going to happen to you! You are going to see the penalty of disobeying me." So I thought if I hit my hand or hurt myself somehow, I must have done something wrong five minutes ago. If something went wrong in my life, I would ask, "What did I say to my mother?" or "What did I do to my dad?" or "What kind of wrong did I do to someone?"

Chains like this are not God's intention for us! God wants to set us free from all these lies so we can live for *Him*. When you live for God, there is freedom in that relationship. There are no crippling diseases of the soul in that relationship. There is true freedom from false guilt and from shame.

Jesus Took Our Shame

Hebrews 12:2 says that Jesus "endured the cross, scorning its shame, and sat down at the right hand of the throne." Jesus took the shame! The Messiah, the Son of God, God in human form, took the shame of being crucified naked alongside criminals. The sinless Messiah never committed any crime, but he bore your shame. Why? *Because the perfect Lamb of God wants to remove your shame from you.*

Shame is not a little thing. It is the heaviest weight there is, heavy enough to kill you. After failing in every area of my life, I started to join my voice with the enemy's. "You're a loser," I would tell myself. "You've failed in everything." I had failed in business. I had failed in relationships. I had failed in two marriages. I had failed in motherhood. I had failed in every area of my life. I accepted the fact and the shame and guilt that came with it. "I failed. I cannot make it in this life."

On the day I was going to kill myself, I was telling myself these

After failing in every area of my life, I started to join my voice with the enemy's.

things. I looked at myself in the bathroom mirror and just repeated it all: "I failed. I cannot make it in this life, and I don't want to carry this shame anymore. I don't want to carry this guilt anymore. I want to be set free from this." I planned to set myself free by killing myself, but instead, Jesus found me that day. He saved my life, and years later, He set me free from the shame as well.

Many of you live your lives with guilt, shame and condemnation, and many of you are raising your children with guilt, shame and condemnation. Your children do things for you because you put guilt on them. This is the way you are operating as a parent because this is what you learned from your parents. You are chained, and you are chaining your children. God wants to set you free!

Healing The Lepers

There are a lot of voices in the world that will put shame on us if they can. In the Middle East, when someone is sick or something bad happens to them, the first thing they say is, "Oh, what have they done? What has she done? What has he done to deserve this?" The first thing we want to do is condemn the sick or afflicted with something. This goes all the way back to Bible times! Job says in Job 10:15, "If I am guilty—woe to me! Even if I am innocent, I cannot lift my head, for I am full of shame and drowned in my affliction." This man had lost ten of his children. He had lost all his possessions. He had lost all his health, and he had lost his position in society. Everyone was pointing their fingers at him. "What have you done that you are going through this? What have you done to deserve this?"

When I read Matthew 8, I can feel the shame in the man with leprosy: "When Jesus came down from the mountainside, large crowds followed him. A man with leprosy came and knelt before him and said, 'Lord, if you are willing, you can make me clean.' Jesus reached out his hand and touched the man. 'I am willing,' He said. 'Be clean!' Immediately he was cleansed of his leprosy" (Matthew 8:1–3).

Recently I heard a testimony about a preacher who was living with people who had leprosy, and was praying and speaking the love of God over them. Lepers around the world have their own communities. You don't see people with advanced leprosy walking around you. Do you know why? It is because they hide. They have shame. They are disfigured, and they don't want other people to see them. They are ashamed of themselves. This little passage in Matthew really breaks my heart when I read it, because I was like that man! Because of my failures, because of my ugliness, because of my infirmities, I was hiding. This leper didn't even think he was worthy to be healed. He didn't even think someone could show mercy and compassion to him because he had already condemned himself.

Lepers are a perfect picture of shame. In the society of Jesus' time, they were covered with guilt and shame. They were unclean. Nobody touched them. People would go and throw leftover food out to them like garbage, and these people would come from the caves where they were hiding and go and eat whatever was thrown to them.

But this leper's story doesn't end in shame and hiding. He is ashamed of himself. He is hiding. And then Jesus comes. The leper barely even has hope, but he goes and kneels before Jesus, kneeling on the ground because he feels like he is nothing. Can you feel his pain? I can, because I have been there! He is full of pain. He kneels before Jesus and says, "Lord, if you are willing, you can heal me."

There is so much in that "if you are willing"! *I know I am not worthy. I know I don't deserve it, Lord. I know I am ugly and despicable in appearance. I am full of shame. I know I am nothing, but if you are willing, you can help me.*

And look at what Jesus did! Jesus was a Jew, and according to Jewish law, he shouldn't have touched that man, because that man was unclean. But Jesus reached out to him and touched him and said, "I am willing. *I am willing.* Be

> ## "If you are willing, you can heal me."

clean." No condemnation, no guilt, no finding fault: just compassion and love. And at that moment, the leper was cured.

Let me tell you, my friends, that healing was not only in the leper's body! It was in his heart too. When I came before the Messiah, the Son of God, the Living Redeemer, He was touched with my weaknesses. When I fell, when I was hurting, He didn't kick me and say, "Look what you have done. Shame on you." No, He said, "Come here. We have some cleansing to do. Come! We have some work to do. Just come!" And He removed my shame.

The labels we carry are about shame. I carried the label "Divorced." I carried the label "Loser." I carried the label "Failure." And Jesus just cleansed me. Today, He wants to do the same thing for you.

I am nothing special. God chooses the weak things of the world to shame the strong. God chooses the foolish things of the world to shame the wise. If you are ordinary, if you are sick with guilt and shame and condemnation, you are a perfect candidate for God to touch and cleanse! He can give you a new heart, a new purpose and a new life, whether you're coming to Him for the first time or you've been a Christian for decades. He is the Master Physician. He is the best doctor I know.

If you have a crippling disease of the soul today, just call Doctor Jesus. If you want to be set free today, if you want to be delivered, call Doctor Jesus. He says, "I didn't come for the healthy. I came for the sick" (Mark 2:17). He came for people like you and me.

No More A Victim

Today, Jesus Christ is telling you, you don't have to live as a victim anymore. I know this from experience. I am not a victim anymore. I am not just a survivor. I *live,* I *thrive* through Jesus Christ! I am a freedom warrior for Jesus Christ. You can be that freedom warrior too.

When that young girl finished sobbing, I gently cleaned her face with a napkin. I lifted up her beautiful face, holding her chin up so she could look me in the eyes. Her tearful eyes were red and swollen from crying. She looked at me, and I saw fear. I saw hurt. I saw a deep wound in her soul, and I knew she felt like she could never recover from this tragedy.

I looked in her eyes straight and strong. She looked down and was in tears again. I lifted up her chin and looked into her eyes and said, "Tell me, do you believe what your father told you? Do you believe, do you truly believe that when you were seven years old, you seduced your father? You were a minor. He was the adult, and he was stronger than you. Now you tell me, is it your fault or not? If you insist on believing in a lie, I cannot change anything. You have free will to believe in whatever you wish. Do you believe what your father told you?"

I don't just survive anymore. I thrive!

She answered, weeping, "No, I don't. I don't. It was not my fault. He was stronger. I was so afraid. He beat me up too before he raped me."

There and then, we prayed. I asked her to pray as well. It is not good enough for people to rely on someone else's faith and relationship with God. You need to open up your own mouth, pray, confess, proclaim, repent and break the agreement you have made with Satan by believing his lies. And she did these things. She completely rejected the lies of the enemy; she proclaimed that she was a child of God and the enemy had no power over her. She repented of making an agreement with her father's deception and carrying the guilt and condemnation he had put upon her. She repented from self-hatred. She asked God's cleansing power to come and completely make her new. At the end, she looked snow white—happy, free and full of hope for her future.

Finally Free

As you've read the stories in this chapter, I hope you are getting a vision for your own freedom from shame. But let me ask you: is it easy to get free from shame?

The answer is *absolutely*. Jesus died on the cross for your freedom from every kind of bondage. He died on the cross and shed his blood to cancel the enemy's assignment in your life. All you need to do is to believe and pray. It really is that easy!

Can this girl lose her freedom and go back to her old thinking? Can she go back to thinking that she was the guilty party in what happened to her and become completely wounded again? Again, the answer is *absolutely*. People get healed and delivered by the blood of the perfect Lamb, and that is easy! But they don't lose their free will. If they start listening to the same lies again and again, soon they will find themselves in the same despair. Many people will then suggest, "Maybe they were not completely delivered or healed at that time." But that is not the case. People do get delivered very easily if they want to and are receptive. But if they are double-minded and weak in their faith, they will go back to their old ways when the enemy starts attacking them again and again.

If you are ready to be finally free, you can pray for healing from shame in your own words and your own way. The following prayer is an example you can use as a starting point if you like.

Dear Lord Jesus,

I open my heart to You right now. You know that what happened to me is devastating me. [Name that abuse or incident that hurt you deeply. Try to articulate it.] I need Your healing touch. I am breaking and rejecting the lies of the enemy: _____ [list those lies]. Please come and cleanse my heart. I receive Your love and healing right now.

"But I will restore you to health and heal your wounds," declares the LORD,
"because you are called an outcast,
Zion for whom no one cares."
JEREMIAH 30:17

The Secret Place

My Love,

I always desire that you come to Me first. I know you have missed Me. I miss you more. I am waiting for you. I am longing for you to abide in Me so I can abide in you. I have been protecting you from things you know not of. I have been closing doors to protect you even though you wanted to enter through them. The way seemed right to you, but in the end it would have been nothing but disaster.

The other day I saw you just stopping for a moment to acknowledge that you were Mine. It brought a smile to my heart and blessed Me more than words can describe.

Do you remember the night you opened your heart to Me and shared the most secret places? I knew all of them from the beginning. But just you sharing them with Me blessed my heart very much. It was the first time you did not go to your best friend or to your mother. It was the first time you came to Me and shared everything that was in your heart. At that moment, I comforted you and took you into My arms. That is the way I desire for us to be always.

You are Mine, and I am yours for eternity.

With My Everlasting Love,

Always Yours,
Your Father

Chapter 18

Broken Heart

The LORD is close to the brokenhearted
and saves those who are crushed in spirit.

PSALM 34:18

My Precious and Beautiful Daughter,

I care for you. I care for your heart. I think of you all the time because of My love for you. I want to heal your heart and make it whole again. Your heart may be broken over many things. The abuse, rejection, betrayal, abandonment, and tragic events have broken your heart. If you feel unloved and unfulfilled, I want to change that right now. If you surrender your heart to Me, even though it may be in a thousand pieces, I will heal your heart and make it whole. All you need to do is trust Me with every corner of your heart and surrender. Allow Me to enter into the very secret places of your heart so I can do my miraculous work and give you a new heart today.

My Dear Lord, My King,

Thank you for loving me unconditionally. For a long time, I was blind to Your love. I couldn't see Your amazing love. I am sorry, Lord. I didn't receive Your love. Instead I sought people's love. And I ended up with a broken heart. Please forgive me, Lord, for not receiving Your love and trusting You to heal my broken heart. Today, I make a decision to trust my heart to Your hands without any reservation. Please search my heart. Please check every compartment of my heart and heal the areas that need Your supernatural touch. Give me a new heart today, Lord, I pray. I pray that You will make my heart whole again. I receive Your love, Lord. No one's love can be compared to Yours, my Maker. In Jesus' name I pray.

Amen.

A Culture of Broken Hearts

*He heals the brokenhearted
and binds up their wounds.*

He determines the number of the stars
and calls them each by name.
PSALM 147:3–4

We live in a culture of broken hearts. So many things that are normal in our day and culture cause hearts to be broken. We are surrounded by people who are deeply wounded, and many of those heart wounds are never really recognized by others.

Divorce = Broken Heart

Recently God revealed to me that every child from a broken home has a broken heart. If you come from a broken home, you have a broken heart.

Every child from a broken home has a broken heart!

Brokenness affects the divorced as well! If you are divorced, you have a broken heart. If your husband abandoned you for another woman, you have a broken heart. Divorce is a form of brokenness, always.

Abused = Broken Heart

Abuse is also rampant in our culture. Parents, relatives school friends, siblings, and peers abuse. If the very people you trusted abused you or raped you or molested you, you have a broken heart. If your parents were brutal to you, you have a broken heart. If you were bullied and outcast, you probably have a broken heart. You are broken, and God sees that broken heart.

So many young people out there are hurting. When my daughter comes to tell me the things her classmates say to each other, it is incredible to hear how cruel they can be. I remember her crying at home because they mocked one of her friends and called her names because she is overweight. My daughter stood up for her, and was called names too, for doing that. These children and teenagers are hurting. They have broken hearts. There are kids who feel like they are not worthy to be loved. They are not worthy to be accepted. They believe a lie. This is why you see a lot of drug abuse, eating disorders, obesity and emotional eating among teenagers. This is why young people are cutting themselves, hating themselves, and thinking they are not worthy to be loved.

Our hearts are supposed to be safe. We are designed to live in relationships of honor, trust and affection. When these things are absent, and especially when someone you love and trust hurts you, your heart breaks. As a result, we carry pain and find ourselves unable to love and trust again, even when we want to.

My daughter's father, my former husband, dumped me on the highway when he was high and drunk, and she was in the car. She was two and a half years old at the time. She was so traumatized that she did not speak until she was four. The day after that incident, with a police escort, I went and picked her up. I was twenty-eight years old, a single mother, divorced twice, and ready to kill myself because I believed anybody could be a better mother for my daughter. We were a pair of broken hearts!

We sin against our children a lot of the time. They are an easy target!

Many of us commit sin most often against our children. They are an easy target. This is very rarely acknowledged, but it is true. During a time of divorce, many parents punish each other by hurting the children. My daughter's father is a very good man right now—God turned his life around, and they have a decent relationship. But for years he punished me by not seeing her. She was four, five, six years old. She had a little Barbie suitcase. She would prepare her suitcase, every week, put it by the door, and sit on that suitcase and wait all morning for her daddy to come, and he would not come. Children go through divorce too, and their pain is never acknowledged enough.

Some of the things my daughter went through in those early days she doesn't remember. Other things she does. But it does not matter whether she consciously remembers or not; her spirit does. Her heart knows that pain. She's been through that rejection.

As her mother, I didn't see until recently how much these things had impacted her. She is a youth leader at church. She is a missionary. I never have to tell her to read her Bible or listen to gospel music. I see her every morning on her knees, just loving Jesus. And as she prays to Jesus, she calls him her daddy. But she has had to deal with the pain of a broken heart. I am married to a wonderful man who raised my daughter, but he's a stepdad. It doesn't matter how good he is or how much he tries, somewhere in the back of her head the enemy will say, "Oh, your real dad doesn't love you. He rejects you. He doesn't call you enough."

Most of the time, people don't hurt us intentionally. The hurt is unintentional, but it still hurts. And we live with an epidemic of broken hearts.

Recently I was dropping my daughter off at school, and she did not want to go at all. I saw the look on her face and asked what was wrong, but she didn't know. She just had this anger and sadness inside, and she didn't know where it all came from.

Well, I realized something as I looked at her. All these years, I had been thinking about how *I* went through a divorce. I would go on platforms and give my testimony, but she went through that too, and I never acknowledged her pain; I just always spoke about my pain. I was thinking all these years, *I went through divorce. I went through all this sorrow and hurt.* But she was there with me, going through all the pain, all the hurt, and all the rejection because of my wrong decisions, and I had never acknowledged it.

I asked her if she wanted to go a café, and she said *yes* just to get out of school. We went to IHOP and ate crepes, eggs and toast, and I started talking about how she had a broken heart because of the past, even because of things she didn't know about her dad and the divorce. My daughter just started weeping. We prayed about it together, and my daughter felt a huge weight lifted off of her. She felt joy and freedom.

"What is wrong with me that my husband left me?"

Betrayal = Broken Heart

"What is wrong with me?" asked Doris. "What is wrong with me that my husband left me for another woman? Where did I fail? What have I done wrong?"

Doris is one of many women I have met who were betrayed and left by their husbands for another woman. The first reaction we feel after abandonment and betrayal is to find fault in ourselves. We feel we must have caused what happened! We cannot simply accept that the other person has a fallen, sinful nature too, and that when he is not walking in obedience and in line with the Word of God, he will fall short and may make the worst mistakes of his life. But of course, the enemy is right there by our side to whisper into our ears his best lies: something is wrong with us that we were abused, rejected, abandoned and betrayed.

I tried to counsel Doris many times that it was not her fault and that she hadn't done anything to deserve her husband's betrayal. Doris was an amazing mother and a faithful wife. She was very beautiful. She loved the Lord. I saw her treating her husband with such love and respect. However, when we would talk, she would try hard to point out her mistakes that had caused her husband to go to other women. Later on, she found out about his many lies. He was living a double life all along, and she felt stupid for believing that he had ever loved her. At that point, she started asking herself how she could be so blind and foolish as to not see her husband's true face! Every time she found out about his lies, she pointed the finger at herself.

For a long time Doris didn't feel beautiful, even though she was extremely beautiful inside and out. Besides her low self-esteem, guilt and self-condemnation, she had one seriously broken heart. Her heart had been stabbed with a knife many times and trampled underfoot, and it shattered into pieces like glass.

Doris suffered with a broken heart for several years until one day she made a decision that the enemy was not going to steal one more day from her. She surrendered all her feelings and the lies of the enemy to Jesus. She confessed and repented from the lies she had believed and asked God to make her heart whole again. And Jesus touched her broken heart and made it whole and brand new.

It's Time To Be Free

You may have a broken heart today. You may have broken a child's heart. You are reading this, and something happened in the past that broke your heart—a breakup, wrong decisions, divorce, abuse, rejection, fears, or betrayal. Maybe your heart is breaking right now, today. Your husband may not be paying attention to your feelings. You feel unfulfilled. You feel alone, even if you are surrounded by people. You are lonely, and this is your heart, shattered. And the enemy just tramples your heart under his feet. You allow him to do it.

God wants to change your heart. He wants to give you a whole new heart. He will do it today. He wants you to receive His healing. He wants to give you a strong backbone, to enable you to face things. You are not alone. Human relationships have broken your heart, but a divine relationship will heal it.

If you have a broken heart, I would like to invite you to pray the following prayer:

> *Dear Lord Jesus,*
>
> *I have come before you confessing that I have a broken heart because of _____ [list what or who broke your heart]. I also confess that because of what happened, I have believed in lies of the enemy, and I have carried guilt and shame. I repent from my false beliefs and the lies. I also forgive those who broke my heart. I ask You to forgive them and bless them. From this moment on, they and the enemy have no power over me. Please wash me clean with Your precious blood, Lord Jesus. I pray that You will heal my heart completely and make it whole again. I receive Your healing, Jesus. I receive Your unconditional love. In Jesus' name I pray.*
>
> *Amen.*

I will give them an undivided heart
and put a new spirit in them;
I will remove from them their heart of stone
and give them a heart of flesh.

EZEKIEL 11:19

Rid yourselves of all the offenses you have com-
mitted, and get a new heart and a new spirit.

EZEKIEL 18:31

Jesus turned and saw her.
"Take heart, daughter," he said,
"your faith has healed you.'
And the woman was healed at that moment."

MATTHEW 9:22

I will give you a new heart
and put a new spirit in you;
I will remove from you your heart of stone
and give you a heart of flesh.

EZEKIEL 36:26

Chapter 19

Freedom from Anger

Everyone should be quick to listen,
slow to speak and slow to become angry.
Because human anger does not produce
the righteousness that God desires

JAMES 1:19–20

My Sweet Daughter,

My love for you has no limits. It has healing power and is always available to you. I want to heal you from your anger. I deeply care for your feelings. I care about the things that cause you to react so badly. I want to help you replace your angry reactions with godly responses so I can lead you to a way of living that is healthy and beneficial for you. The devil, the very enemy of your soul, knows the things that make you angry. He has studied you to provoke you to anger so you may lose your blessings and be destroyed. But I have come to destroy his plans and schemes in your life. I want you to be a conqueror. I want to remove the anger in your heart from its roots so it will not destroy you or hurt you. Then you will enjoy your life, full of love and peace. Today, you just need to let Me do the work in your heart so you will be free from anger.

> *Dear Lord,*
> *Thank You for always being there and listening. Even though there are times I do not listen to You, You are still caring and listening to me. You are so good to me and always merciful. You are slow to anger and abounding in love. I want to be like You. I open my heart to You, Lord. You know the areas in my heart that need Your healing touch to be delivered from anger. You know very well, dear Lord, the root and the cause of the anger in my heart. Please remove it from its roots. I confess my unrighteous anger and my foolish and hurtful behavior because of it. I don't want to act in anger anymore. Please cleanse me, Jesus, with Your precious and powerful blood from all of my anger. I pray in Jesus' name.*
> *Amen.*

A Culture of Anger

Love is not easily angered.
1 CORINTHIANS 13:5

I come from a culture where anger is one of the most dominant feelings. Anger is part of the Muslim world, and it was blended into my DNA. In Turkish culture we get easily angered, and I grew up in a very angry and hostile environment. My parents constantly yelled and cursed at each other. They slammed doors and broke things. I was accustomed to that kind of behavior.

I share my stories openly on TV with a Muslim audience, and many write asking me to pray to get rid of their anger. But until I point it out, most of them do not recognize that anger is a problem. Once I bring awareness to the issue, many Muslims respond in desperation to get rid of the anger that is such a dominant force in their belief systems and daily lives.

It is part of Islam to be angry at things that are not of Allah, so Muslims often justify their anger. But the Bible makes it clear that hostility, hatred and demonstrated anger are from the devil and from our sinful nature. In my TV programs, I tell angry Muslims that if they are acting upon hatred and anger, if they are beating up their wives or children, it is not of God. The Quran says you can discipline your wife using violence. This is not of God. If this is what you believe, then you need to look for the true God.

Learned Behavior

Many of us learn anger from other people, as well as inheriting it from our parents and the culture we grew up in. Most of us become like the very people we once claimed we would never become. It seems like the more we don't want to be like someone, the more likely we are to become just like them!

This would take another book to explain fully, but I can tell you one thing: our parents are our first teachers, and they set up a standard and show us a code of behavior that is most natural for us to follow.

"I will never become like my mother," I said . . . and I became just like her.

Mockers stir up a city,
but the wise turn away anger.
PROVERBS 29:8

When I was about nine years old, my father bought several nice shirts from an expensive store. He wore one of them when he was going to work in the morning. When he came home late that day, he complained that something was wrong with the shirt and it had bothered his neck all day long. As he took the shirt off and investigated, he and my mom noticed there was a defect on the shirt—one side of the collar was shorter than the other side and didn't fit right. Well, my father was upset that after he'd paid a large sum of money, a fancy store would sell a defective shirt. So he told me to get ready, as he wanted to take me back to the store with him. I didn't want to go. I knew how it was going to end up! As I trembled with fear and anxiety, he ordered my mother to get me ready. As he was driving back to the store, he was cursing and screaming at other drivers. I was quiet and scared as always.

After he parked his car, he started walking fast while pulling me harshly. He stormed into the store with the shirt in a bag in his hand. He went to the salesclerk and complained about the defective item. The salesclerk apologized and took the bag from my dad to investigate the shirt. After looking at it, he told my father that he was right, but he could not accept the shirt as a return or exchange because it was dirty from being worn all day. My father started yelling at the clerk, "Who cares if it was worn or not? You cannot sell a defective shirt! It took me all day to notice it! I want my money back!"

The clerk tried to be calm. He kept a plastic smile mixed with fear on his face as he explained once again the store policy for the worn merchandise. My father's voice was like a thunderstorm this time, as he could not put up with the clerk's stupidity. You could feel his anger growing. He asked to see the manager. The clerk was happy to leave and call the manager. Meanwhile, I started walking away and looking for a place to hide in the store. I didn't want anyone to know he was my father. I always wanted to be invisible during times like these.

Finally the manager came, and he too told my father the company policy. At that time in Turkey, the customer was always wrong. They didn't have policies that would protect consumers. Even though I was very young, I could see my father's point. But his behavior made him the bad guy as usual. After the manager insisted that they had to follow their company policy, my father took the same shirts from the shelves to show the manager they were all defective. And they were.

The manager stood his ground and repeated the same line once again. At this, my father completely lost it. He took all the shirts and started ripping them one by one and screaming and going completely crazy. Everybody was looking at him. I was hiding behind the coats and shaking with fear. After he ripped the shirts, he threw them at the manager's face. The manager attempted to call the police and told my father they didn't want a customer like him. My father started looking for me. Oh, how I wished I didn't belong to him! He yelled my name, and I came out of my hiding place. He pulled me violently by my hand, and we left the store.

These angry outbursts were normal behaviors in our family. They could happen anywhere. My father would throw things in a restaurant or curse on the street. Any day could start out normal and calm and end in fighting and turmoil. What I remember the most is having a fear of the unexpected. I remember a deep fear of being embarrassed.

I didn't know that the anger routine I hated was going to be a big part of my own life one day. When I grew up, I too would be controlled and consumed by anger.

Do not be quickly provoked in your spirit,
for anger resides in the lap of fools.
ECCLESIASTES 7:9

Going To The Root

Later in life, I learned that anger outbursts had been part of the daily life in my family for many generations. My father told me one day that he had been beaten up severely by his mother and cursed and yelled at for most of his childhood. He was molested by maidservants when he was five years old. At that time, his family was rich. They were living in a castle close to the Russian border in the northeastern part of Turkey. Then his father lost everything in gambling, and my father's parents got divorced. My father had to start working at age seven to help support the family. That rough life added to his anger.

My mother's anger issues were rooted in growing up without a father, and being bullied and called names by kids on the street. Later on, my father's unfaithfulness brought deeper and more intense anger into her life, which she released on me by physically and verbally abusing me.

If you are dealing with an anger problem today, pray and ask God to show you the root of that anger problem. Recognizing roots allows us to break ties with family curses and our agreements with lies we have believed. It shines light into the dark places where our anger is coming from and allows us to bring truth and freedom into those places.

The Bible has a lot to say about anger and how it brings destruction into our lives.

A gentle answer turns away wrath,
but a harsh word stirs up anger.
PROVERBS 15:1

Do not make friends with a hot-tempered
person;
do not associate with one easily angered.
PROVERBS 22:24

In your anger do not sin: Do not let the sun go
down while you are still angry.
EPHESIANS 4:26

But now you must also rid yourselves of all such
things as these: anger, rage, malice, slander,
and filthy language from your lips.
COLOSSIANS 3:8

Therefore I want the men everywhere to pray,
lifting up holy hands without anger or
disputing.
1 TIMOTHY 2:8

What Makes You Angry?

When I was a Muslim working at a company where my boss was a Christian, it made me very angry when he would share his faith with me. He would talk about Jesus as the Son of God, which was complete blasphemy according to my faith at the time. His love for Jesus made me angry too. He was a sweet man, and had so much goodness in him. He helped me

The name of Jesus made me angry.
His name was an offense to me.
One day I had to face that offense,
and I had to make a decision.

more than I could ever tell you, but it made me so angry that he called Jesus his Lord and Savior—his God. He didn't come against me when he witnessed to me; he wouldn't offend me or say terrible things about my faith, but *his* faith made me angry.

My boss didn't know much about Islam, but he knew one thing: he knew his God well. He knew his Jesus well. He had a personal relationship with his God. And that made me more angry, because I never had a relationship with my god. He was not performing the rituals I was, yet he was claiming that he had a relationship, a personal relationship, with this God.

One day he started asking me questions. He said, "Işık, you need to ask yourself: can this be God who says beating up a woman is okay or even required? Can this be God?" He said, "Just ask the questions. Is it okay? Is it of God that a man can have more than one wife? Just ask these questions." Well, those challenges made me even more angry!

Truth we don't want to hear can make us angry too!

One day he said to me, "Işık, you are a very lost woman." I got so angry in my heart I almost wanted to quit my job at that time—and believe me, in those days I really needed that job! But I went home. I looked in the mirror and cried, and said, "Yes, I am a very lost woman."

People get angry for many reasons. But you remember what I always say—the problem is not the problem. With drugs and alcohol and other addictions, there are always things beneath the addictions that are causing that problem. The same thing is true with anger. An angry response comes from something underlying that needs to be dealt with and healed.

Abuse results in anger! If you were victimized, you may have a serious anger problem.

Abuse results in anger. Not only did I inherit angry behaviors from my parents and from the Islamic culture, but I grew a lot of my own anger as a result of the abuse I went through. There are many angry people who try to hide the anger within them for a long time. However, sooner or later the sleeping lion wakes up. A reaction that looks sudden and unexpected to you may be the result of years of abuse and frustration.

If you watch and observe them enough, you don't need to be a prophet to see who has an anger problem

You don't have to be a prophet to see people who are angry inside.

inside. You can see it in the way they act. You can see it in the way they try to control themselves for a short while. You can see it in their behaviors. And you know it if there's anger inside of yourself. It's like a disease.

Let me ask you, friends: Don't you want to get rid of this? Forget the self-control part of it; don't you just want to be anger-free?

There are so many people walking on the streets, in the supermarkets and in our churches who are like walking, ticking bombs. Their anger is because of something or someone else, but if you accidentally cross them, they just vomit and puke everything inside of them onto you. Sometimes we say, "Wow, what did I ever do to you?" But most of the time it is nothing to do with you or me. And I am not talking from the other side of the fence! I am talking as a person who really knows what violent anger is. I received it, and I gave it out.

If you are carrying more than you are supposed to, *you get angry!* If you don't have a voice and you are oppressed, *you get angry!* If you are burnt out, *you get angry!*

Burnout can be another cause of anger. Some people are simply doing more than God is asking them to do, and they get angry because they feel so trapped and exhausted.

Rejection, abandonment, and betrayals also cause anger. King David didn't see his son Absalom for two years. This caused anger in Absalom, and later on he rebelled against his father and tried to divide the kingdom. Ishmael was sent away with his mother, Hagar, by Abraham. Ishmael's anger and hostility are still heavily on display in the Muslim world.

Getting Free From Anger

As believers in Christ, first we have to become aware of our anger, then we can acknowledge it and repent from it. We need to depend on God to do the miraculous work in us. The truth of the matter is, it may not happen in one day, or even in one year or two. It takes dedication, in many cases desperation, and the Holy Spirit's power to be free from anger.

My anger didn't just disappear as soon as I gave my life to Christ Jesus. God had to do much work in me. It took years, and still God has to work in my heart! I'll say "Oh, I am completely delivered of this," but then he'll show me a person or a circumstance that makes me angry, and it is humbling to see how I still need God's help. I may not be acting upon anger the way I used to, and those who know my entire life story—like my parents—will say, "Wow, what a change you've had!" But there are times I still have to say, "Well, Lord, thank you for showing me that I am not completely perfect in this area and I still need your help."

When we are humble and repentant about anger, the Lord will deliver us from it day by day. Our freedom from anger begins with being related to God in the right way. Pride will get in the way, and so will refusal to admit the truth.

Prideful Anger!

I used to get angry at angry people. That was not a good place to be! I also had another type of anger, where if I counseled someone and told them the right way to go and they did not listen to me, I would get very angry. That's an anger that comes from pride. Or, if someone doesn't acknowledge you or give you the honor you think you deserve, and you get angry, that's a prideful anger again. Insecure people who have issues related to rejection, get angry when people don't return their calls or text messages. Many people hold grudges because of that.

Many kids I know are angry because their fathers left them or their parents neglected them. Years later, people get into marriages still carrying anger problems rooted in early years of childhood, and most of them don't know where the anger is coming from. In most cases, anger is a symptom of a deeper problem. Whatever the cause of your anger, I encourage you to look within and see where it is originating. The Holy Spirit wants to set you free. You need inner healing, emotional healing.

Becoming An Empty Vending Machine

After I received Jesus Christ as my Lord and Savior, I still had anger in my heart—not as much as I used to have, but still a good amount! I wanted to get rid of it, but it still flared up, especially when I was put down or treated like a doormat.

I was getting counseling that first year from my pastor and his wife, who were speaking into my life and teaching me the Word of God. At the time, my former husband would have our daughter every other weekend, and we had to do an exchange at the end of the weekend in the parking lot of a shopping plaza or some similar place. When he would bring her back with her belongings, it was also the time for him to give me the child support check.

One night after the weekend was over, when I was only a few months old in the Lord, he brought our daughter and didn't give me the check. As I was putting our little girl in the car, I reminded him about it. He took the check out, cursed me, and just threw the check at me. It flew into the air and disappeared—the wind must have blown it away. He got inside his car like nothing had happened and started driving away.

Well, I ran into my car and started chasing after him. The road was divided by a landscaped median with trees and flowers. I was so angry I drove over the median with my car, passed him, and blocked the road in front of him. I got out of my car and started toward him. I wanted to open his door and beat him up. I don't know what I was thinking! He worked out three hours a day. He was in his best shape, and I was at my worst. But it didn't matter at that point, because I was not thinking with a sober mind. I was blinded by my anger. He just sat in his seat, looking at me, smiling and mocking me.

When I reached his door, I suddenly became aware of the noises I was hearing, and looked around. On the opposite side of the road, a tourist bus had stopped, and all the Japanese tourists were taking my picture or looking at me in shock. There was a sign on their bus that said, "Welcome to America."

Realizing how foolish I must have looked, I stopped at once and went back to my car. I could hear my ex-husband yelling after me, "Christian, huh? You will never change! Look at you!"

At that moment, I completely agreed with him. I left that place feeling completely defeated. As I was driving, I cried violently. My daughter was in the back seat, witnessing everything in shock. I felt like I had failed once again as a mother, and this time as a Christian too. Was my former husband right? Was there no hope for me? Was it true I would never change?

Of course, the enemy wanted me to believe all of that. And I was in agreement with the enemy.

"You must become an empty vending machine!"

It was late at night, but I called my pastor. He and his wife said, "Just come here, Işık."

I went all the way there crying. I told them everything. I told them how terrible and stupid I'd acted and how I'd failed the Lord. I told them how ashamed I was, and was just weeping. "He told me I will never change. Nothing will change me. I am a hypocrite."

My pastor listened patiently, then said, "This is exactly what the enemy wants you to believe. He wants you to believe there is no hope for you and that you're a failure. Yes, you failed. But that is not the end of it. You fall and you get up. You fall and you get up. You never give up."

Then he smiled like something was funny, and I got even more angry. *Why is he laughing at me?* I thought. *I have a serious problem. I have a crisis here!*

Smiling, he continued, "We are just like vending machines."

"Vending machines?" I asked.

"Yes," he said. "You know, one of those machines you put money into and then take a Coke out. You see, the enemy knows what to put in you and which button to press to get whatever he wants out of you. The devil knows your buttons. He knows what makes you angry, such as degrading you, belittling you, and verbal abuse and insults. He is a good psychiatrist, and he knows all about your childhood. He knows all your weaknesses and what words and situations will upset you. Then he uses people to press your buttons to get the ugliest behavior from you. Moreover, after he gets what he wants out of you, like he did tonight, then he comes and condemns you and brings discouragement and hopelessness into your heart so that you will give up.

"Now I am going to tell you this," he continued. "The more you trust Jesus and allow him to work in you and change you, the more you surrender to God, the more the vending machine will be empty. That is dying to self. The enemy will try to push your buttons, but nothing will come out of you. One day you will give no reaction to the same insults and belittlement, because whatever your ex-husband says will not change your identity or worth in Christ Jesus. One day, that vending machine will be empty; there will not be any soda left. One day you will be so dead to self that your ex-husband or your father can say whatever they want and it will not hurt you or make you angry."

My pastor was right. As I followed Jesus closely and sought God's help and guidance, my vending machine became emptier and emptier. After awhile my former husband saw that no matter what he did to provoke me, he would get nothing out of me—so he quit provoking me. It took awhile for him to accept that I had changed and had made serious progress.

After two years from that night when I lost my temper, my ex-husband called me out of nowhere one night and said, "I want to ask your forgiveness for everything I have done and said to hurt and insult you. You are a woman of God. Jesus truly did a work in you. Please forgive me."

That was a turning point in our relationship that affected our daughter in a positive way as well. From that time on, we had peace and respect for each other. Even though he did not choose to give his life to Jesus, still he respected me for doing so.

Who Are You Representing?

We are all representing our faith in one way or another. We are all preaching a message with our behavior more than with the words we speak or declare. When you start to make progress in any area, people notice! They don't need you to be perfect, but you are a good witness when they can see you growing and changing. The more we seek God's help and abide in Jesus, the more the results will be lasting and remarkable.

Today Jesus wants to set you free from anger. He wants to empty your vending machine. It is possible for you to be completely delivered from your anger by God's supernatural touch.

Baby elephants throw themselves into the mud when they are angry. I wonder how many people are still stuck in the mud just because they got themselves into it out of anger, bitterness, unforgiveness and sadness. Maybe today is the day for you to be hosed down and washed from all your stinky attitudes! It may not be obvious on the outside, but you are stuck in the mud. If that's you, it's time to go to your daddy, your heavenly Father. You are his princess, after all! It's time to get cleaned up and beautiful again.

Just say a simple prayer:

> *Dear Lord,*
>
> *I have been in the mud for so long, and I don't want to be there anymore. Please forgive me of my stubbornness, anger and rage. I ask you, Lord Jesus, to cleanse me from anger. Please, Lord Jesus, remove my anger at its roots. I repent from all my anger, bitterness, unforgiveness and sadness. I receive your deliverance, freedom and joy. In Jesus' name I pray. Amen.*
>
>

An angry person stirs up conflict,
and a hot-tempered person commits many sins.
PROVERBS 29:22

part three

Stay Free

Living Out Your Freedom In Christ

Chapter 20

Doing All Things in Christ

For I can do everything through Christ,
who gives me strength.
PHILIPPIANS 4:13NLT

Apart from me you can do nothing.
JOHN 15:5

My Beautiful Daughter, Apple of My Eye,

Cling to Me and remain in Me. I desire for you to seek My face daily and spend time with Me. If you make Me your source of strength and wisdom, you will be more productive and prosperous in everything you do. In everything I have called you to do, I will give you success if you make Me the center of your life. Stay with Me longer and longer. The more time you spend with Me, the more you will have for the assignments I have given to you. You will see time and the fruit of your labor multiply as you come to Me to abide each day.

Dear Lord,

I cannot live one day without Your presence in my life. I desperately need You every moment of my life. I remain in You. I stay with You and dwell in Your presence. I cannot survive in this cursed world without Your help. I acknowledge my continuous need to be connected to You by spending time with You every day. Please forgive me for the times I have tried to run this race by myself without seeking Your face first. I fail each time when I try to carry my workload without You. Please give me divine strength, health and wisdom to do what You have called me to do. In Jesus' name I pray.

Amen.

A Successful Godly Life Starts with Clinging to God

Remain in Me, as I also remain in you.
No branch can bear fruit by itself; it must remain in the vine.
Neither can you bear fruit unless you remain in Me.
I am the vine and you are the branches.
If you remain in Me and I in you, you will bear much fruit; apart from Me you can do nothing.

JOHN 15:4–5

It was almost unbearable to listen to the man dining beside me at a Christian event. He was in his late fifties. We were seated at the same table, and he was going on and on about the ministry and God. He had been almost everywhere in the world and knew all of the mission work on Planet Earth. He had worked intensely in the mission field and raised funds for many missionary organizations and projects. But there was no presence of the Holy Spirit in his talk. The dryness in his speech hurt the deepest part of my soul. I finally said to myself, *I cannot take this torture anymore.* He was so dry and disconnected that I wondered how he was able to breathe with such spiritual dryness. He said many things that were very profound to him, but they sounded like rubbish to me.

After half an hour, I couldn't stand it anymore. I didn't want to be rude, but I couldn't keep smiling out of politeness. I excused myself from the table and hurried away, wondering how he had ended up so spiritually bankrupt.

The Holy Spirit answered me, "He doesn't abide. He doesn't know My voice. He does his things. He doesn't want to listen to Me. He likes to listen to his own mind, where the voice of the enemy dwells."

I felt sick to my stomach. You see, I immediately realized that I was not immune to this same problem. We all need God. And we are all able to get disconnected from Him. This was one of the events where God shook me and made me realize how much I needed Him in my walk and ministry.

Paul said that we can do all things through Christ who strengthens us (Philippians 4:13). Jesus said that nothing will be impossible for us (Matthew 17:20). But the key is abiding in Christ and continually being connected to Him so we can grow in freedom, in power and in maturity.

So far in this book we have seen that it is God's will for us to be free. We've seen that our identity, purpose and healing are found in Him.

Ultimately, freedom does not do us much good if we do not continue to grow.

We've looked at many specific kinds of bondage and the freedom that is available to us. But ultimately, freedom does not do us much good if we don't continue to grow. We will lose freedom unless we learn to do all things in Jesus.

This final section of the book will look at spiritual growth and how we can stay free and live in the freedom we have found. But the secret to doing this is really not a secret! We just need to remain in Him.

Today, I invite you to cling to God. Make Him your best friend. Acknowledge Him as your only source of strength and wisdom. Worldly wisdom is dry and meaningless. We need oil in our lamps, and without it we run dry. This is why we need to remain in God every day and even many times during the day.

God has set us free. Now, let's learn how to stay free, live free and grow free.

Chapter 21

God is For You, Not Against You!

What, then, shall we say in response to these things?
If God is for us, who can be against us?
ROMANS 8:31

My Sweet Daughter,

I am always with you and for you. Whatever you are going through, I am by your side. To the degree you want Me in your life, I guide you and direct your path. Read My Word and delight in My presence daily. Seek My face and My will to learn from your circumstances. But in everything you face, know that I am for you, not against you. I always want your very best. Draw near to Me, and I will draw near to you. Remember I am God who is near. I love you with an everlasting love.

Dear Lord,

I am very grateful You are near. I know You are with me. This is the most important thing I need to know. Even in the times when it feels like You are distant and are not answering me, I know You love me unconditionally and protect me from things that I don't even know. Please help me to respond to my circumstances in Your way, not my way. Help me to learn from my trials. Help me to pass the tests to please and honor You. In Jesus' name I pray.
Amen.

The God Who Is Near

Psalm 145:18 says, "The LORD is near to all who call on Him, to all who call on Him in truth." When I was a new believer in Christ, I had a hard time understanding and accepting that God was always near and that He was always for me. I think I carried with me the God of Islam, who

One of God's names is "Near."
He is a good God!

wanted to "get" me and punish me. I had an unhealthy fear that God wanted to punish me, teach me a lesson, or discipline me.

It took me a long while to be set free from the punisher God! Instead, I learned the true character of the God who loves me, who is full of grace and mercy. He is a very patient God who is slow to anger and abounding in love.

Many Christians lack a healthy fear of God, and I have addressed this in my other books, but right now, I want to focus on Him being for us, not against us.

> *But now in Christ Jesus you who once were far away have been brought nearby the blood of Christ.*
> EPHESIANS 2:13

When Jesus was on the earth, He spent time with sinners. It made the religious people angry! But He told them that He had come to seek and to save the lost (Luke 19:10). He was always for them, not against them! Paul told us the same thing. In Romans 8:31–32 he asks, "If God is for us, who can be against us? He who did not spare His own Son, but gave Him up for us all—how will He not also, along with Him, graciously give us all things?"

This means that God is never against us. Sometimes He might be against our attitudes. Sometimes He might be against our actions. But He is always *for us*. He wants to set us free from attitudes and actions that harm us. He wants us to walk in our full identity as His daughters, His beloveds, His beautiful princesses. He hates anything that makes us walk in the ugliness and pain of slavery and shame.

Romans 8:28 also says that God works all circumstances for good to those who love Him. So not only is God for you, but all your circumstances are for you too! No matter what happens in your life, it will work to your good if you love God.

Because God is for us and has died to pay for our sins, nothing we can do will turn God's heart against us. We don't have to come in fear before Him, hoping He will be for us this time. His grace is always covering us. He always welcomes us and wants us to come. His desire is for us to live as His beloved.

When we settle in our hearts that God is for us and we start to declare and believe it, it will make a difference in how we experience life. The truth will set us free!

The Battle Cry

In 2 Chronicles 20, the Israelites won a big battle against a vast army just by praising God and singing to Him. They sang and shouted, "Lord, you are good, and your love and mercies endure forever!"

I win many of my battles by declaring God's goodness.

I have learned to fight my battles from that portion of Scripture. When there is an attack of the enemy or a difficult time, I sing at home and praise Him. I have seen many of my spiritual wars end in victory when I praised God in this manner. When I believe that God is for me, it makes a difference in how I approach Him and how I deal with everything that comes my way!

We Don't Tell God Enough How Good He Is!

God doesn't need to hear from us how good He is. But it blesses His heart to hear it from His children. I remember one Father's Day when I called my father. He was very angry at me for a couple of years for becoming a follower of Christ. When I called home, most of the time, he didn't want to talk to me. My mother always answered the phone and told me he was not available or not at home.

One Father's Day, I called my parents' home. My father answered the phone. I said, "Dad, I just called to tell you that you are the best father in the whole world. I love you. You are a good dad, and I just want to thank you for being a good dad. You provided shelter for us. You worked hard and took care of our needs. Thank you for being such a good dad."

My father broke down in tears. That was a breakthrough between us. If you know my testimony, you know that my father had many faults that brought tragedy and misery to our family. But that day, I made up my mind to tell him all the good things he did. My words melted his heart, and we were reconciled.

Now, imagine how much more our God deserves our acknowledge-ment of His goodness! He is the perfect Father. He is a great dad. He deserves all our thanksgiving and praise.

I usually praise God out loud simply by listing His names. I have seen great victories in my life just by calling God by His names! At the end of this book, I have made a list of His names available for you. Every morning, start your day with praise, thanksgiving, and worship. Start praising His names. You will see that you defeat the enemy more easily when you start your day exalting God.

> *No, the word is very near you; it is in your*
> *mouth and in your heart so you may obey it.*
> DEUTERONOMY 30:14

Not a Single Day Without Appreciation!

I don't want to miss out on life, on all of its days, by letting it go by without appreciating each and every moment, including trials. In my home, we don't let a day pass without acknowledging God's goodness, His love, and His undeserved mercies. Husband, wife and child, we all make a point of showing appreciation to God and to each other as well. That encourages us and brings out the best in us.

Many people ask me, "After all you have been through, how can you be so joyful?" My joy comes from gratefulness. I am grateful to my Lord Jesus for bringing me out of darkness and giving me joy that surpasses all understanding. Knowing that I am loved, blessed and protected by my Creator fills my heart with joy. That is a miracle in itself!

God Is Near, and He Knows What He Is Doing!

Sometimes we tend to tell God what He is supposed to do with our lives. We expect Him to act or move a certain way on our behalf. We even treat Him like our servant and tell Him what we want Him to do. The scariest thing is that we make our own decisions without consulting and seeking Him, and then we want Him to follow us in the direction we decide to go!

At its root, this kind of behavior comes from not believing that God is really for us. We think we have to be for ourselves and figure everything out because he won't do it or take proper care of us otherwise. I know several single people who couldn't wait for the person God had chosen for them to marry. As their loneliness grew thicker and joined to the enemy's voice, they went into an unequally yoked relationship. Many of them ended up marrying an unbeliever. After the honeymoon was over, they faced the sad reality of having a companion who didn't care for their God. Then they placed their unbelieving husbands on every prayer list possible for salvation. This is making a decision without God's approval and then telling God to fix our ungodly choices.

Two ladies I know recently got divorced after several years of marriage to unbelieving husbands. One of them had insisted so much that this man was from God even though he didn't surrender his life and heart to

Christ. After ten months into the marriage, she called me one day and burst into tears. She was going through a nightmare. She was fifty-two years old, in a second marriage, and completely miserable.

This woman got divorced again after two years, and became bankrupt spiritually, emotionally and financially. It took her ten years to recover. When she was fifty-six, she looked like an eighty-year-old—destroyed, wounded and damaged. Sometimes our disobedience costs us more than we can fathom.

Trust God when you are lonely! Trust God when you are hurting!

We can rely on God no matter what our circumstances are. Trust Him with *all* your heart. Don't rely on yourself. Don't rely on Him only when you like what He's saying. Rely on the One with ALL the answers ALL the time. God can make a way even when it seems impossible. *He is for you.*

The apostle Paul said that when we are weak, then we are strong in Christ. One day when Paul was trying to be strong, God told him, "My power is made perfect in weakness" (2 Corinthians 12:9). Let that power come into your weakness and strengthen you in all ways. You are more than a conqueror through Christ! His grace is sufficient for you to move mountains!

Being strong is overrated! When you are weak, then you are strong in Christ!

God doesn't leave any story unfinished. He always brings a completion of what He started. God is the author and finisher of our story. He loves us, and

He's busy taking care of all that we need. So if you are in the midst of a trial, just know that your Author has written pages of divine victory for you. He will turn this around!

You are God's unique creation. You are an amazing masterpiece! You were handmade by a brilliant Artist! There is nobody else like you. And there is something very important God has set aside that only you can fulfill—a divine purpose for your life.

Ask God for revelation today. Trust him to show you what He has for you to do and who you are in His sight. Trust Him to work through your circumstances and take care of you. He is for you.

The Power of Thankfulness

Thankfulness attracts miracles.
Thankfulness opens the door of our hearts
to welcome joy.
Where there is a grateful heart,
there you will find abundant joy and
the supernatural at work.
Joy and gladness will be found in her,
thanksgiving and the sound of singing.
ISAIAH 51:3

Thankfulness unlocks the treasure box in heaven. Thankfulness is powerful because it brings us into alignment with truth about God and about ourselves. The truth is that no matter what difficulties we may face, God is for us! Thankfulness acknowledges that. Thankfulness refuses to agree with the enemy or listen to his lies. Thankfulness keeps us plugged into God and trusting Him.

From them will come songs of thanksgiving
and the sound of rejoicing.

I will add to their numbers,
and they will not be decreased;
I will bring them honor,
and they will not be disdained.
JEREMIAH 30:19

"I will give thanks to you, Lord, with all my heart;
I will tell of all your wonderful deeds."
PSALM 9:1

Do not be anxious about anything,
but in every situation, by prayer and petition,
with thanksgiving, present your requests to God.
PHILIPPIANS 4:6

Give thanks in all circumstances;
for this is God's will for you in Christ Jesus.
1 THESSALONIANS 5:18

Are You Still a Prisoner?

Awhile ago, I prayed over a woman who had spent several years in prison and gave her life to Christ there. She knew the Word of God very well, and God had changed her life drastically. Now she was trying to minister to others, but it was not working out well. She was intimidating others with her way of communication. God said to me, "It is an inmate spirit." I recognized it immediately. She called it "self-confidence and security." She hated insecurity and could preach against it for days. In the beginning, she also called it "authority in Christ" and said that was just the way she was. But her pride blinded her to what was really going on with her.

Hatred of insecurity is the first sign of an inmate spirit. Even though she was not in prison anymore and looked very feminine and pretty, she carried a "tough guy" personality. It amazes me how the enemy can be so influential once he finds an open door for deception!

I asked her why she was not being able to minister as she was called to do. Soon, the Holy Spirit showed her that without meekness in Christ, there is no power. The truth is the opposite of what the world believes. The more you humble yourself, the more you are elevated by God. Her "tough guy" persona was her way of surviving in life. But she needed to let go of it and allow God to be for her instead.

Once the truth was revealed, she was set free and didn't have to look so tough or act so confidently. The need to do so was a chain in her life! Now she is enjoying life and friendships without her inmate tough mask.

If you come from a rough life, you need to examine yourself to see if you have that prisoner spirit. (You don't have to have been in prison to have it.) Pray to be set free, because it is a prison in itself.

> *Do not fear, for I have redeemed you;*
> *I have summoned you by name; you are mine.*
> *When you pass through the waters,*
> *I will be with you;*
> *and when you pass through the rivers,*
> *they will not sweep over you.*
> *When you walk through the fire,*
> *you will not be burned;*
> *the flames will not set you ablaze.*
> ISAIAH 43:1–3

The Freedom of Trust

When we believe that God is for us, we are free to walk in joy and peace. We don't have to look out for ourselves. We don't have to cringe away from God in an unhealthy fear of Him. Instead, we can honor and thank Him in everything.

Trust is amazing freedom. Trusting God makes us able to walk in our true identity as His precious daughters.

Pray this prayer and thank God today!

Dear Lord,

You are for me! I declare this with gratitude and joy. Thank you for giving Your Son so that I might be Your daughter. Thank you for showing me in Your Word that Your heart toward me is always good. Lord, I confess that I have sometimes doubted You. I have thought You were against me. I repent from believing this lie. From this day forward, I want to walk in the confidence and joy of knowing You are entirely for me and working all things for my good. In Jesus' name.

Amen.

After consulting the people,
Jehoshaphat appointed men
to sing to the Lord and to praise him
for the splendor of his holiness
as they went out
at the head of the army, saying:
"Give thanks to the Lord,
for his love endures forever."
2 CHRONICLES 20:21

Chapter 22

It's All About Eating
And Eating the Right Thing

I have food to eat that you know nothing about.
My food is to do the will of him who sent me
and to finish his work.
JOHN 4:32, 34

My Precious Daughter,

I want to feed you with My heavenly manna. I want to fill you with My Holy Spirit. Earthly nourishment is good for you a little. However, My Word and heavenly blessings are far more fulfilling than earthly food. When you read My Word, spend time in My Word, and obey My Word, you will find greater fulfillment in your life than you ever have before. You will grow spiritually and in power to do My will. Today I invite you to eat at My table. Today I invite you to feed yourself with My heavenly food.

Dear Lord,

Please fill me with Your love. By Your Holy Spirit and your Word, I ask You to fill every area of hunger in my heart and life that earthly food cannot fill or satisfy. I am hungry and thirsty for Your righteousness. I want to do nothing but what pleases You. Please forgive me for my selfishness and for seeking to satisfy my own flesh rather than focusing on what pleases You. Please give me an obedient and a wholly devoted heart. In Jesus' name I pray.

Amen.

What You Feed Yourself Matters

I am the bread of life.
Whoever comes to me will never go hungry,
and whoever believes in me will never be thirsty.

JOHN 6:35

Food has an important place in the Bible.

- The first sin was because of eating! And eating the wrong thing!
- Israel grumbled and sinned because of food!
- Esau sold his birthright because of food.
- Joseph was hired to stock the food to prepare a nation for famine.

- Ezekiel ate the scroll of prophecy.
- Jesus' first temptation was about food.
- Jesus broke bread and said it was his body!
- Jesus fed thousands of people.
- Jesus cooked fish and fed His disciples.

These are just a few examples out of the many places food is mentioned in the Bible. It is important symbolically and in other ways, but the most important principle is this one:

What you feed yourself is important!

After a Sunday morning service, the pastor of the church was greeting people at the door as they were leaving. He saw one of the members of the church and asked him, "How are you doing, Brother Mark?"

The church member responded honestly, "Not too good, Pastor. It feels like there is a war in me between two people. One wants to do what is right and good. The other one wants to do what is bad and wicked."

The pastor asked, "So which one is winning?"

Brother Mark replied, "The one I feed the most."

Even though you may have heard this story before, it has a valuable point to get our attention. Our flesh and spirit are in a constant fight within us. The one that we feed the most will win the fight.

Flesh gives birth to flesh,
but the Spirit gives birth to spirit.
JOHN 3:6

Do not work for the food that spoils,
but for the food that endures to eternal life,
which the Son of Man will give you.
JOHN 6:27

It is written: "Man shall not live on bread alone.
But on every word that comes from the mouth of
God."
MATTHEW 4:4

What We Eat Is a Daily Choice!

As believers, we have a daily decision of what to feed ourselves and whether to feed our flesh or our spirit. When we sit in front of a TV for hours, which are we feeding? When we go out shopping, which are we feeding? When we are in the middle of nonsense chatter, gossip or slander, which are we feeding?

I know you can't spend twenty-four hours a day reading your Bible. Yes, there are some activities that we are obliged to do each day, and there are other things that are not bad in and of themselves. I'm not saying you can never shop or watch a movie!

> "Everything is spiritual,"
> I told Brother John.

However, I would suggest that you start reevaluating your daily diet. Take an inventory of the things you do, and find out how much time you actually spend feeding your spirit person.

We have a brother who works for our ministry who recently got married. A few days before he made a lifetime commitment, I told him, "Brother John, if you will allow me, I would like to give you a piece of marriage advice." He kindly welcomed me to share my mind. I said, "I just want you to know that every problem you face in your marriage will be spiritual." He just looked at me and smiled. I don't know how seriously he took me, but I am very serious! *Every problem you face in life is spiritual,* whether it is rooted in the spiritual to begin with or will be tested in the spiritual eventually.

Not the things themselves, but the way we handle them is spiritual. The more you feed your spirit person, the better you handle life.

How you react or respond to things shows where you are spiritually. For example, if you are facing financial challenges, it is spiritual. This is why many marriages fall apart after a few trials and tribulations. This is why people lose their jobs and become suicidal or go into depression. How you handle your finances or how you handle unemployment is spiritual.

If you are tested with your health, it is sooner or later spiritual. How you trust God is spiritual. The attitude of your heart is spiritual. If you are going through a conflict at your workplace, how you react or respond is spiritual. If for some reason your spouse cannot fulfill his or her marital duties to you sexually, how you keep yourself pure, understanding, and still loving, is spiritual.

The bottom line is that everything in the physical and tangible realm we face, and how we react to it, is spiritual. Our responses demonstrate our depth and fullness in the Spirit in our walk with Christ.

> *Those who live according to the flesh have their minds set on what the flesh desires; but those who live in accordance with the Spirit have their minds set on what the Spirit desires. The mind governed by the flesh is death, but the mind governed by the Spirit is life and peace. The mind governed by the flesh is hostile to God; it does not submit to God's law, nor can it do so. Those who are in the realm of the flesh cannot please God.*
> ROMANS 8:5–8

Connecting to God

When we look at the history of Christianity, we see that Jesus had the most successful ministry that has ever existed in the last two thousand years. He ministered on earth for only three years. He had no social media, no TV, no radio and no mobile apps. He started as one man and changed the entire course of mankind. How did He do this?

Today, so many churches and Christian organizations will show you in ten or twelve steps how to save the world. Many Christians and missionaries attend programs and seminars to learn about these methods and strategies to change the world. But they may fail to see the perfect example standing in front of their eyes in all His simplicity and power.

> *Whoever claims to live in him must live as Jesus did.*
> 1 JOHN 2:6

> *For the kingdom of God is not a matter of talk but of power.*
> 1 CORINTHIANS 4:20

When Jesus told God the Father in the garden of Gethsemane, "Not my will, but your will be done," he showed us the power behind his ministry: obedience.

> "He who fears God fears no man," said the preacher.

The more we crucify our flesh in obedience to God, the more powerful our spirit person becomes.

Only a strong communion and fellowship with God can provide a healthy fear of God, as well as an ongoing experience of His power and presence. If you are disconnected, you are running on an empty gas tank. We cannot afford to go on without God's presence! We cannot live or minister without seeking His face and eating His Word daily. There are days I feel God's presence stronger than other days. There are days I don't feel a lot. But my feelings don't change my devotion to seeking Him. I am ministering at a conference as I am writing this book, and after each meeting today, I took an hour's break and came to my room to pray and rest in His presence. I pursue God. I go after Him and His Word. I strongly suggest that you discipline yourself to go to Him daily, even several times during the day.

Going To The Well

Reading the Bible, the Word of God, is absolutely essential to growing as a Christian and remaining in God at all times.

> Reading a book is one drop of water to your thirsty soul.
> But reading the Word of God is Niagara Falls.

Go to the well. Go to the source. Many Christians read other Christian authors and get fed through others' revelations. Other books cannot be compared to the Word of God. I promise you, you will not grow enough just from other books! You will grow through the Word. Seek the leading of the Holy Spirit to understand what you are reading.

Let the Word of God sink into you deeply. Read the Scriptures, pray them, and speak them. I read one or two verses in a chapter and stop and meditate on them. I pray through the Scriptures. I pray Paul's prayers for the early churches. I pray Jesus' prayers. I pray Daniel's and Nehemiah's prayers. They are beautiful prayers. Sometimes I pray psalms. Don't be stuck on one way or one thing while God is offering you many meal options. Don't eat too fast. Taste fully, chew slowly, and digest the Word of God.

Blessed are those who hunger and thirst for
righteousness for they will be filled.
MATTHEW 5:6

Making the Word of God your food is the secret of being fruitful. People often ask me, "How do you do the things you do? Where do you find time to do everything? How can you be so fruitful?" God does it all when we surrender. We bear much fruit if we remain in Him. I eat His Word at least three meals a day, and then I remain in Him and meditate in His Word. I can't even think of a life without Jesus and daily living with Him.

The Miraculous Power of Obedience

If you love me, keep my commands.
JOHN 14:15

And this is love: that we walk
in obedience to his commands.

As you have heard from the beginning,
his command is that you walk in love.
2 JOHN 1:6

Jesus replied, "Anyone who loves me
will obey my teaching.
My Father will love them, and we will come to them
and make our home with them."
JOHN 14:23

Do not merely listen to the word,
and so deceive yourselves. Do what it says.
JAMES 1:22

There is a miraculous power in obedience and submission. You feed your spiritual person as you obey God.

Spending time in God's Word and prayer is incredibly important to feeding our spirit person. But ultimately, the Word of God will not benefit us unless we obey it. *Obedience is the first step to dying to self!* When you start dying to your flesh, the Spirit's power will start filling you and your life more and more. Unless you empty yourself, you cannot be full of the Spirit. The flesh must be crucified. If you do not obey the Word and die to self, the results will be anything but fruitful.

Dying to self does not mean denying who God made you to be, or choosing to do things that make you miserable. It just means that you give up your own ways, your sinful habits and your generational behaviors, and surrender to Jesus. You allow Him to work in your life and your heart. As we have already seen, He is for us! So dying to self actually brings us more fully into ourselves as God meant us to be. Jesus said if we lose our lives, we will find them (Matthew 16:25).

When we do not die to self in surrendering to Jesus, it only hurts us and makes our lives unfruitful. For example, when you don't forgive in a marriage, you build invisible walls between you and your spouse. Those walls get taller and stronger throughout the years. The end result is two strangers who hate or dislike each other. Those walls can be destroyed only through love. Love is a decision, not a feeling.

Obedience is a willful act of committing to do what is required without grumbling or delay. We obey to exalt the One who commands us—God himself. Obedience can be painful or sacrificial, but it's also humbling, worshipful and powerful! When we love God, obedience is a joy.

> *Does the LORD delight in burnt offerings and*
> *sacrifices*
> *as much as in obeying the voice of the LORD?*
> *To obey is better than a sacrifice,*
> *and to heed is better than the fat of the rams.*
> *For rebellion is like the sin of divination*
> *and arrogance like the evil of idolatry.*
> 1 SAMUEL 15:22–23

There is miraculous power in obedience. When I was a young Christian, God called me to serve Him through an American minister who spoke in tongues, and I heard everything in Turkish. I didn't know anything about tongues, but God was doing a miracle! This preacher looked at me in the eye and said, "Sister, I don't know what I said. But you know what I said. Take God seriously. He is going to use you mightily." And it was true. As I have learned to obey God, I have seen Him do miracles in and through me also.

Learn to Hear, Then Learn to Obey!

In Greek, the word for "obey" actually means to hear or listen. Over the years, I have learned to obey God's voice at once, the first time I hear Him. Believe me, I have missed a lot of opportunities because of my late obedience! Many times God will stretch you and get you out of your comfort zone. But if you discipline yourself to obey Him right away, you will have amazing experiences in life, and He will take you to the next level of glory.

Jesus is our example in this. Paul describes Him:

"Being in very nature God, [Jesus] did not consider
equality with God
something to be used to his own advantage;
rather, he made himself nothing
by taking the very nature of a servant,
being made in human likeness.
And being found in appearance as a man,
he humbled himself by becoming obedient to death—
even death on a cross!
Therefore God exalted him to the highest place
and gave him the name that is above every name,
that at the name of Jesus every knee should bow,
in heaven and on earth and under the earth,
and every tongue acknowledge
that Jesus Christ is Lord,
to the glory of God the Father."
PHILIPPIANS 2:6–11

In my life, my main goal must be to please God. My attitude determines whether I am pleasing God or not. As a believer in Christ, my ultimate goal is to be Christ-like. That pleases God.

What does it mean to be like Christ? Even though He was God in human flesh, He gave up all his rights and power to become a servant. Moreover, He was obedient to His Father to the point of dying on the cross, a shameful death. How much more do I need to exercise humility and serve others, following His example?

> *Do nothing out of selfish ambition or vain conceit.*
> *Rather, in humility value others above yourselves,*
> *not looking to your own interests*
> *but each of you to the interests of the others.*
> PHILIPPIANS 2:3–4

When we are living selfishly and always thinking about ourselves and trying to make ourselves happy, we are going farther than God is willing to go with us. He is for us, but He knows that our striving to selfishly make ourselves happy will not make us happy! It will just put us back into slavery to our flesh. However, when we think of, and care for others, we do what He said: "Love your neighbor as yourself." We are becoming more like Jesus. A selfless life is a God-like, content and happy life. When we are living like this, we can trust God to take good care of us.

When we make sure our spirit person is eating the right things—the food of the Word, the Spirit, obedience and love—we will live a healthy, growing spiritual life.

Dear Lord,

I want to walk a blameless and an upright life, just like many giants of faith in the Bible. I want to please You and bring a smile to You because I love You. I want You to be the first, and I will take the second place after You. I want to be able to say, "Not my will, but Your will be done" and crucify my flesh to live as a living sacrifice. Please forgive me for my disobedience. Please help me to walk in obedience to You. I admit that I need Your help. Please give me a yielding and obedient heart. In Jesus' name I pray. Amen.

Chapter 23

Learning to Rest in God

Tiredness and burnout opens the door to the enemy.
You must teach yourself to rest in God!

Come to me,
all you who are weary and burdened,
and I will give you rest.
MATTHEW 11:28

My Beautiful Princess,

I feel your tiredness. I feel your weariness. Come to Me to be strengthened by Me. Come to Me so I can fill you with My joy and give you more strength to go on. When you run the race in your own strength, you will be out of energy quickly. The enemy loves for you to run the race without staying connected to Me and receiving your strength from Me. I want to fill your cup. Come to Me before the fatigue leaves you almost lifeless. Your mind, your body and your soul need to enter My rest to be recharged and renewed. I lift you and raise you up when you feel like you cannot go on.

Dear Lord,

I come to you to be strengthened. You are my source of rest and strength. You are everything I need. I need Your rest. I need Your strength to go on. Please forgive me for trying to do everything with my own strength. I am sorry for trying to fix things, circumstances and people in my own way, which gets me tired easily. I am tired of fighting my battles by myself. I need to rest in Your presence. I am surrendering all my weight and burdens to You right now. Thank You for lifting up the weight from my shoulders and carrying my burdens. I receive Your divine strength, Your wisdom and rest from You. In Jesus' name I pray.

Amen.

The Dangers of Burnout

Truly my soul finds rest in God;
my salvation comes from him.
He truly is my rock and my salvation;
he is my fortress, I will never be shaken.

PSALM 62:1-2

There was a woman in a valley by a very high mountain who prayed day and night for God to use her. She prayed for God to give her an assignment that she would gladly do. She had great passion to serve Him.

After much prayer, God answered. He said, "Take a bag of food to a village on top of the mountain. There is a starving family who needs that food." The woman was so happy that God had given her a job to do! With great joy and enthusiasm, she started walking and climbing the mountain with that bag of food.

While she was walking her way up the mountain, she came across an old man who was carrying a box. She asked the old man where he was going. When he told her he was taking the box to the same family, she offered to take it so he wouldn't have to climb the mountain anymore. So she carried the bag God had given her and the box she had volunteered to carry for the old man.

While she was carrying the box and the bag of food, she saw an old lady who was carrying a bag of potatoes. When our woman learned that the old lady was taking the sack of potatoes to the same family, she offered to take the sack as well. The old lady gladly handed the potatoes to our woman.

As the woman of our story climbed more and more, the weight she was carrying got heavier and heavier. She started getting angry at the people who gave her all the stuff she was carrying for them, and she got angry at God for giving her such a difficult task.

Right before she reached the village, she gave up, dropped everything to the ground, and started complaining to God, "I wanted to serve you, God, but this is more than I can carry. I am tired. I am spent. Look at me. I don't think it is fair that I am carrying all of this. I am afraid you have chosen the wrong person for the task."

God asked her, "What did I give you to take to the starving family?"

She exclaimed, "You gave me the bag of food. But then he gave me a box and she gave me a sack of potatoes. I cannot possibly do this anymore."

God responded, "I only gave you the bag to carry. You yourself volunteered to carry the box and the potato sack. I didn't give them to you to carry. I gave them to my other servants. But you hindered their service to me and also your own. You should have carried only what I gave you."

Many people try to carry more than they are supposed to. The enemy somehow convinces them to do more than they can. Then they become bitter and lose their joy. Most people miss life and God's blessings just because they work themselves so hard.

> "I want to live on top of a mountain all by myself!" she exclaimed.

A lot of people tell me, "I want to live on top of a mountain alone. I am tired of this life." I tell them this is a sign of being burned out. If you want to live alone in the middle of nowhere, you may already be burned out! If you are feeling this way, you need time off.

On a weekly basis, God gave us a Sabbath day to rest. If you cannot rest one single day every week, all the stress and weariness will accumulate. I have been there. It is a discipline to say no for one full day instead of "go, go, go" and "do, do, do." You need it. I need it.

Take a little vacation with Jesus. You need His rest.

We Make More Mistakes When We Are Tired!

"What is wrong with me?" I asked. "Why am I feeling the way I'm feeling? Why am I reacting the way I'm reacting?"

My husband answered, "Are you really wondering what is wrong? It's serious if you cannot see what is wrong, as easy as this is to see."

I asked, "Tell me. Please tell me. I need to know."

He smiled kindly and said, "You are exhausted. That is the reason you are feeling like this. You have been working nonstop. Then you have been facing a lot of warfare and responding to people who watch your show who live in darkness, depression and misery. Then you receive persecutions, death threats and insults. You have been traveling, praying over hundreds of people all over the world, and trying to take care of the housework and family. And you are still asking what is wrong with you? Plain and simple, honey, you need a good rest! You also need to stop working so hard to try to save the world. It is God's job."

Saving the world is God's job.

How come I couldn't see that? It was very simple, but I couldn't see it. When we are so entangled and occupied with life's daily assignments, it can become very difficult to see even the little and simple truths. Sometimes we need others who love us to point them out plainly.

After my husband told me that, I stayed in bed for three full days. I couldn't move. Fatigue overtook me and my body. My husband brought food to my bed, and I was without strength. I had no fuel to continue. I was truly exhausted and burned out, and it was important for me to realize it.

Everybody Has A Limit

Elijah was a man of God. But he was a human being too. After a huge victory, where God answered his prayers and fire came down from heaven and then rain started falling after three years of drought, he ran for his life for fear of a woman called Jezebel. He found a spot under a tree and prayed for God to take his life. He wanted to die. He had come to the end of his rope. He was suicidal.

Elijah, a mighty man of God, had no strength or desire to continue. Everybody has a limit. I don't care how spiritual, how powerful you are in the Lord. You may even be like Elijah, but if you continue to run your life depending on your own strength without proper rest, you will hit bottom.

"I can't do this anymore. I am just so tired."

"I can't do this anymore," Susan cried during one of our counseling sessions. I told her, "You are right, dear. You cannot do this anymore. But God can. You need to stop fighting your own battles. You need to take a break and let the Lord God of the universe fight it for you."

She looked at me as if I'd told her the most profound mystery in history. It is simple. We do not have to do God's job. That is the truth, but somehow we run without taking a break. This is a trap of the enemy. It is a lie of the devil that God wants us to work ourselves into the ground and we can never take a break. The devil loves for us to work nonstop. He loves for us to get weary and burned out, because when we are tired, we are more prone to making mistakes.

I get upset easily when I am tired. When I was burned out, I was just snapping at my family all the time. I had no patience to listen to anyone. I'm telling you, I was just out of fuel to go on! But I didn't know it. I didn't know why I was so irritated all the time. When we are tired, we get upset easily. And it goes beyond that. We make some of the worst decisions when we are exhausted. Some of you are even tired of thinking and making mental lists. Take a break and enjoy your rest in God's presence!

God Rested. Why Not You?

God created his masterpiece in six days and rested on the seventh day. Did God need a nap? Of course not. Psalm 121:4 says that God never sleeps nor slumbers. But God *rested*. Why can't you? Are you better than God?

Rest has a different meaning in the Hebrew language than just lying down or sleeping. Rest means pausing. Rest means stopping and reviewing the work that is done in such a way that you can delight in the things you have accomplished or created. It is digesting; it is gazing at the work you have done. Rest provides the enjoyment of a job well done. Rest brings joy and peace to renew our strength. It gives us the needed time to think through life and the things we may be facing or trying to accomplish.

The enemy hates for you to take a break and will try anything to interrupt your rest. It took me awhile to get this. Whenever I took time to get some rest, the enemy brought distraction to steal my time with Jesus. Finally I learned his wicked game. Just like everything, the thief wants to steal your time of rest. He knows that if he steals your rest, you will not be very fruitful. He wants to devastate your vacation and your holiday season with your family. You need to be aware of his tricks and his attempts to interrupt your time of rest, and not give in.

Setting Boundaries

"But this is an emergency," said Bill. "We need to get this done today to meet the deadline for the grant proposals. Our whole ministry is depending on this final paperwork."

I didn't ask, "Where were you before now?" I already knew how the enemy uses people to steal my time with Jesus. Instead, I said, "Then ask for an extension." That emergency plea had already stolen my peace at that moment, of course. But it was within my will to choose not to allow the thief more.

It's important to set boundaries in our lives. Many people don't like people with boundaries. They are offended by them. Your boundaries silently rebuke those who don't have strong principles. They are intimidated by your borders and the lines you draw. But I'll tell you what: the more you are secure in your identity in Christ, the more people will despise your guts. This is the truth. Once you stand your ground, it will

I want freedom, not obligations.

bother others. You need to stand your ground anyway.

I hate being obligated. Obligation is a force that makes you do something you don't want to do. It makes your work mandatory. It's a chain you want to get rid of, that has been put on you by someone else. How do you know you are obligated to do something? You know it when you are not doing the task with love. You are doing it just to please some person, not God. God doesn't obligate us. He wants even our obedience to come out of love. Religion obligates. Love sets free.

I wanted to shout, "Lady, just leave me alone!"

"Please give me my freedom to spend my time with my Lord," I said firmly to a very controlling lady. I was a guest in her house. She had overbooked me and was trying to assign me to many obligations. I was exhausted from several prior trips, and I needed one full day with Jesus.

Believers who don't spend regular time with Jesus may not like seeing you so disciplined. Some just don't like to receive "no" as an answer. I don't know what this woman's problem was, but finally I hit my limit. I was tired. When I am tired, I get frustrated easily. I said to her, "I think I am saying NO with an accent. You don't seem to understand it."

Finally she backed off. But I was already upset. I said to myself, *I will never come to stay here again under her dictatorship.* I went to my room and threw myself into the arms of Jesus and stayed there for a full day and night.

Know Your Limits

Everybody has a limit. I said it earlier, but I am going to say it again. Believe me when I say this! Everybody has a limit, even prophets and pastors. We are all human, and we all have physical limitations, even though some people act like they don't. That is a dangerous place. The moment I start feeling that I am getting frustrated and easily upset, is the time I most likely need to take a break. You need to have an awareness of when it is your time to take a break.

Not taking a break is an offense to God.

Have you ever stopped to think that when you are going nonstop, telling yourself that if you don't do the work no one else will, or that without you the world would stop turning, it is an offense to God? By not taking a break, you are saying that you cannot trust anything to God and you are the one in charge who must take care of everything. Ouch!

When you stop being Ms. Fixer, God is pleased to fix things, and He will do a better job than you! If you are a fixer, a workaholic or a controller, you may have a hard time taking a break. Remember, the world is turning without you, and if anything happens to you today, the world will still turn. Stop making excuses for not taking a break!

Jesus said that whoever wants to follow Him has to pick up the cross. Following Jesus takes self-denial. In the same way, when God spoke about the Sabbath, He said people had to deny themselves any work on

the day they took their break! That denial looks like this: "You want to do something very much. You need to take care of something that is very important, yet you choose to spend time with God and take a break."

Keeping the Sabbath day is self-denial, because it requires obedience.

Of course, real emergencies can come up that you need to respond to—if your child is suffering with a fever and needs to go to the emergency room, go! But you don't need to do the laundry. You don't need to spend a few more hours at the office. You are already exhausted with the things you have done all week, and you know that you need to take a break.

> *It is a day of Sabbath rest,*
> *and you must deny yourselves;*
> *it is a lasting ordinance.*
> LEVITICUS 16:31

Almost everyplace I go, there are many people who want me to meet their Muslim neighbors or abused women in their neighborhood. Everyone knows at least a couple of people whom I need to meet so I can rescue them. I used to try to please everyone and attend to everyone's requests. I almost burned out. People will kill me by dragging me around if I let them.

I finally started telling people that they are responsible to witness and minister to their neighbors. Of course, this is not an answer controlling people like to hear! I have learned to focus on pleasing God rather than pleasing people.

> **People will judge you or make you feel guilty if you take a break.**

Doormat or Servant?

God doesn't want any of his children to be a doormat. Being a doormat is to be abused and to be under the dictatorship of someone else. A doormat doesn't have the liberty to say *no*. She has to say *yes* to everything she is asked to do. Being a doormat is slavery. People who are doormats are bitter and angry inside. They hate what they do, but they don't have the strength or freedom to stop doing it. They operate by fear and condemnation.

On the other hand, a servant is a person who does the work willingly, gladly and with love. There is no obligation or manipulation for her to do anything. She does it with a happy heart. Unfortunately, work-centered ministries often manipulate people to work like a slave and turn them into

> **A servant operates from love and freedom, not obligation or manipulation.**

doormats by manipulation. "If you love God, you will do this and that."

When I was a new believer, I wanted to please everyone in the church. I wanted everyone to like me. I wanted to gain everyone's approval. And I will be honest: it also fed my ego when I was the only one running to somebody's aid, when no one else was helping. It gave me a hidden pride.

Even as I write this, I am saying, "Lord, forgive me for my foolishness! What was I thinking?" Every time someone was sick, I was the one to cook for the sick person and her family. I did it with a glad heart for so many years. I was a single mother and struggling at the time, but found delight in bringing food that I couldn't afford to eat myself, to a family in need.

As my work hours and responsibilities changed over time and God started calling me into a different ministry, I started telling people very kindly that I couldn't cook anymore. I faced a lot of condemnation, and people started putting a lot of guilt on me. I yielded many times to church people's guilt trips, and my daughter suffered the consequences, as I couldn't spend much time with her due to trying to juggle too many things.

I served out of obligation, not because of love. I regret those years that I felt obligated and became a church doormat to please others. Now there are days when I don't text or call someone just because I am taking a time of rest. If I let people, they will be all over me. If I allow people to schedule my life, they will kill me or get me sick. I can't tell you the ridiculous things people want to book for me to do without any wisdom or the Holy Spirit's guidance. They would work me to death if I said yes to everything!

When you look at it this way, you can clearly see how ridiculous it is. And yet, many people judge me for taking time off. Many times I take Tuesdays off because I have a live TV program to the Middle East on Wednesdays. It doesn't seem to mean anything to many people who know that I spend my Tuesdays with Jesus—they try to reach me anyway. But it is not their duty to protect my time with Jesus. It is my responsibility to set healthy boundaries and give them a consistent message that my yes is a yes and my no is a no.

When you set boundaries and you become strong about them, even the most secure-looking people around you will get bothered. I have been judged and criticized many times for taking "too much" time to spend with the Lord. I have become subject to many people's sarcastic comments, even from friends. Your standing firm hurts others. It convicts. You have guts, and it offends their compromise in how they waste their time. They persecute you in their hearts, if not in their speech. But the more I stand firm, the more people have to respect my boundaries. It is not easy, but God has given me a titanium backbone.

People want and like the anointing upon me, but they despise what it takes to protect it. There is a price tag and a cost to serving God. I cannot attend many social gatherings and events that people invite me to. For example, I have three colleagues in ministry whose wives are pregnant. They are all expecting on dates that are close to each other. My assistant asked me what we were going to do about their baby showers. I told her, "I cannot do baby showers. We will bless them with gifts, but not baby showers." I get invited to many things, and I say no to the majority of them.

I was recently in an area to hold a conference when I called a friend who lived there to tell her I was in town. She invited me to spend time with her and her friend, but I couldn't fit her in specially, so I told her I was there for a conference and if she could come, I could see her. I didn't want to leave without saying hello to her.

Well, she got offended. She wanted me to change my schedule. But I was on God's assignment. My life is not mine anymore, and if I will live for Him, I have to be prepared for immature people to get offended.

If you try to be everything, you will be nothing!
ANONYMOUS

Dealing With Time Eaters

"She comes to my cubicle and doesn't leave for a long time. I don't know what to do," my assistant told me. I told her I had the same problem with the same individual. With her, the smallest subject, that should take less than a minute to address, would easily take from half an hour to an hour. I told my assistant that I'd learned to set boundaries with people like this and that she had to do the same. She had to learn to deal with time eaters.

The enemy uses time eaters to make you unproductive and unfruitful. He is the thief and uses people to steal your time. And yes, it is stealing.

Time eaters are people who somehow come into your life and steal your time from the very important things, such as God, His calling on your life, and your family. They almost suck the life out of you with their nonsense or complaints. The word *brief* is not in their dictionary. They have a victim mentality, and their focus is only on themselves. They are stuck in "I" and "me." You don't see them serving, ministering or helping others.

I have met many time eaters in my life. They all have two things in common: they are selfish and they are miserable. Are you good with boundaries? Because time eaters are not. They don't respect your time, your space, or your feelings. Get ready: if you put up boundaries with time eaters, you will go through some rejection.

Most of the time, lonely people become time eaters. They don't have anyone to talk to. They don't have much to do, and when there is a small opportunity, they will take it all the way to the extreme. You give them an inch and they take miles. I know people who tell me, "I need two minutes of your time. It will be very short," and it is a big fat lie.

I had a production manager working for me when I was a CEO in the secular business world. He used to request two-minute meetings that would last what felt like an eternity. He would write such long reports that I couldn't find time to read them. When I would meet with him, I couldn't get any work done that day. He would go on and on.

One day as I was talking with him, I asked the Lord to show me why this man needed to write and talk way too long. The Holy Spirit revealed to me that he had a troubled marriage. So one day when he was speaking, I stopped him and said, "I want you to know I am praying for your marriage." He looked startled and asked, "Why?"

Now I felt that I was in trouble, and had to tell him the truth. These were my immature years of handling situations like that! But in the moment, I thought that after all, I was his boss. If anyone had authority to tell him, it was me. Moreover, he was stealing my time and others' in the company, and it needed to be addressed. I know now that to address it starting with such a personal matter was a mistake, but back then I didn't have that wisdom.

I said, "I have been noticing that you always come to my office requesting two-minute meetings and end up taking hours. And the things you want to talk about shouldn't take more than a few minutes. I notice the same thing with your e-mails. This has been bothering me, so I started praying. Jesus revealed to me that you have no voice at home. You don't have healthy communication with your wife. You compensate for it at work and outside of home."

Well, even as I was saying this, I was immediately aware of my fault. I shouldn't be mentioning his personal life, and I didn't know how to fix it. I thought the best thing was to apologize.

The man was quiet. I said, "I am very sorry. I shouldn't bring up your personal life."

He responded, "No. I am just speechless. You are right. My marriage is suffering. My wife and I have become two strangers. My previous boss threw my reports in the trash can in front of everybody during a meeting. I've been warned before about my communication skills. But what you said about the root of it is shockingly true. I never thought of it."

He stayed in my office for awhile, and we talked. He allowed me to pray for him. I suggested that before he send me an e-mail, he review it and try to downsize it. I also asked him to put his thoughts in order before each of our meetings. He made a drastic and amazing improvement after that.

If you have to prioritize your life to spend more time with family and God, you may need to do a major cleaning of time eaters out of your address book. If you need to focus on God's calling on your life, you need to put up boundaries. Yes, we have to love people and have much compassion for them. I have so much love and compassion for the hurting, the outcasts and the lost. You can even have compassion for time eaters, but that does not mean playing into their unhealthy habits. Jesus loved the Pharisees, but refused to play their games or share their values. Your time is precious. Are you a good steward of your time? It may be time for you to tell the time eaters, "Get behind me, Satan!"

The enemy wants to distract us so we will not fulfill our calling and responsibilities. The time eater's spirit is against the Spirit of God. We don't treat people as our enemies, but we need to recognize when the enemy is working through someone and cut him off.

Stealing time is as bad as stealing money. Even worse!

If we truly understand what stealing means, we will be very careful with other people's time, and will protect our time as well. There are time thieves everywhere we go. The devil loves to steal our time, which is more precious than money. Money cannot buy time. Money cannot give your years back. Only God can restore what has been lost.

We must be good stewards of our time. We need to use it wisely. If you are wise, you won't waste your time. If you are wise, you don't say, "I have some time to kill." You recognize that your time must be invested in what matters most, and that includes being focused on your calling, taking joy in life, and getting rest when it's necessary.

Blessed Are The Brief

Jesus is the best communicator of all time. He took the least amount of time to deliver the best messages of any preacher ever, and they changed mankind. His sermons are still being preached, studied at Bible schools and seminaries, and turned into commentaries, devotionals and books, over two thousand years later. Jesus was simple and brief. Why can't we do that? I have met many people who were told they had five minutes to testify, and they were upset that the time given them was too short. Five minutes is one and a half pages long. You can tell much in five minutes!

I have had to make the decision in my time management that I will be most effective and productive for the kingdom of God. You need to make the same decision. You don't have to have a big ministry to make planning and time management a priority. The enemy loves for you to waste your time. He loves for you to waste your years running around. He wants you to be empty, burned out and ineffective.

We all need to make a decision whom we serve today. Joshua said, "As for me and my house, we will serve the LORD" (Joshua 24:15). He made a decision and let others know about it. Joshua took a stand. He proclaimed that his only and utmost desire was to serve God and please Him.

What about you?

Am I now trying to win the approval of human
beings or God? Or am I trying to please people?
If I were still trying to please people, I would not
be a servant of Christ.
GALATIANS 1:10

Chapter 24

Living in Victory

You can be a winner only with Jesus!

In all these things we are more than conquerors
through him who loved us.
ROMANS 8:37

My Dear Daughter,

If you live with and through Me, if you do everything with and through My Spirit, You will be living in victory and will be a conqueror in everything you do. But it has to be through My Spirit. Remain in Me, and I will remain in you. No branch can bear fruit by itself; it must remain in the vine. Neither can you bear fruit unless you remain in Me (John 15:4). You, dear child, are from God and have overcome the spirit of antichrist and evil spirits, because the one who is in you is greater than the one who is in the world (1 John 4:4).

The evidence that you are filled with my Holy Spirit is the fruit of My Spirit. If you are lacking these fruits in your walk with Me, pray to Me to be filled continuously. Being filled with the Holy Spirit is an ongoing work. It doesn't end. Being filled is not a one-time event. Many of My children are deceived into thinking that if they are filled once, it will last all of their lives. This belief comes from the enemy's voice, not Mine. Today, I invite you to seek Me and listen to My voice closely. I want to fill you again and again so you can be my witness with the fruit of the Holy Spirit in your daily walk.

Dear Lord,

I want to do everything through You. I don't want to do anything by myself, but with You and through You. I submit all my concerns, fears, dreams and emotions to You. Thank You for loving me so much. Christ is living in me through His Spirit, which is the most powerful spirit in the universe—far greater than any evil spirit. I must live my life with this assurance. Thank you for giving me Your Spirit, who resides in me. I believe the Holy Spirit is active and powerful in me, and I have the authority over spirits that are not of You. I pray I will be always aware of the Holy Spirit's presence in me and exercise my authority as a believer against any evil spirit. I can do everything that Jesus gives me the ability and strength to do. Only through Him will I be able to do everything I am called to do. I acknowledge my dependence on Jesus.

I love You, and I want to walk closely with You. I want to be sensitive to Your voice and be filled continuously with Your Holy Spirit. His fruit will be the first and foremost evidence that I am filled. I ask You to increase the measure of love, joy, peace, patience and other fruits in me. I want to live, speak and walk in love. I need Your help to demonstrate the fruits of the Holy Spirit. I want to be an effective witness, and for others to see the fruit in my life. I want to be full of love, joy and peace.

I can do all things through Christ who gives me strength!

Depending on God Is Not a Weakness, but Strength!

Nothing pleases God more than when we are depending on Him. When we admit our dependency on God, He will be happy to move on our behalf. Every day I tell Jesus, "I am depending on You to do everything You have called me to do. I can only do all things if You are my source of strength and power. I need Your help and presence all the way." I don't start my day without acknowledging my nothingness and His power to do all things in my life.

Before I knew Jesus Christ as my Lord and Savior, I tried to win my battles with my intellect, worldly wisdom and human strength. And I failed. I failed in every area of my life every time! I tried harder and harder. Each time it cost me more energy, more emotion and more resources to fight my battles alone.

I learned a big lesson when I hit the bottom. I am hardheaded, but I finally learned. And I don't want to repeat the same class over and over again! I want to pass. I have no time to lose.

Maybe today God is giving you another chance to pass the test, give up your own will and way, and become a good student. Go to a new level. Spend some time with Him after reading this chapter and acknowledge your need and dependency on Him.

When we try to do anything without seeking God and asking Him to be in it, we fail. If we do not fail in the short run, we will fail in the long run. Even though we may think we have achieved something, it will take much more from us since it will not have God's anointing and blessing. We get more tired and weary than we otherwise would, because we do it with our own strength.

I tried to be strong and
act strong. I pretended to be strong.
It didn't work.
Being strong is overrated!

When I was trying to be strong, I was collapsing inside. After I became weak, I received my strength from Jesus Christ. Being strong is overrated. There is nothing stronger than a woman in tears at the altar surrendering her life, her will, and her all to Jesus.

When I am weak, then I am strong.
2 CORINTHIANS 12:10

What Does It Mean To Abide?

Jesus said that if we are to be fruitful in our lives, we must abide (remain) in Him. My dictionary defines it this way:

> *Remain/Abide: Staying connected. Holding on tightly and focused on a certain state. 1. To remain stable or fixed in a state, 2. To continue in a place. Synonyms: Obey, Observe, Follow, Hold to, Conform to, Adhere to, Stick to, Stand by, Uphold, Heed, Accept, Acknowledge, Prospect, To wait for.*

If I abide in Jesus, He is my source of power. He is my source of protection, godly change, maturity and strength. He is like an electric plug, and I am the electric cord. When I am connected, I can achieve more than I can imagine. The moment I am unplugged, in that moment I am powerless, useless, and going on my own strength, which will not last long!

Imagine a baby in his mother's womb. He can only survive and grow if he is connected to his mother through the umbilical cord. When we are depending on God and connected to Him as our power supply and source, we can do more than we can with our own strength. Tell Him today, "I don't want to do a single thing without You. I stay with You. I remain faithful to You and connected to You. I want to do everything in fellowship and unity with You."

I am the vine; you are the branches.
If you remain in me and I in you,
you will bear much fruit;
apart from me you can do nothing.
JOHN 15:5

How Much Fruit Do You Have?

But the fruit of the Spirit is
love, joy, peace, forbearance,
kindness, goodness, faithfulness,
gentleness and self-control.
Against such things there is no law.
GALATIANS 5:22–23

Jesus said,
"The Holy Spirit will come upon you
and you shall receive power
and be my witnesses."
ACTS 1:8

If we abide in Jesus, the fruit of His Spirit will grow in our lives. Holy Spirit–filled people are easy to be around.

Carla was upset at Jessica, the new girl at her workplace, who was asking her a simple question about the location of the file cabinet. Jessica was shy and didn't know where it was. Carla snapped, "They hire people here and don't teach them a thing as simple as how to file or where the file cabinet is! They think it is my job to train you. You don't even work for my department!"

The young girl was quiet, waiting this trial to be over. She had learned a big first-day lesson: never ask Carla anything again! Julia, the administrative assistant in the office, pitied the girl and kindly showed her the file cabinet.

Over time, Jessica noticed that everyone was quiet around Carla. Everyone was scared of her. She would answer her coworkers sarcastically or rudely. There were good days and bad days, but it was not easy to guess what mood she would be in today!

The sad thing was, Carla had been a Christian almost all her life. She could quote the Bible right and left. There were days she would speak in tongues under her breath and give lectures to others about what it was to be a Spirit-filled Christian. She was moody. She'd had a rough life and had her own reasons for "being that way," and because of that, many people tolerated her with patience and kindness while she intimidated and bullied those around her. She was lonely and often complained that people never cared for her or prayed for her. But she knew her Bible well, prayed all the time, and spoke in tongues.

This is a real-life story—one I witnessed. We all know believers like this—people who are almost unbearable to be around. We try to avoid such people, even though we know they are hurting. Sometimes we may try to help, but they don't let anyone survive within their thirty-yard radius.

Unfortunately, the Christian world is full of mean, intimidating and harsh people. Now, I am going to suggest this to you: the more someone is Spirit-filled, the easier it is to be around that person! The first evidence of the filling of the Holy Spirit is love, joy, peace, patience, kindness, goodness, faithfulness and self-control. These are all qualities that are a pleasure to be around.

Ending Misconceptions

In the charismatic Christian world, how to know whether someone is filled with the Spirit or not is a hot topic. People have a lot of different answers, but I'd like you to think about this and maybe question your beliefs: we can see the filling of the Spirit more in the *fruit* than we can in the *gifts*. People who demonstrate the fruit of the Spirit in their daily walk are easy to be around and represent Christ in every way. People who lack the fruit of the Spirit are difficult to be around and to live with. When we see love, joy, peace and kindness in a person's actions, we see Christ. That is evidence of being filled with the Holy Spirit! When people are difficult to be around, rude to others, impatient, unkind, unloving and lacking love, the filling of the Holy Spirit in their lives is questionable, even if they can speak in tongues or prophesy.

Unlike many others, I believe the first evidence of the Holy Spirit taking residence in you is the fruit of the Spirit.

> *Every good tree bears good fruit,*
> *but a bad tree bears bad fruit.*
> MATTHEW 7:17

Jesus said we will recognize His disciples by their fruit (Matthew 7:16). In Acts 1:8 Jesus said, "The Holy Spirit will come upon you, and you shall receive power and be my witnesses." The very word "witness" implies that you know Christ, you know His changing power, and you experience God. And that witness bears fruit. How can you be a witness while living in bondage and darkness?

What kind of witness would you like to be? When people look at you, can they say, "I want to be like her. I want what she has"? Or when they see you, do they want to run in the opposite direction?

Love Is Kind

The very first fruit of the Spirit is love. In 1 Corinthians 13, Paul puts a crown on his discussion of spiritual gifts by talking about love as the supreme gift! He says that if we don't have love, everything else we do is worthless—even if we give all our money to God or even get martyred for Him.

When you look at Paul's description of love in 1 Corinthians 13, it sounds a lot like the fruit of the Spirit in Galatians 5! Love is patient. Love is kind. Love is not self-seeking or rude.

One of the major areas where we need to have the fruit of the Spirit is our mouth. How many of you get in trouble because of your mouth? Are your words patient, kind, gentle? Read the Love Chapter, and before you say anything that comes to your mind, put it to the test. Exercise the fruit of the Spirit: self-control.

> *Whoever does not love does not know God,*
> *because God is love.*
> 1 JOHN 4:8

To the same measure that we have love in us, we have God in us. The more we are full of God, the more the love of God will overflow in us. Love has its source in God. God equals love—"God is love."

It is God's will that His perfect love will *dwell* in us—will stay, reside and take permanent residence in our lives.

> *So that Christ may dwell in your hearts through faith.*
> *And I pray that you, being rooted and established*
> *in love, may have power, together with all the Lord's*
> *holy people, to grasp how wide and long and high and*
> *deep is the love of Christ, and to know this love that*
> *surpasses knowledge—that you may be filled to the*
> *measure of all the fullness of God.*
> EPHESIANS 3:17–19

Chapter 25

Rise Above

The surest way to win your battles is to rise above!

Do not be overcome by evil, but overcome evil
with good.
ROMANS 12:21

My Precious Daughter,

Even though you are going through many trials and tribulations, your faith is growing stronger in Me instead of drifting away. Thinking of My future plans for you, I am smiling, because I want the very best for you. I want you to rise above and act godly despite the evil that is being done to you. I want you to leave judgment to Me. I will vindicate you. But I don't want you to vindicate yourself. Do good to those who have hurt you and done evil to you. Do it not because they deserve it; do it unto Me. Because when you didn't deserve it, I still showed My kindness and mercy to you.

My beautiful daughter, I AM love. My love is unending. My love has miraculous power. It is bigger and higher than faith. It has the number one place among the gifts, and it has the number one place among the fruits of the Spirit. There is nothing more important or more valuable than love. It is my *agape* love. It is not rude, impatient, jealous or self-seeking. It is kind and protecting. It is limitless. I want to shower you and fill you with that kind of love. My love heals and casts out all fear. My love builds up, encourages and changes. Today I offer you My unconditional love. Will you receive it? Will you embrace it?

Dear Lord,

You are the lover of my soul. It is not easy to comprehend Your endless love. There is no human being able to offer me love like Yours, my Lord God. Please fill me and shower me with Your love. I want Your love to overflow through me to others. Please forgive me for falling short of loving You and others. I need Your help. You are my source of true love. No one can love me like You do. No one else would die on the cross for me. I acknowledge Your unconditional love. I don't deserve it, Lord. But I receive it. Please make my heart Your home.

Please help me to love my enemies and forgive those who hurt me. I need your supernatural power to rise above the situation and demonstrate kindness and forgiveness despite the evil behavior done toward me and my loved ones. Please give me grace and spiritual strength to do good to those who hurt me. I can only love my enemies through Your help. Without you, Lord, I will act in the flesh and react instead of responding appropriately by Your Spirit. Please forgive me for entertaining in my thoughts the idea of hurting those who hurt me. I need You every minute of my life. In Jesus' name I pray. Amen.

Rising Above

Love your enemies, do good to those who hate you.
LUKE 6:27

I was very hurt to hear that a dear sister in Christ was speaking ill about me to others. One of the ladies who worked part-time for my ministry happened to hear what this minister lady was saying about me, and she came to tell me about it.

At first, I was naïve enough to listen. Later on, I had to make a decision that I would not listen to an evil report. It was affecting me and poisoning me. God also brought to my attention that the lady who was carrying this report to me was doing this many times in other situations as well, and that was a problem in itself.

It is very hard not to receive an offense when it is directed against you. I learned three lessons from this incident. First, the person who is bringing the word may not necessarily be a good friend. Second, I shouldn't be listening when someone brings a negative word that was spoken about me. Third, if I was naïve enough to hear the negative report in the first place, I should respond in love and godliness and not allow the report to poison me further so that I react in the flesh. As a matter of fact, I should do something good to the person who hurt me.

That is called rising above or slaying the devil. *Mature believers can rise above anything done to them or said about them and respond with love and kindness.* This is a way of dying to self that leads to abundant life!

Do the Opposite of Your Flesh

Not many people can do the opposite of what their flesh wants to do. You need to train and discipline yourself to walk in the Spirit. If you do the opposite of your flesh, your flesh will starve. We call this "dying to self."

The devil loves for you to react to circumstances in the flesh. Your flesh and the enemy side together. Why? Because our sinful nature gravitates toward the enemy's voice. We are more prone to listen to the enemy than to the Holy Spirit. But when we are able to crucify the flesh and act in a godly way, then maturity starts.

After making the mistake of not stopping the friend who brought the bad report to me, I had to make a decision about how to respond to the offense. It was not easy. My heart was heavy from hearing that someone I respected and loved was speaking very negative things about me out of jealousy.

After I prayed, God told me to overcome evil with good. My flesh didn't want me to do good! My flesh wanted revenge. My flesh wanted vindication. My flesh wanted to teach her a lesson. But nothing good, nothing that would please God, could come out of my flesh.

If you don't have a disciplined prayer life, it is almost impossible to conquer your flesh. You need to abide in God to be able to have victory. After much prayer, I came to a place of peace and love. This is supernatural. You need God's supernatural power to bring you to a place of love and peace for the person who hurt you.

Bounce Back Quickly

The more you seek the Lord, the more quickly you can come to a place of peace and love. In this situation, it took me several hours to get there. But at least it was in the same day! I remember it used to take days, weeks, and even months. That night, I decided to give that person a very nice gift the next day. I went to bed in perfect peace, knowing the perfect will of God for me.

The next day, I wrapped an accessory that I had received from the Middle East for this sister, wrote a very encouraging card for her, and gave it to her. She was very surprised and touched by my gesture. As I gave her my gift, I felt that love was restored between us, shackles were broken, and the enemy was slain.

Don't Receive An Evil Report

After a few months, the very same sister who had brought the gossip and story of slander about me brought me another one. I told her I was not interested, and asked her to never bring me a negative word again. She was hurt, but received it well.

As curious as you may get, know that if you don't open a door and welcome an evil report, people will stop bringing them to you! When the Scripture says not to give the devil a foothold (Ephesians 4:27), that also applies to receiving an evil report. The very moment you allow a person to give you an evil report, you drink the poison and it's in your system. It is better not to listen to it than to listen and then have to fight to get it out of your system.

Overcoming By Rising Above

Overcome: Defeat, successfully dealt with or conquered, gaining superiority in battle, rising above.

When evil is done to us, we are harmed and hurt by others, intentionally or unintentionally. Our first reaction is to dislike them, hate them or hurt them back. But when we behave or feel that way, we are operating in the same spirit and feeding its evil purpose. The Scripture tells us not to be defeated and not to be conquered by evil (Romans 12:21). That part of the verse is passive. However, it also tells us to be *active* in overcoming (conquering, successfully dealing with, even gaining superiority over) evil with good.

For me, good is godly. Years ago I made up my mind that whenever I heard something gossiped about me or slandered against me, I would give a gift to the person slandering—something I would really, really like for myself. I cannot tell you the testimonies of victory that followed!

Slaying the Devil

There are several ways to slay the work of the devil in your life.

1. The most powerful way is to do the opposite of your flesh, as I shared with you earlier. If your flesh wants revenge, give a blessing. If your flesh wants to gossip back, speak good things. If your flesh wants to punch someone in the face, give them a gift instead!

2. Asking someone's forgiveness, even though you believed that person was totally and utterly on the wrong side, is powerful. Just saying, "I am sorry. I love you" will slay the devil.

3. Another effective way is to give them gifts with a nice and encouraging note. I also find something positive and good to say about them, both to say *to* them and to say to others when they are absent.

4. I had another minister sister whom I heard was speaking nonstop evil

about my ministry. I donated a nice sum to her ministry. She didn't know about it and never learned that I'd made a contribution. But the devil's work was slain in my life, and I was blessed just by obeying the Lord.

5. Confront the people who carry evil reports. Clean your address book of people who are gossips and slanderers. For a time, I had several people around me and even working for me who were bringing gossip and slander that was affecting me negatively. I had to confront them to the point of cutting ties with them. You would be surprised to hear how people justify their wrong behavior in bringing dissension and strife in the body of Christ. This should not be tolerated.

6. Pray for those who do wrong to you. Pray for God's abundant blessings upon them and their family. That will also help you to forgive them.

Yielding to God's Authority

Submit yourselves, then, to God.
Resist the devil, and he will flee from you.
JAMES 4:7

Acquaint now yourself with Him
[agree with God and show yourself to be
conformed to His will]
and be at peace;
by that [you shall prosper and great] good
shall come to you.
JOB 22:21AMP

James 4:7 tells us exactly how we can rise above the devil. First, we yield to God. I am willing to yield and commit to God's authority, which includes trusting Him. I am submitting to Him, trusting His character. To *submit* is to willingly yield, surrender, commit to yield oneself to the authority to another, remain in him.

How can you submit to God? Live and respond to circumstances according to His Word and His promises in His words. When Jesus was tempted in the wilderness, He responded to the tempter with the Word. He submitted to the Word. Then the next part is to resist the enemy. To *resist* is to strive to not give in. It is pressing on so that the negative thing will not affect, move or shake you. It is remaining strong and not allowing the force of the devil's work to get into your system. This can happen when someone calls us to gossip and we submit to God's Word and remain righteous and don't give in to the temptation.

Finally, the devil will flee from us! He will run away, hurry away and fly away.

The Miraculous Power of Love

You have heard that it was said,
"Love your neighbor and hate your enemy.'
But I tell you, love your enemies and pray for
those who persecute you, that you may be chil-
dren of your Father in heaven."
MATTHEW 5:43–45

Whoever does not love does not know God,
because God is love.
1 JOHN 4:8

Recently, a Muslim man wrote to me. His picture was on Facebook, and he was wearing a commando outfit and had a bandana saying "Allahu Akbar" on it. He was holding two machine guns in the picture, right there on Facebook! He wrote to me and said, "I hate you, and it is my mission to find you and kill you, until the last drop of my blood and my last breath. This is my life's mission. I am going to rid the earth of you."

"Until the last drop of my blood and my last breath, I will find you and kill you."

Well, I struggled. I mean, if you just saw the man in this picture! It was like something from a horror movie. Sometimes people send me my image in Photoshop, how they would cut me in pieces. Those threats are all demonic.

I got that message, and the Holy Spirit whispered into my heart with His gentle voice: "No weapon formed against you shall prosper" (Isaiah 54:17).

I went to a prayer meeting right after I received this message and asked for prayer. But at that moment, more than fear, I was sad in my heart that someone could hate so much. The hatred and the evil in that man hurt my soul.

The prayer time was not enough. I went to my office and started praying for him, and said, "Jesus, you give me the answer. How should I answer him?"

Jesus said to me, "Go and write to him and say, 'You told me until the last drop of your blood and until your last breath you will find me and kill me, and I am committed to love you unconditionally until my last breath and until my last drop of blood, because my Lord Jesus says to love your enemies.'"

That is freedom! That is rising above. I felt free and full of love. This is called walking in the supernatural.

God is love.
God = Love.
The more you have God in you,
the more love you have in your heart.
It is simple math!

The Freedom of Love

Loving your enemies is freedom. Great men, great women cannot hate. So I wrote this man: "My Lord Jesus says 'Love your enemies,' so I will be loving you. If you are hungry, let me know; I will make sure to send you aid. If you are thirsty, let me know."

> "I don't think you understood me. I really wanted to kill you."

He didn't answer me back for two weeks. After two weeks he wrote me again, and said, "Lady, I don't think you understand." But then he called me *baci*, which means "sister." Wow, from enemy to baci!

His message continued. He said, "I don't think you understood me. I really wanted to kill you. I read about your life. You are a highly educated woman. I know you understand. And you told me that you love me and that you want to help me. Don't you know that I am a very dangerous man? I have murdered and raped. I have done terrible things. I can do anything to you that I have done to other people, and I wouldn't even blink my eye. It wouldn't move a thing in me, but what you said to me moved something in me. What kind of God can love me and tell you to love me?"

> "I heard you too were a Muslim like me. How did you become a Christian?"

Finally he wrote, "I heard you once were a Muslim like me. How did you become a Christian?"

What an opportunity to share what Jesus had done for me! I wrote my testimony to him, my entire life in very much detail. I told him that I understood his anger. I told him that once I was like him, full of hatred, hostility and anger. I told him about the abuse I went through and my failures. I shared about my depression and suicidal thoughts. Then I explained to him that on the day I was contemplating suicide, Jesus revealed Himself to me in a miraculous way so that I knew He was the Son of God who died for me on the cross to save me from hell.

Unconditional love requires unconditional forgiveness!

I received no responses for a couple of weeks. Then one day I found another message from him in my inbox. He confessed to me all his sins. He said he had a wife, and he was cheating on her every day and beating her up. Moreover, he was a very violent man. Everybody around him was afraid of him. He said, "I don't think your God can love me. Or forgive me."

We start writing to each other, and I wrote him, "Unconditional love entails unconditional forgiveness. You cannot tell someone, 'I love you unconditionally' and then go and say, 'I cannot forgive this.' If you completely and truly love someone, you will forgive whatever it is. You can forgive them. You cannot do it with your own strength; this is supernatural."

We wrote back and forth for awhile, and then one day he wrote me one thing, one sentence: "I am ready." In the morning, I opened my Facebook and saw his message, and there was his phone number underneath.

I called him, and he was weeping and weeping and weeping and weeping. He was like, "What should I do? Should I go on my knees? I want to do everything right. Tell me what to do, Sister."

And I said, "Do whatever feels comfortable. This is not a religion. You are leaving religion, and you are entering into a relationship."

So he did. He went on his knees, as Muslims will mostly do. One day every knee will bow, every tongue will confess, and it's better on this earth than later!

As he was on his knees, he was crying so hard he couldn't even repeat the sinner's prayer. All he said was, "Yes, yes, yes."

Later on he wrote me. He had been beating up his wife so badly, but that night as she was washing the dishes, he told her, "Move aside." Of course she followed his order, and he started washing the dishes. And he turned to her and said, for the first time in twenty years of marriage, "I love you." He is a changed man. After that, he started protecting me on social media. He would write and say, "Be careful with this group. Be careful with that group." That is the supernatural power of the love of God.

Who shall separate us from the love of Christ?
Shall trouble or hardship or persecution
or famine or nakedness or danger or sword? . . .
No, in all these things we are more than conquerors
through him who loved us.
For I am convinced that neither death nor life,
neither angels nor demons,
neither the present nor the future,
nor any powers, neither height nor depth,
nor anything else in all creation,
will be able to separate us from the love of God
that is in Christ Jesus our Lord.
ROMANS 8:35–39

For this reason I kneel before the Father,
from whom every family in heaven and on earth
derives its name.
I pray that out of his glorious riches
he may strengthen you
with power through his Spirit in your inner being,
so that Christ may dwell in your hearts through faith.
And I pray that you, being rooted and established in love,
may have power, together with all the Lord's holy people,
to grasp how wide and long and high and deep
is the love of Christ, and to know this love
that surpasses knowledge—
that you may be filled to the measure
of all the fullness of God.
EPHESIANS 3:14–19

Chapter 26

Seeking Him First

Seek first his kingdom and his righteousness,
and all these things will be given to you as well.

MATTHEW 6:33

My Dear Child,

The more you seek Me, the more I will pour down My blessings on you. I want you to always seek the Giver, not the gift. I want you to come to Me for Me. I want to be the priority in your life. I want to be the first on your list. When you put Me first, everything will fall into the right place in your life. When you seek Me and My righteousness first, you will see that your life will be victorious in every way. Even though you may have many needs, know that if you seek Me first, I will provide for them all. Come to Me and seek Me every day and every moment in your life.

Dear Lord,

I come to You. I seek Your face. I acknowledge my need for You. Please come and fill me with Your righteousness. I need Your righteousness. I need Your presence in my life. Without You, everything falls apart. Everything is meaningless without You. I want You in my life in increasing measure. Please forgive me for the times I didn't seek You first but asked of You many things You could do for me. You are more important than anything in my life. You have the first place. Thank you for Your love and grace. Thank you for always wanting the best for me. In Jesus' name I pray.

Amen.

Seek First The King And The Kingdom

Seek: Look toward, go after, look for, pursue, discover.

In Jeremiah 29:13, God promises us that we will find Him if we seek Him with all of our hearts. There are two key points here that make our relationship with God a success: seeking Him—that is, pursuing Him—and doing the pursuing with all of our hearts. We need to seek and pursue Him with all of our hearts to the point that we have no other desire.

Love the Lord your God
with all your heart and with all your soul
and with your entire mind
and with all your strength.
MARK 12:30–31

If only these two Scriptures were fulfilled in our lives, everything else would fall into the right place. We would have the most victorious walk with God that is possible.

Many of us fall short of the first two commandments (love the Lord with all your heart and love your neighbor as yourself). Then our relationship with God suffers, and our relationships with others suffer as well. When we love God as described, being "sold out" to Him, it changes everything about our lives. You may need to stop here and pray to love Him and seek Him with all your being. We need to prioritize *everything* in our lives, even our prayers!

Prosperity Through Faith?

One of the biggest stumbling blocks of the Western gospel to the world is the so-called "prosperity gospel." It promotes seeking materialistic comfort and achievements instead of seeking God. This unbiblical teaching sees giving as an investment in the stock market and focuses on the hundredfold return, taking the Scriptures about giving and tithing out of context.

According to this teaching, "planting the seed" of tithing or giving is part of an investment deal with God. We try to serve Him for what we can get out of it, instead of serving Him for Himself and for His kingdom.

Instead of pursuing God's righteousness first, most Christians are still at the "wanting first" stage. There is nothing wrong with wanting and wanting something from God. However, when wanting is more important than pursuing and seeking God, then that wanting becomes an idol and God becomes our second priority.

Almost 50 percent of Christians believe in financial prosperity through faith in Jesus Christ.

Finding Jesus In The Small Things

Are you waiting for a big thing to happen so that you can be happy? Many miss life this way. If we seek God instead of the next "big thing," our eyes can be opened to the small things He is always doing for us and the many little ways He loves us.

In a marriage, the husband can't always be taking his wife on a second honeymoon to the Bahamas or buying her million-dollar diamond rings. In fact, if that was all he ever did for her, and didn't show her kindness or affection in daily life, she would probably not even feel loved. But a husband who loves his wife in small, continual, daily ways really shows his love for her.

It's the same with God's love for us. Our eyes just need to be opened to see His love!

Do not despise these small beginnings,
for the Lord rejoices to see the work begin.
ZECHARIAH 4:10NLT

When I received Jesus as my Lord and Savior, I was a single mother just trying to survive. My daughter was four years old. Since I had just become a Christian, it was our first Christmas. We were part of a Christmas play at our church, and I had $29 saved up for Christmas shopping. I asked my daughter what she wanted for Christmas. She said, "Mom, I want a big Christmas tree with lights, colors and everything on it." Well, I said, "Just pray, honey. Just pray to Jesus." I knew I couldn't afford what she wanted.

A couple of weeks before Christmas, one morning she woke up and said, "Mom, Jesus told me He is going to give us the tree today." I smiled. I didn't want to discourage her faith. But to be honest, in my heart I had no hope about the tree.

After I picked her up from school that day, we were in the car driving home. She exclaimed, "Mom, stop the car! This is the store where we are going to get the tree."

Now, you have to understand that my daughter never insisted or cried for a toy or anything. At almost age four, she knew our situation and never asked for anything. This was the first time, and she was so passionate about the tree. She begged me, "Mom, please, please, this is the store." It was Sears, so we had been there before, and I thought that was why she wanted to stop there.

I couldn't resist her pleading, so I parked the car, trying to figure out what I was going to do when we got in there. My credit was in bad shape, so I couldn't use my credit card. But somehow, I followed this four-year-old girl who was full of faith, believing we were going to walk out of the store with a huge Christmas tree. She was holding my hand and dragging me.

We got to the tree department, and the trees were hundreds of dollars. My daughter stopped in front of this big, beautiful Christmas tree that was already decorated and had beautiful ornaments and lights on it. She shouted, "This is the tree I want!"

At that moment, my heart was bleeding. I felt so guilty for obeying her and feeding into her dream. I was about to choke into tears. I said, "Honey, this is for next year. This year, we will get a small one. Not from this store." I had a thrift store in mind—I thought maybe, just maybe, we could find something there.

Then one of the workers came and asked, "Is there anything I can help you with, ma'am?" I said, "No, thank you. We are just looking." But no. My daughter said, "Yes, this is the tree we want to buy."

The salesclerk smiled and looked at me. I said, "I am sorry. She has her own mind today. We cannot afford this tree. Next year." I just wanted this to be over!

But then, to my shock, the clerk said, "Ma'am, I am sure we can do something about it." Before I said anything, she continued, "I am the manager. And this tree is a demo. Whatever you can afford to pay, it will be yours."

I took the money from my purse and showed her. "This is all I have." She said, "Then the tree is yours." She called two associates and ordered them to put everything in boxes and carry it to my car. She said, "MERRY CHRISTMAS!"

I was in tears. My daughter was just giggling and rejoicing. She said, "I told you, Mom. Jesus promised me."

I said, "I know, darling. He always keeps His promises!"

Our God is for us! He loves us. We are His daughters, and we are precious to Him. When we seek Him first, we don't have to be afraid that He will enslave us, that He will fail to care for us, or that He will put us back into bondage. He desires to care for us. And He knows even the smallest needs and desires of our hearts.

Jesus Cares For The Smallest Desires of Your Heart!

Recently I needed some jackets for my TV programs. I keep the same black pants and only change my jackets, so I often need new ones. I went to a thrift store, and as soon as I walked in, I noticed twelve jackets, all of them brand new and exactly my size. They had their original tags on. Each was $3.99. The only thing missing was a note: "From Jesus, who loves you and supplies all your needs."

I picked up all of the jackets and went to the register, and the cashier said, "Today is a half-off day. So you will get 50 percent off each jacket. I just wanted to hug her. I paid for the jackets and couldn't stop saying, "Thank you, Jesus! Thank you, Lord! All good gifts come from you."

Every day you can experience His presence and goodness. You only need to walk by faith, not by sight.

When wanting is more important than seeking God first and foremost, our walk with him suffers.

We all have many needs and wants. We all have dreams and desires. If we go after God first, if we pursue knowing Him on a personal level and being like Him, then He will reward us by revealing Himself . . . and He promises to care for our other needs as well.

Press on! All we need, desire, and want will be given to us. Solomon asked for wisdom, and *everything* was given to him. But during the process of going after Him, pursuing Him and seeking to know Him more, our desires, dreams and wants will change. We will walk in total freedom and desire God above everything else.

David wrote, "The LORD is my shepherd; I shall not be in want" (Psalm 23:1). Paraphrasing in my own words: *I am completely satisfied, content and fulfilled just because the Lord God is my shepherd. I don't need anything else.*

Dear sisters, fellow princesses of the King, may this be the prayer of all our hearts.

Dear Lord,

I want You more than anything in my life. I want to know You more. I want to get closer to Your heart. Please draw me nearer to You. Bring me closer to Your heart.

Amen.

I know what it is to be in need,
and I know what it is to have plenty.
I have learned the secret of being content
in any and every situation . . .
I can do all this through him who gives me
strength.

PHILIPPIANS 4:12–13

Names of God

1. **Abba: Daddy:** The Spirit you received does not make you slaves, so that you live in fear again; rather, the Spirit you received brought about your adoption to sonship. And by him we cry, "Abba, Father." **Romans 8:15**
2. **Adonai-LORD/Master:** The Headship Name: But Abram said, "Sovereign Lord, what can you give me since I remain childless...?" **Genesis 15:2**
3. **Advocate:** My dear children, I write this to you so that you will not sin. But if anybody does sin, we have an advocate with the Father—Jesus Christ, the Righteous One. **1 John 2:1**
4. **Almighty:** The sound of the wings of the cherubim could be heard as far away as the outer court, like the voice of God Almighty when he speaks. **Ezekiel 10:5, Genesis 17:1-2**
5. **Alpha and Omega:** I am the Alpha and Omega, the First and the Last, the Beginning and the End. **Revelation 22:13**
6. The **Amen:** To the angel of the church in Laodicea write: These are the words of the Amen, the faithful and true witness, the ruler of God's creation. **Revelation 3:14**
7. **Ancient of Days:** I beheld till the thrones were cast down, and the Ancient of days did sit, whose garment was white as snow, and the hair of his head like the pure wool: his throne was like the fiery flame, and his wheels as burning fire. **Daniel 7:9**; Until the Ancient of days came, and judgment was given to the saints of the most High; and the time came that the saints possessed the kingdom. **Daniel 7:22**

8. **Apostle:** Therefore, holy brothers and sisters, who share in the heavenly calling, fix your thoughts on Jesus, whom we acknowledge as our apostle and high priest. **Hebrews 3:1**

9. **Architect:** For he was looking for the city which has foundations, whose architect and builder is God. **Hebrews 11:10**

10. **Author and Perfecter of Faith:** Fixing our eyes on Jesus, the author and perfecter of faith. For the joy set before him he endured the cross, scorning its shame, and sat down at the right hand of the throne of God. **Hebrews 12:2**

11. **Beginning and the End:** I am the Alpha and Omega, the First and the Last, the Beginning and the End. **Revelation 22:13**

12. **Beloved:** "Behold my servant, whom I have chosen; my beloved, in whom my soul is well pleased: I will put my spirit upon him, and he shall show judgment to the nations. **Matthew 12:18**

13. **Beloved Son:** And a voice from heaven said, "This is my Beloved Son, in whom I am well pleased." **Matthew 3:17**

14. **Bread Of Life:** Then Jesus declared, "I am the bread of life. Whoever comes to me will never go hungry, and whoever believes in me will never be thirsty." **John 6:35**

15. **Bridegroom:** The bride belongs to the bridegroom. The friend who attends the bridegroom waits and listens for him, and is full of joy when he hears the bridegroom's voice. That joy is mine, and it is now complete. **John 3:29**

16. **Bright and Morning Star:** "I, Jesus, have sent my angel to give you this testimony for the churches. I am the Root and the Offspring of David, and the bright and Morning Star." **Revelation 22:16**

17. **Builder:** For every house is built by someone, but the builder of all things is God. **Hebrew 3:4**

18. **Chief Cornerstone:** "...Built upon the foundation of the apostles and prophets, Jesus Christ himself being the chief corner stone." **Ephesians 2:19; 1 Peter 2:6**

19. **Chief Shepherd:** And when the Chief Shepherd appears, you will receive the crown of glory that will never fade away. **1 Peter 5:4**

20. **Chosen One:** A voice came from the cloud, saying, "This is my Son, whom I have chosen; listen to him." **Luke 9:35**

21. **Comforter:** And I will pray the Father, and he shall give you another

Comforter, that he may abide with you forever. **John 14:16**

22. **Consuming Fire**: for our "God is a consuming fire. **Hebrews 12:29**

23. **Creator**: (1) Do you not know? Have you not heard? The Lord is the everlasting God, the Creator of the ends of the earth. He will not grow tired or weary, and his understanding no one can fathom. **Isaiah 40:28**; (2) They exchanged the truth about God for a lie, and worshiped and served created things rather than the Creator—who is forever praised. Amen. **Romans 1:25, 1 Peter 4:19**

24. **Dayspring**: Because of the tender mercy of our God, by which the Dayspring from on high has visited us. **Luke 1:78**

25. **Deliverer**: (1) And in this way all Israel will be saved. As it is written: "The deliverer will come from Zion; he will turn godlessness away from Jacob. **Romans 11:26**; (2) The Lord is my rock, my fortress and my deliverer; my God is my rock, in whom I take refuge, my shield and the horn of my salvation, my stronghold. **Psalms 18:2**

26. **Desire of all Nations**: And I will shake all nations, and the desire of all nations shall come: and I will fill this house with glory, saith the Lord of hosts. **Haggai 2:7**

27. **Door**: Therefore Jesus said again, "Very truly I say to you, I am the door of the sheep." **John 10:7**

28. **Elohim**: The strong creator: In the beginning God created the heavens and the earth. **Genesis 1:1**

29. The **Eternal**: The eternal God is your refuge, and underneath are the everlasting arms. He will drive out your enemies before you, saying, 'Destroy them!' **Deuteronomy 33:27**

30. **Eternal Immortal Invisible King**: Now to the King eternal, immortal, invisible, the only God, be honor and glory for ever and ever. Amen. **1 Timothy 1:17**

31. **Everlasting GOD**: For this God is our God for ever and ever; he will be our guide even to the end. **Psalms 48:14**

32. **Expected One**: he sent them to the Lord to ask, "Are you the one who is to come, or should we expect someone else?" **Luke 7:19**

33. **Faithful And True**: I saw heaven standing open and there before me was a white horse, whose rider is called Faithful and True. With justice he judges and wages war. **Revelation 19:11**

34. **Faithful Witness**: And from Jesus Christ, who is the faithful witness, the firstborn from the dead, and the ruler of the kings of the earth. To him who loves us and has freed us from our sins by his blood. **Revelation 1:5**

35. **Father**: "This, then, is how you should pray, "'Our Father in heaven, hallowed be your name..'" **Matthew 6:9**

36. **Father Of Glory**: "...That the God of our Lord Jesus Christ, the Father of Glory, may give you the Spirit of wisdom and revelation in the knowledge of him. **Ephesians 1:17**

37. **Father Of Lights**: Every good and perfect gift is from above, coming down from the Father of Lights, who does not change like shifting shadows. **James 1:17**

38. **Father of Mercies**: Praise be to the God and Father of our Lord Jesus Christ, the Father of Mercies and the God of all comfort. **2 Corinthians 1:3**

39. **Father Of Spirits**: Moreover, we have all had human fathers who disciplined us and we respected them for it. How much more should we submit to the Father of spirits and live! **Hebrews 12:9**

40. **First And The Last**: I am the Alpha and the Omega, the First and the Last, the Beginning and the End. **Revelation 22:13**

41. **Firstborn From The Dead**: and from Jesus Christ, who is the faithful witness, the firstborn from the dead, and the ruler of the kings of the earth. To him who loves us and has freed us from our sins by his blood. **Revelation 1:5**

42. **Firstborn Of All Creation**: The Son is the image of the invisible God, the firstborn over all creation. **Colossians 1:15**

43. **Fortress**: Lord, my strength and my fortress, my refuge in time of distress, to you the nations will come from the ends of the earth and say, "Our ancestors possessed nothing but false gods, worthless idols that did them no good." **Jeremiah 16:19**

44. **Glorious Sword**: Blessed are you, Israel! Who is like you, a people saved by the Lord? He is your shield and helper and your glorious sword. Your enemies will cower before you, and you will tread on their heights. **Deuteronomy 33:29**

45. **God in Heaven**: When we heard of it, our hearts melted in fear and everyone's courage failed because of you, for the Lord your

God is God in heaven above and on the earth below. **Joshua 2:11**

46. **God Of Abraham, Isaac And Jacob**: 'I am the God of your fathers, the God of Abraham, Isaac and Jacob.' Moses trembled with fear and did not dare to look. **Acts 7:32**

47. **God of Glory**: (1) The voice of the Lord is over the waters; the God of glory thunders, the Lord thunders over the mighty waters. **Psalms 29:3**; (2) To this he replied: "Brothers and fathers, listen to me! The God of glory appeared to our father Abraham while he was still in Mesopotamia, before he lived in Harran". **Acts 7:2**

48. **God of Peace**: Now may the God of peace, who through the blood of the eternal covenant brought back from the dead our Lord Jesus, that great Shepherd of the sheep. **Hebrews 13:20**

49. **God of Righteousness**: Answer me when I call to you, my righteous God. Give me relief from my distress; have mercy on me and hear my prayer. **Psalms 4:1**

50. **God Sees Me**: She gave this name to the Lord who spoke to her: "You are the God who sees me," for she said, "I have now seen the One who sees me." **Genesis 16:13**

51. **GOD that Avenges**: He is the God who avenges me, who subdues nations under me. **Psalms 18:47**

52. **God's Mystery:** My goal is that they may be encouraged in heart and united in love, so that they may have the full riches of complete understanding, in order that they may know the mystery of God, namely, Christ. **Colossians 2:2**

53. **Good Shepherd:** "I am the good shepherd. The good shepherd lays down his life for the sheep." **John 10:11**

54. **Great High Priest:** Therefore, since we have a great high priest who has ascended into heaven, Jesus the Son of God, let us hold firmly to the faith we profess. **Hebrews 4:14**

55. **Head Of The Body, The Church:** And he is the head of the body, the church; he is the beginning and the firstborn from among the dead, so that in everything he might have the supremacy. **Colossians 1:18**

56. **Head Over All Things:** And God placed all things under his feet and appointed him to be head over everything for the church. **Ephesians 1:22**

57. **Healer:** He said, "If you listen carefully to the Lord your God and do what is right in his eyes, if you pay attention to his commands and keep all his decrees, I will not bring on you any of the diseases I brought on the Egyptians, for I am the Lord, who heals you." **Exodus 15:26**

58. **Heir Of All Things:** But in these last days he has spoken to us by his Son, whom he appointed heir of all things, and through whom also he made the universe. **Hebrews 1:2**

59. **Helper:** Surely God is my help; the Lord is the one who sustains me. **Psalms 54:4**

60. **Holy One:** But you have an anointing from the Holy One, and all of you know the truth. **1 John 2:20**

61. **Horn of Salvation:** The Lord is my rock my fortress and my deliverer; my God is my rock, in whom I take refuge, my shield and the horn of my salvation, my stronghold. **Psalms 18:2**

62. **I AM:** "Very truly I tell you," Jesus answered, "before Abraham was born, I am!" **John 8:5;** "And God said to Moses, 'I AM THAT I AM': and he said, thus shalt thou say unto the children of Israel, 'I AM hath sent me unto you.' " **Exodus 3:14**

63. **Image Of The Invisible God:** The Son is the image of the invisible God, the firstborn over all creation. **Colossians 1:15**

64. **Immanuel: (God with us):** "The virgin will conceive and give birth to a son, and they will call him Immanuel" (which means: God with us). **Matthew 1:23, Isaiah 7:14**

65. **Jealous God:** You shall not bow down to them or worship them; for I, the Lord your God, am a jealous God, punishing the children for the sin of the parents to the third and fourth generation of those who hate me. **Exodus 20:5**

66. **Jehovah: The LORD:** God also said to Moses, "I am the Lord. I appeared to Abraham, to Isaac and to Jacob as God Almighty, but by my name the Lord I did not make myself fully known to them." **Exodus 6:2,3**

67. **Jesus: (Salvation):** Who Saves People From Their Sins: For God so loved the world that he gave his one and only Son, that whoever believes in him shall not perish but have eternal life. **John 3:16**

68. **Jesus of Nazareth:** Then he went out to the gateway, where another

servant girl saw him and said to the people there, "This fellow was with Jesus of Nazareth." **Matthew 26:71**

69. **Judge**: I have not wronged you, but you are doing me wrong by waging war against me. Let the Lord, the Judge, decide the dispute this day between the Israelites and the Ammonites. **Judges 11:27**

70. **Judge Of The Living And The Dead**: He commanded us to preach to the people and to testify that he is the one whom God appointed as judge of the living and the dead. **Acts 10:42**

71. **King Of Israel**: "Let this Messiah, this king of Israel, come down now from the cross, that we may see and believe." Those crucified with him also heaped insults on him. **Mark 15:32**

72. **King Of Kings And Lord Of Lords**: On his robe and on his thigh he has this name written: King of Kings and Lord of Lords. **Revelation 19:16**

73. **King Of The Jews**: Above his head they placed the written charge against him: this is Jesus, the King of the Jews. **Matthew 27:37**

74. **King Of The Nations**: ...And sang the song of God's servant Moses and of the Lamb: "Great and marvelous are your deeds, Lord God Almighty. Just and true are your ways, King of the nations." **Revelation 15:3**

75. **Lamb**: In a loud voice they were saying: "Worthy is the Lamb, who was slain, to receive power and wealth and wisdom and strength and honor and glory and praise!" **Revelation 5:12**

76. **Lamb of God**: When he saw Jesus passing by, he said, "Look, the Lamb of God!" **John 1:36**

77. **Last Adam**: So it is written: "The first man Adam became a living being; the last Adam, a life-giving spirit." **1 Corinthians 15:45**

78. **Lawgiver And Judge**: There is only one Lawgiver and Judge, the one who is able to save and destroy. But you—who are you to judge your neighbor? **James 4:12**

79. **Life**: Jesus said to her, "I am the resurrection and the life. The one who believes in me will live, even though they die." **John 11:25**

80. **Light**: The Lord is my light and my salvation— whom shall I fear? The Lord is the stronghold of my life—of whom shall I be afraid. **Psalms 27:1**

81. **Light Of The World**: When Jesus spoke again to the people, he

said, "I am the light of the world. Whoever follows me will never walk in darkness, but will have the light of life." **John 8:12**

82. **Lily of the Valleys:** I am the rose of Sharon; and the lily of the valleys. As the lily among the thorns, so is my love among the daughters. **Song of Solomon 2:1,2**

83. **Lion Of Judah:** Then one of the elders said to me, "Do not weep! See, the Lion of the tribe of Judah, the Root of David, has triumphed. He is able to open the scroll and its seven seals." **Revelation 5:5**

84. **Living God:** But you must not mention 'a message from the Lord' again, because each one's word becomes their own message. So you distort the words of the living God, the Lord Almighty, our God. **Jeremiah 23:36; Joshua 3:10; Daniel 3:26;** You show that you are a letter from Christ, the result of our ministry, written not with ink but with the Spirit of the living God, not on tablets of stone but on tablets of human hearts. **2 Corinthians 3:3 & 6:16**

85. **Living Water:** "But whoever drinks the water I give them will never thirst. Indeed, the water I give them will become in them a spring of water welling up to eternal life." **John 4:14**

86. **Lord:** If you declare with your mouth, "Jesus is Lord," and believe in your heart that God raised him from the dead, you will be saved. For it is with your heart that you believe and are justified, and it is with your mouth that you profess your faith and are saved. As Scripture says, "Anyone who believes in him will never be put to shame." For there is no difference between Jew and Gentile—the same Lord is Lord of all and richly blesses all who call on him, for, "Everyone who calls on the name of the Lord will be saved." **Romans 10:9-13; Joel 2:32**

87. **Lord God of Israel:** Praise be to the Lord, the God of Israel, because he has come to his people and redeemed them. **Luke 1:68;** Praise be to the Lord, the God of Israel, from everlasting to everlasting. Amen and Amen. **Psalms 41:13**

88. **Lord Is There:** "The distance all around will be 18,000 cubits. "And the name of the city from that time on will be: the Lord is there." **Ezekiel 48:35**

89. **Lord Mighty In Battle:** Who is this King of glory? The Lord

strong and mighty, the Lord mighty in battle. **Psalms 24:8**

90. **Lord of All the Earth**: See, the ark of the covenant of the Lord of all the earth will go into the Jordan ahead of you. **Joshua 3:11**

91. **Lord of Hosts**: Restore us, O God of Hosts; make your face shine on us, that we may be saved. **Psalms 80:7, Jeremiah 35:17 & 38:17;** Year after year this man went up from his town to worship and sacrifice to the Lord of Hosts at Shiloh, where Hophni and Phinehas, the two sons of Eli, were priests of the Lord. **I Samuel 1:3**

92. **Lord Strong and Mighty**: Who is this King of glory The Lord strong and mighty, the Lord mighty in battle. **Psalms 24:8**

93. **Lord that Smites**: I will not look on you with pity; I will not spare you. I will repay you for your conduct and for the detestable practices among you. Then you will know that it is I the Lord who smites you. **Ezekiel 7:9**

94. **Majestic Glory**: He received honor and glory from God the Father when the voice came to him from the Majestic Glory, saying, "This is my Son, whom I love; with him I am well pleased." **2 Peter 1:17**

95. **Majesty:** The Son is the radiance of God's glory and the exact representation of his being, sustaining all things by his powerful word. After he had provided purification for sins, he sat down at the right hand of the Majesty in heaven. **Hebrews 1:3**

96. The **Man:** When Jesus came out wearing the crown of thorns and the purple robe, Pilate said to them, "Here is the man!" **John 19:5**

97. **Man of Sorrows:** He is despised and rejected of men; a man of sorrows, and acquainted with grief: and we hid as it were our faces from him; he was despised, and we esteemed him not. **Isaiah 53:3**

98. **Master: Chief, Commander:** The disciples went and woke him, saying, "Master, Master, we're going to drown!" He got up and rebuked the wind and the raging waters; the storm subsided, and all was calm. **Luke 8:24**

99. **Mediator:** For there is one God and one mediator between God and mankind, the man Christ Jesus. **1 Timothy 2:5**

100. **Messiah:** The first thing Andrew did was to find his brother Simon and tell him, "We have found the Messiah" (that is, the Christ). **John 1:41**

101. **Mighty GOD:** For to us a child is born, to us a son is given, and

the government will be on his shoulders. And he will be called Wonderful Counselor, Mighty God, Everlasting Father, Prince of Peace. **Isaiah 9:6**

102. **Most High**: But they put God to the test and rebelled against the Most High; they did not keep his statutes. **Psalms 78:56, Genesis 14:18, Daniel 3:26**

103. **Only Begotten Son**: This is how God showed his love toward us: He sent his Only Begotten Son into the world that we might live through him. **1 John 4:9;** No man hath seen God at any time, the only begotten Son, which is in the bosom of the Father, he hath declared him. **John 1:18**

104. **Passover Lamb**: Get rid of the old yeast, so that you may be a new unleavened batch—as you really are. For Christ, our Passover lamb, has been sacrificed. **1 Corinthians 5:7**

105. **Potter**: Yet you, Lord, are our Father. We are the clay, you are the potter; we are all the work of your hand. **Isaiah 6:8**

106. **Power**: "I am," said Jesus. "And you will see the Son of Man sitting at the right hand of Power, and coming on the clouds of heaven." **Mark 14:62**

107. **Priest Forever**: And he says in another place, "You are a priest forever, in the order of Melchizedek." **Hebrews 5:6**

108. **Prince**: God exalted him to his own right hand as Prince and Savior that he might bring Israel to repentance and forgive their sins. **Acts 5:31**

109. **Prince Of Life**: You killed the Prince of Life, but God raised him from the dead. We are witnesses of this. **Acts 3:15**

110. **Prince of Peace**: For to us a child is born, to us a son is given, and the government will be on his shoulders. And he will be called Wonderful Counselor, Mighty God, Everlasting Father, Prince of Peace. **Isaiah 9:6**

111. The **Prophet**: Questioned him, "Why then do you baptize if you are not the Messiah, nor Elijah, nor the Prophet?" **John 1:25, Deuteronomy 18:15**

112. **Provider**: So Abraham called that place The Lord Will Provide. And to this day it is said, "On the mountain of the Lord it will be provided." **Genesis 22:14**

113. **Rabbi**: Teacher, literally "my great one": "But you are not to be called 'Rabbi,' for you have one Teacher, and you are all brothers. **Matthew 23:8**

114. **Redeemer**: Then all mankind will know that I, the Lord, am your Savior, your Redeemer, the Mighty One of Jacob. **Isaiah 49:26 & 60:16;** For I know that my Redeemer lives and that he shall stand at the latter day upon the earth. **Job 19:25**

115. **Refuge**: Trust in him at all times, you people; pour out your hearts to him, for God is our refuge. **Psalms 62:8;** God is our refuge and strength, a very present help in trouble. **Psalms 46:1**

116. **Resurrection**: Jesus said to her, "I am the resurrection and the life. The one who believes in me will live, even though they die." **John 11:25**

117. **Righteous One; Righteousness**: My dear children, I write this to you so that you will not sin. But if anybody does sin, we have an advocate with the Father-Jesus Christ, the Righteous One. **1 John 2:1;** In his days Judah will be saved and Israel will live in safety. This is the name by which he will be called: The Lord Our Righteous Savior. **Jeremiah 23:6**

118. **Rock**: The Lord is my rock, my fortress and my deliverer; my God is my rock, in whom I take refuge, my shield and the horn of my salvation, my stronghold. **Psalms 18:2**

119. **Root And Offspring Of David**: "I, Jesus, have sent my angel to give you this testimony for the churches. I am the Root and the Offspring of David, and the bright Morning Star." **Revelation 22:16**

120. **Rose of Sharon**: I am the rose of Sharon, and the lily of the valleys. **Song of Solomon 2:1**

121. **Sanctifier**: "Say to the Israelites, 'You must observe my Sabbaths. This will be a sign between me and you for the generations to come, so you may know that I am the Lord who sanctifies you.' " **Exodus 31:13**

122. **Savior Of The World**: They said to the woman, "We no longer believe just because of what you said; now we have heard for ourselves, and we know that this man really is the Savior of the world." **John 4:42**

123. **Seed of the Woman:** And I will put enmity between thee and the woman, and between thy seed and her seed; it [the seed of the woman] shall bruise thy head, and thou shalt bruise his heel. **Genesis 3:15**

124. **Servant:** Indeed Herod and Pontius Pilate met together with the Gentiles and the people of Israel in this city to conspire against your holy servant Jesus, whom you anointed. **Acts 4:27**

125. **Shaddai: Lord Almighty:** And, "I will be a Father to you, and you will be my sons and daughters says the Lord Almighty." **2 Corinthians 6:18**

126. **Shepherd:** The Lord is my shepherd, I lack nothing. **Psalms 23:1**

127. **Shepherd And Guardian Of Our Souls:** For "you were like sheep going astray," but now you have returned to the Shepherd and Guardian of your souls. **1 Peter 2:25**

128. **Shield:** But you, Lord, are a shield around me, my glory, the One who lifts my head high. **Psalms 3:3;** Blessed are you, Israel! Who is like you, a people saved by the Lord? He is your shield and helper and your glorious sword. Your enemies will cower before you, and you will tread on their heights. **Deuteronomy 33:29**

129. **Son Of God:** But Jesus remained silent. The high priest said to him, "I charge you under oath by the living God: Tell us if you are the Messiah, the Son of God." **Matthew 26:63;** So if the Son sets you free, you will be free indeed. **John 8:36**

130. **Son Of Man:** "You have said so," Jesus replied. "But I say to all of you: From now on you will see the Son of Man sitting at the right hand of the Mighty One and coming on the clouds of heaven." **Matthew 26:64, Daniel 7:13**

131. **Source:** From him the whole body, joined and held together by every supporting ligament, grows and builds itself up in love, as each part does its work. **Ephesians 4:16**

132. **Sovereign:** When they heard this, they raised their voices together in prayer to God. "Sovereign Lord," they said, "you made the heavens and the earth and the sea, and everything in them. **Acts 4:24**

133. **Stone:** The stone the builders rejected has become the cornerstone; **Mark 12:10**

134. **Strength**: The salvation of the righteous comes from the Lord; he is their stronghold in time of trouble. **Psalms 37:39;** May these words of my mouth and this meditation of my heart be pleasing in your sight, Lord, my Strength and my Redeemer. **Psalms 19:14**

135. **Sunrise From On High**: Because of the tender mercy of our God, by which the rising sun will come to us from heaven. **Luke 1:78**

136. **True God**: Now this is eternal life: that they know you, the only true God, and Jesus Christ, whom you have sent. **John 17:3**

137. **True Vine**: I am the true vine, and my Father is the gardener. **John 15:1**

138. **Vinedresser**: I am the true vine, and my Father is the gardener. **John 15:1**

139. The **Way, The Truth, And The Life**: Jesus answered, "I am the way and the truth and the life. No one comes to the Father except through me." **John 14:6**

140. **Who was and Is, and Is to Come**: "I am the Alpha and the Omega, says the Lord God, who is and who was, and who is to come. The Almighty." **Revelation 1:8**

141. **Wisdom Of God**: But to those whom God has called, both Jews and Greeks, Christ the power of God and the wisdom of God. **1 Corinthians 1:24**

142. **Wonderful Counselor**: For to us a child is born, to us a son is given, and the government will be on his shoulders. And he will be called Wonderful Counselor, Mighty God, Everlasting Father, Prince of Peace. **Isaiah 9:6**

143. **Word**: In the beginning was the Word, and the Word was with God, and the Word was God. **John 1:1**

144. **Word Of God**: He is dressed in a robe dipped in blood, and his name is the Word of God. **Revelation 19:13**

145. **Word Of Life**: That which was from the beginning, which we have heard, which we have seen with our eyes, which we have looked at and our hands have touched—this we proclaim concerning the Word of life. **1 John 1:1**

146. **Yahweh**: "I AM." And God said to Moses, I AM THAT I AM: and he said, thus shalt thou say unto the children of Israel, 'I AM hath sent me unto you." **Exodus 3:14**

Dream Church

IN 2016, AFTER A TERRORIST ATTACK in Orlando, I had a simple social media broadcast that went viral. People started sending me thousands of messages asking what was the next step to take. They were in desperate need of instructions. I felt led to call for a 40-day fast, which included a live Facebook broadcast for each of the forty days. So together with my audience we entered into a forty-day fast. My fast consisted of only one meal per day, and each day I preached whatever message God had given me. These messages made a significant change in the lives of many. At the end of the fast, during the 40th-day broadcast, my audience was sad that it was over. During that very broadcast, Holy Spirit impressed on my heart to continue doing these broadcasts under the *Dream Church* umbrella.

God's Dream Church is where all people, all nations, all tribes, all colors and cultures are welcomed. People started joining me at every service, from Afghanistan, Iraq, Egypt, United States, Pakistan, England, Kenya, Malaysia, Singapore, Ethiopia, Lebanon, Turkey, Australia, New Zealand and more.

We continue to receive countless testimonies and praise reports from people all over the world who are part of Dream Church.

Ministry Overview

TV Programs

Sound of Love, The Way, Embracing New Life **and others**

- Broadcasting in 160 countries and 5 continents
- Total households reached internationally and nationally: approximately 384 million households that represent approximately 758 million people
- A library of 600+ television programs in 5 languages: Arabic, Farsi, Urdu, Turkish, and English.

Social Media Outreach

- Millions of followers on Facebook in multiple languages
- Our followers are from Egypt, Iran, Iraq, Indonesia, Pakistan, India, Turkey, Morocco, Saudi Arabia, Afghanistan, Yemen, Lebanon, Jordan, Libya, and more.
- Hundreds of thousands of monthly video-views and downloads
- Thousands of monthly messages and comments handled by dozens of online missionaries

Radio Programs

- Began airing *Embracing New Life* revival messages on radio networks

Ministry Overview Continued

- Işık's Turkish radio programs, titled "Ask IŞIK," air in Turkey and beyond, multiple times daily.

Songs

- Işık and her husband wrote and composed the songs "I Just Said Yes" and "He'll Never Leave You." They have also written other songs that are being translated into multiple languages.

About the Author

IŞIK ABLA (pronounced Ishyk) was born in Istanbul, Turkey. She was raised—and verbally and physically abused—in a Muslim home, only to escape into even more severe abuse by the Muslim man she married.

Işık entered college when she was just sixteen, earning a bachelor's degree in literature, followed by an advanced business degree. She worked in high-ranking executive positions for some of the largest corporations in Turkey, and traveled throughout Europe.

In 1996 she fled to America from her violent Muslim husband after he tried to kill her. After years of struggling to start her career over again in a foreign country and failing in many areas of her personal life, Işık fell into a deep depression and became suicidal.

On the day she was planning to end her life, she had a personal encounter with God. That day, she surrendered her life to Jesus and received the supernatural healing and redemption of Jesus Christ. From that moment on, her life changed miraculously for the better.

After receiving the Lord's call to full-time ministry, she attended Ambassador's Commission School of Ministry, and soon after graduation, became an ordained minister. She studied Masters in Divinity and attended both Yale and Harvard Universities for further training and courses.

In 2009, Işik began hosting a satellite TV program, which generated an overwhelming public response. Two years later, she began a live call-in program, simulcast on Turkish and Farsi TV channels throughout the Middle East and Europe. The responses started multiplying as the lives of Muslims were being transformed.

Today, Işik's programs are broadcast in 160 countries, on five continents, and in five languages: Turkish, Arabic, Farsi, Urdu and English, reaching an audience of more than 750 million viewers, and engaging more than six million followers through social media. On Facebook alone, she has millions of followers.

In 2016, she focused on social media engagements hosting weekly Facebook Live videos called *Dream Church*. She was awarded the National Religious Broadcaster's International Impact award for demonstrating a strong personal commitment to proclaiming Christ through electronic media, and working with integrity and faithfulness to influence a culture for Christ.

Her message of hope, love and redemption, found only in a loving God, resonates and continues to reach the Muslim world for Christ. As a Muslim-background believer, she is uniquely poised, knowing the culture, language and social norms, to authentically and relationally share the good news of Jesus Christ to Muslims.

54809143R00212

Made in the USA
Columbia, SC
08 April 2019